"I was hoping to get another dance with you," Parker said.

Molly gave a happy laugh. "All you had to do was ask."

He pulled her to a stop, then pointed above her head. "I'm asking," he said, his voice suddenly thick.

She looked up to catch a brief glimpse of mistletoe, just before his lips came down on hers.

Parker had meant the gesture to be friendly, but before he had reached her mouth he knew that it was going to be more than that. He kissed her once, before releasing her as if he'd been burned. Molly stood watching him for a long moment.

He put his arm back around her waist. "I...ah...could try it again."

She stepped backward and shook her head. "No. Then I'd have to fire you."

"So if I kiss you again, I lose my job? Hmm." The decision took him about three seconds before he snatched her against him again....

Dear Reader,

Ana Seymour's seventh book for Harlequin Historicals, *Lucky Bride,* is a sequel to *Gabriel's Lady.* When ranch hand Parker Prescott discovers that his boss might be forced to marry a dangerous con man, he sets out to save her... only to fall in love with her in the process in this delightful Western set in Wyoming Territory.

Romance Writers of America RITA Award nominee Gayle Wilson is back with *Raven's Vow,* a haunting Regency novel about a marriage of convenience between an American investor and an English heiress. Elizabeth Mayne, another March Madness/RITA Award nominee author, is also out this month. *Lord of the Isle* is a classic Elizabethan tale featuring an Irish nobleman who unwittingly falls in love with a rebel from an outlawed family.

Our fourth title for the month, *The Return of Chase Cordell,* is a Western from Linda Castle, who is fast becoming one of our most popular authors. It's a poignant love story about a war hero with amnesia who rediscovers a forgotten passion for his young bride.

Whatever your taste in reading, we hope you'll enjoy all four of these terrific stories. Please keep an eye out for them wherever Harlequin Historicals are sold.

Sincerely,

Tracy Farrell
Senior Editor

Please address questions and book requests to:
Harlequin Reader Service
U.S.: 3010 Walden Ave., P.O. Box 1325, Buffalo, NY 14269
Canadian: P.O. Box 609, Fort Erie, Ont. L2A 5X3

ANA SEYMOUR

LUCKY BRIDE

Harlequin Books

TORONTO • NEW YORK • LONDON
AMSTERDAM • PARIS • SYDNEY • HAMBURG
STOCKHOLM • ATHENS • TOKYO • MILAN
MADRID • WARSAW • BUDAPEST • AUCKLAND

ISBN 0-373-28950-2

LUCKY BRIDE

Books by Ana Seymour

Harlequin Historicals

The Bandit's Bride #116
Angel of the Lake #173
Brides for Sale #238
Moonrise #290
Frontier Bride #318
Gabriel's Lady #337
Lucky Bride #350

ANA SEYMOUR

has been a Western fan since her childhood—the days of the shoot-'em-up movie matinees and television programs. She has followed the course of the Western myth in books and films ever since, and says she was delighted when cowboys started going off into the sunset with their ladies rather than their horses. Ms. Seymour lives with her two daughters near one of Minnesota's ten thousand lakes.

In memory of my grandmother
Jane Lovene Eiler
my ever-present example of a woman of spirit

Chapter One

Wyoming Territory
November, 1876

Parker Prescott pushed back the brim of his lucky Stetson and grimaced as he surveyed the dusty street. Whoever had named this place Canyon City must have had a darn good sense of humor. This sure as hell wasn't Parker's idea of a city. And the closest thing he'd seen to a canyon in the brown plains he'd just crossed was the collapsed prairie dog hole that had lamed up his horse.

He sighed. It appeared the livery was at the far end of town, past a row of three saloons, a bathhouse and a tonsorial parlor. He took a step back and gave his mount a pat. "Just a little farther, Diamond," he told the animal. "Then you can give that leg a nice long rest."

Parker had walked the last few miles into town, and the thought of that bathhouse was appealing. He'd see to Diamond, then head back and try to soak away his aches and his gloomy mood in a steaming tub. The aches would disappear faster than the gloom, he reckoned.

Diamond seemed to sense that her limping journey was just about over. She tossed her head and followed willingly as Parker started up the street. His horse's mishap was the last in a string of plain bad luck that had set Parker to wondering why he'd ever left New York City in the first place.

He'd headed out of Deadwood in Dakota Territory in October and had intended by now to be clear to the West Coast, trying his luck in the dying gold fields of California. But he'd been hit by an early fall snowstorm and had had to hole up in a cave until his supplies were gone, forcing him to double back to Lead to restock. When he'd finally gotten out of the Black Hills and hit the vast, rolling plains, he'd lost the trail, wandering like an idiot for days. He'd never be a mountain man, he'd decided ruefully. There'd been no need to learn to steer by the stars in the busy streets of Manhattan.

And now Diamond had come up lame, forcing Parker to abandon the idea of making it across the mountains before winter. But he wasn't about to get stuck for the season in Canyon City. There had to be someplace in Wyoming Territory where a man could find some of life's amenities—a thick steak and a pretty girl would do to start.

He passed the third saloon, taking a step away from the wooden sidewalk as a cowboy out front spewed a poorly aimed wad of tobacco in his direction. Perhaps he could make it to Cheyenne for the winter, Parker mused. Surely the territorial capital would offer some...

His head spun around. As if conjured up by his thoughts, directly across the street from him stood the two prettiest females he'd seen since his last stroll down Park Avenue.

Diamond gave a slight whinny of protest as her owner tugged on her reins. Parker hesitated a moment. Diamond needed attending to, but by the time he made it to the livery and back, the two visions across the street might have disappeared. He reached over to tie the horse to the saloon hitching post, then gave a halfhearted swipe to the dusty front of his clothes. His appearance couldn't be helped. He gave a self-deprecating chuckle. If the ladies had any sense, they'd be able to see through the dirt to the sterling qualities of the man underneath.

He strode across the street and planted himself in front of the two women, scooping his hat off his head and giving a little bow. "Morning, ladies," he said politely. Their pastel dresses were as fresh and pretty and sedate as an Easter church service. The two were obviously not the kind of women who sold themselves in the upstairs rooms of saloons. Too bad. Parker wasn't much interested in decent women these days. But it still would be a pleasure to hear a feminine voice.

"Excuse my taking the liberty of addressing you two ladies without an introduction." He flashed the easy smile that never failed to charm and tried to keep from staring at two sets of golden lashes fluttering over two sets of enormous blue eyes.

"The name is Parker Prescott, at your service," he continued with another slight bow. "I'm new in town, and I wondered if I might prevail on you ladies to help a weary traveler with a bit of information." He made his speech New York-formal and his manner as elegant as if he were wearing cutaways at the opera instead of buckskins in the middle of a godforsaken cow town.

His efforts appeared to have some effect. The taller of the two gave him a shy, dimpled smile and said, "What kind of information, sir?"

This time Parker's grin was genuine. The girl's smile was the loveliest thing he'd seen in a month of Sundays. And her voice would stand out in an angel chorus. After a fascinated moment he managed to say, "I've had an accident with my horse and am in sore need of a hearty meal and a good hotel."

"There's just the one place for both," the girl answered, pointing to a faded yellow clapboard building behind her. A sign over the double doorway said Grand Hotel.

Parker's smile dimmed, but he recovered and continued. "Perhaps you ladies would join me for a meal? I've had a long, lonely trip, and I'd surely appreciate a bit of company."

The girl who had answered him looked at her companion. They had to be sisters. Their delicate features were nearly identical, noses tilting upward and cheeks pink with a natural blush. The shorter one spoke for the first time. "Don't even think of it, Susannah. You know nothing about this man."

Susannah tossed her head, sending her blond curls bouncing under the silk-ruched bonnet. "If we have to sit around all afternoon waiting for Molly we might as well be comfortable in the café with a nice cup of tea."

"She's right, you know," Parker said, addressing the shorter sister with a serious expression. "You shouldn't be out here on the street waiting for your companion. It would be much better to wait inside enjoying a nice piece of apple pie.''

The girl's face brightened a bit at this suggestion, but she still looked skeptical. ''Molly would throw a fit,'' she said slowly to the girl she had called Susannah.

''Oh, pooh. She's not our mother, you know, for all she tries to act like one.''

''You ladies are sisters?'' Parker asked.

Susannah nodded and held out a gloved hand. ''Susannah and Mary Beth Hanks. Molly's our older sister. She's over at the Feed 'n' Seed.''

Parker took the offered hand and held it in both of his. For a moment he lost track of his thoughts in the depths of Susannah Hanks's blue eyes. ''I'm pleased to make your acquaintance, Miss Hanks,'' he said finally. Lord almighty, it had been entirely too long since he'd been around decent women. He felt as tongue-tied as a schoolboy at his first afternoon social. Where was that glib Eastern patter that had set all the ladies back in Deadwood to sighing? Of course, the ladies of Deadwood hadn't exactly been ladies.

He dropped Susannah's hand and turned to her sister. ''And yours, Miss Hanks. I can hardly believe my good fortune at meeting two such lovely examples of Wyoming aristocracy.''

Mary Beth gave a little giggle and slowly offered her hand. ''I reckon that's the first time the Hanks sisters have been called aristocracy,'' she said.

Parker took the girl's hand. It was plumper, smaller than her sister's. He lifted it toward his lips. ''It isn't hard to recognize—'' he began, then froze as he felt the cold pressure of a gun barrel against the back of his neck.

"Take your hands and your eyes off my sisters or I'll blow that fancy-talking tongue clear out of your head."

The voice behind him held nothing of the melodious grace of her sisters. Parker held one hand in the air and with the other carefully reached behind his head to grasp the end of the gun and move it away. "I assure you, Miss Hanks," he said smoothly, "I mean no disrespect to your sisters or to you."

He turned around and tried to keep his astonishment from showing in his expression. The woman he faced was as unlike the two pastel confections behind him as a rattler from a pair of buttercups. She stood like a man with her feet planted apart, a mean-looking buffalo rifle cradled easily in her arms. At least it was no longer pointed at him. She wore denim pants that hung on her like a half-empty flour sack and a bulky buckskin jacket, also several sizes too big. An oversize man's felt hat was pulled down over her hair, but he could see from the wisps that escaped along each side that, unlike her sisters' blond tresses, her hair was a nondescript brown. Her cheeks were chapped and roughened by the wind.

"You can be on your way," she said, swinging the rifle barrel in the direction of his horse. "We're not interested in talking with any traveling sidewinders."

He felt a surge of irritation, but hid it behind a smile. "My own sister has called me worse things at times, Miss Hanks, but she never really meant them. She has a right feisty temper when she gets riled. I believe it was my homesickness for her that emboldened me to address *your* lovely sisters."

Molly Hanks's expression did not soften. "There's a telegraph at the end of the street. Why don't you go send your sister a wire and leave mine alone?"

Parker turned back toward Susannah and Mary Beth, but they were both staring down at the ground. "I didn't mean any harm, ladies," he said.

Susannah looked up quickly, and he thought he detected a hint of apology in her eyes before she shifted them downward again.

"I just might take your advice, Miss Hanks," he said softly, turning back to the oldest sister. With a last glance at her rifle, he clapped his hat on his head and headed across the street toward Diamond.

His delight at the unexpected encounter with the two lovely sisters had faded, and a wave of homesickness hit him. Perhaps he *would* send Amelia a telegram, let her know where he was. She and her new husband, Gabe Hatch, would be back in New York City now, with Gabe taking over the family banking position that Parker had so detested. He grinned as he thought about his former mining partner turning on the charm for all the reformer friends of Parker and Amelia's mother. He wondered if the true story would be revealed—that his bluestocking sister had gone to Deadwood to save Parker from the evils of the Wild West...and had instead fallen head over petticoats for a wickedly handsome professional gambler.

He found the telegraph office and sent his message, then went back out into the street with a lump the size of a potato in his throat. All of a sudden, winter was looking mighty long.

As he stepped off the sidewalk, the three Hanks sisters exited from a doorway across the street. All three turned their heads his way. He gave a little bow and tipped his hat, but as the two younger sisters started to smile at him again, the oldest grabbed each by an arm and tugged them in the opposite direction.

"He was being a regular gentleman, Molly," he heard the tall, pretty one say in a loud, angry whisper.

Molly didn't bother to lower her voice. "There's no such thing as a gentleman, Susannah. Leastwise, not in Wyoming Territory." She uncocked her rifle and passed it to her left hand. "I'm finished here. Let's get home."

She turned and marched up the street toward a wagon parked out in front of the feed store. Susannah looked across to where Parker stood with Diamond, watching them. She gave him a furtive wave, to which he tipped his hat and winked. Mary Beth nervously grabbed her sister's arm. "C'mon, Susannah. Molly says we have to go."

Parker watched them leave with a sigh of regret. He'd best put the beautiful Hanks sisters out of his mind. If their older sister was such a tigress, he'd hate to imagine what their father or brothers would do to guard their virtue.

Parker eased his shoulders into the steaming, soapy water. It felt even better than he had anticipated. He hadn't had bathwater this hot since he'd headed west. Perhaps Canyon City would do for the winter after all. The Grand Hotel, despite its unimpressive exterior, had yielded a prime sirloin the size of a serving platter. The liveryman who was tending to Diamond appeared to be a proper expert in horseflesh. And then, of course, there were those intriguing Hanks sisters.

He'd promised himself to put them out of his head, but the rest of his body kept bringing up the subject. If he could just get the two younger ones alone, preferably the taller one, Susannah... He closed his eyes and pictured them, standing there in the dusty street. Her eyes had been the color of his mother's prize china. Cornflower blue, it was called.

"I ain't about to fish you outta there if you fall asleep, sonny."

Parker jumped at the strident voice. He sat up with a slosh. A large woman had come in at the far end of the room carrying a load of towels. She was as tall as Parker and twice as wide. Parker looked down at the water in consternation. The last of the bubbles had gone over the side of the tub when he sat up, leaving him fully exposed to view.

"Don't worry," the woman said, following the direction of his gaze. "You ain't got nothing in there I ain't seen before." She lowered the towels and craned her neck to peer at the water. "Though it don't look too bad for a pilgrim like you."

Parker felt his skin grow hotter than the temperature of the water. "I don't believe I've had the pleasure, ma'am," he said, masking his discomfiture.

"Maxine McClanahan," she said, her voice booming. "Most folks just call me Max. I thought you'd need a towel."

"Much obliged." His embarrassment faded at the woman's brisk manner. He met her steady gaze. Her hair was shot through with gray, but she was definitely not the grandmotherly type. She had a no-nonsense air about her. Max. It suited her.

He sat back and allowed her to finish her un-abashed perusal of him. "Do you work here?" he asked.

She shook her head. "Own the place."

Parker lifted his eyebrows in surprise, eliciting a chuckle from Max.

"So what, pilgrim? You don't think a woman can own a respectable business? I thought you'd be a mite smarter than the usual drifters we get through here. The only time they feel comfortable givin' money to a woman is when she's lying on her back." She gave a little huff and deposited the towels on the room's only chair.

Parker grinned. "I'll be happy to give you my money, ma'am. What was it you called me? A pilgrim?"

"Yup. A pilgrim. A tenderfoot," she clarified.

"How'd you know I was a tenderfoot?"

She glanced at the jumbled heap of Parker's things. "The clothes, for one. Ain't a gent in Canyon City who'd wear a silk vest like that one. 'Cept maybe Harvey Overstreet. And that's 'cause he's been ex-pectin' to die for the past ten years and wants to look pretty in his coffin."

"Back in Deadwood there were lots of men with vests like mine," Parker protested.

"Deadwood's a boomtown—gamblers and scala-wags and fancy dreamers." Her grimace left no doubt as to Max's opinion of the quality of Deadwood menfolk. "Out here's the *real* West. Honest-to-goodness cowpokes who wouldn't know a silk shirt from a burlap bag."

"And who don't like women in business," Parker added.

Max put her hands on her ample hips. "That's for *darn* sure. They've near run poor Molly Hanks out of the territory."

"Molly Hanks?" Parker pushed himself farther out of the water and felt the sudden chill on his skin.

Max nodded. "After her pappy died, none of these pea-brained cowhands would work for her. They say a woman's got no business running a ranch."

"That particular woman looks like she could run just about anything," Parker said under his breath.

"Molly's a tough one," Max agreed with another rumbling chuckle. "But if she don't get some of them to change their minds by spring roundup, I'm afraid she ain't got a sinner's chance in heaven of making a go of it."

Parker shivered. He looked over at the stack of towels, just out of reach. "Ah... would you like to hand me one of those?" he asked.

Max leaned her back against the wall and let a broad smile cross her face. "Come on, pilgrim. At my age there just ain't that many pleasures left in this life, so I take 'em where I can get 'em. And from what I've seen so far, a nice long look at you would be pure pleasure."

Trying not to feel self-conscious, Parker stood, letting the dirty water sluice down his lean body. His eyes met Max's. She watched him with a brief flicker of a nearly forgotten hunger, then it was replaced by her sardonic humor. "Pure pleasure is right," she said with a wink as he grabbed a towel and began to dry himself. She looked him up and down without self-consciousness. "You can bathe here any time you want, pilgrim. Half price."

Parker laughed. Canyon City was definitely proving to be much more enjoyable than he had suspected. "Is there work hereabouts?" he asked.

Max cocked her head. "Not this time of year, I wouldn't think. Except out at the Lucky Stars, of course."

"The Lucky Stars?"

"Hanks's place. Ol' man Hanks named it after his three girls. He always called them his lucky stars."

"They didn't have any brothers?"

"Nope. Just the three fillies. Sarah Hanks died on the last one and Charlie Hanks never got over it. Not 'til the day he died."

"So the three girls are running the ranch now?"

"Molly is. Can't say as the other two are much help."

Parker tied the towel around his waist. "Where might I find their outfit?"

Max pushed away from the wall and started to walk toward the door, a secret smile on her face. "You plannin' to sign on out there?"

"I might give it a try."

Max shook her head. "Head straight north out of town. You can't miss it."

"Thank you, ma'am," Parker said with a smile and a nod. "And thanks for the, ah . . . company."

Max started out the door, her broad shoulders shaking with silent laughter. "Lord almighty," he heard her say as she disappeared into the front room, "that's all Miss Molly needs . . . a gol-danged pilgrim with the body of a prize stallion."

He'd found the canyon. It wasn't much of a canyon, but it sliced deep enough so that the horse he'd exchanged for Diamond tossed her head and looked reluctant to start down.

Parker dismounted and walked to the edge, looking for a path. A pilgrim, Max had called him. At the moment he was ready to add some epithets of his own to the description. When he left Canyon City he could have sworn he was heading due north, but he'd been riding a good portion of the afternoon and hadn't seen the Lucky Stars ranch. Nor had he seen anything of the Hanks sisters. To make matters worse, the wind that had been brisk when he left town was now downright nasty. He hunched into his sheepskin jacket. Max hadn't said anything about having to cross a canyon. Maybe he should turn back to town. If, indeed, he knew which way was back.

"What do you think?" he asked the swaybacked sorrel. The animal had been a sorry trade for Diamond, but the liveryman had insisted that Diamond might never heal up, in which case *any* trade was a good one. Parker didn't know enough about horses to argue.

The animal looked at him reproachfully, as if to remind him that finding the right road was the rider's responsibility, not the horse's. He took another look into the canyon. The riverbed at the bottom was dry. There'd be no problem crossing. And the slope up the far side looked more gentle than the one he was standing on. If he could make it down, he should be all right.

"Ah, hell," he said aloud. He grasped the horse's reins firmly in one hand and started down the slippery side of the cliff, pulling the balky animal after him. Now that he was on his way, it didn't look so formidable. And the wind cut a little less once he was within the shelter of the rocks. A few ominous white flakes whipped by him, but he ignored them and concentrated on his footing.

"Just one foot after the other," he said under his breath. One *tender*foot after another, he silently corrected, remembering his encounter with Max. He grinned in spite of himself.

Chapter Two

❦

"Papa must be a-rollin' in his grave to see me like this," Susannah said with disgust, tearing off the oversize gloves and looking at her chapped hands. "My skin's going to be as tough as shoe leather."

"People don't roll in their graves," Molly replied. "Once they're dead, they're dead."

"Can't we go back now, Molly? I'm half-froze."

Molly pulled off her own gloves and huffed on her numb fingers. The storm was getting worse, and if they hadn't found the blamed mule by now, they probably weren't going to. They could only hope that the poor nag had found a place to take shelter. Beatrice was too old to weather a storm like the one kicking up just to the west of them. Too old to be of much use around the ranch, either. She'd been their father's favorite—the only animal he could afford when he'd first come West back in '50. He'd been on his way to join the California Gold Rush, but had fallen in love with the wide open skies of Wyoming and had never left. Molly still felt the pain like a piece of glass in her throat every time she thought about him. She reckoned she owed it to Papa not to let Beatrice freeze to death alone in a snowstorm.

"We'll look along the canyon," she told her sister. "If we can't see any sign of her there, we'll have to head back."

Susannah wheeled her horse toward the west. She was actually the best rider of the three sisters, but she played down her skill, not wanting Molly to assign her more tasks around the place. "Hurry up with it, then. That's a blizzard coming," she called back to her sister. "I don't see what's so all-fired important about an old mule. She won't even let any of us ride her."

"She misses Papa, just like the rest of us. One of these days she'll calm down."

Susannah frowned and let Molly pull up alongside her. "You talk about her as if she were a member of the family."

"Don't be stupid. You and Mary Beth and I are the family. The only family we have left."

They'd been riding toward the edge of Copper Canyon, an unexpected gap that opened up in the middle of the prairie like a crack in a smooth pan of cake. It was named not for any particular mineral content but for its burnished red color when the sun hit it right. Susannah reached the edge first and pulled up, holding her hat down on her head as the wind tore into her. "She's not going to be down here, Molly," she hollered. "Papa never took Beatrice into the canyon."

Molly squinted to keep the snow from her eyes. The big flakes were coming down harder, and it was becoming difficult to see. She flipped her horse's reins over its head and handed them to her sister. "Hold on to Midnight. I'm going to take a look."

"I don't think . . ."

Before Susannah could finish her protest, Molly had jumped from her horse and was walking toward the edge of the cliff. As she reached the rim, her heart gave a little jump. Through the snow she could make out the distinct shape of an animal, just a few yards down into the canyon. "She's here!" she yelled to Susannah as she scrambled over the side.

"Be careful. The ground's slippery," her sister warned.

In fact, the footing was more treacherous than Molly had anticipated. The snow had formed an icy coating over the rocks. She turned around and began to climb down backward, holding to the side as she went. From beneath her came a gentle whinny. She straightened up in surprise and looked over her shoulder. She knew the mule's throaty sound. The animal below her was not Beatrice.

Her body sagged a moment with disappointment, then she straightened her back. It was *someone's* animal, and it didn't belong stuck here on the side of a canyon. She faced the rocks once again and continued down until she reached the horse. Close up, it didn't look as if it was worth saving, but there was a fancy tooled saddle on its back and bulging saddlebags.

She looked around. Where in blazes was the rider? The gale tore at her, threatening to blow her off the side of the cliff. She clutched at the horse for support. "What are you doing here, you old nag? Where's your owner?" The animal tossed its head and gave another whinny of complaint.

Molly twisted around to survey the surrounding area, but the canyon was fast turning into a sheet of white. She could barely see the ground right next to her own feet. She started to feel an ominous cold from the inside out. If the owner of this horse was lying hurt or wounded somewhere near here, they might not find him until after the storm, and by then it would surely be too late.

"Susannah, come help me!" she shouted.

She could barely hear her sister's reply over the wind's howl, and she could no longer see to the top of the cliff. She grabbed the horse's reins. The leather was frozen stiff. "Halloo! Is anyone there?" she called out.

The snow blew into her mouth and stung her eyes. Leading the horse, she started to climb down into the canyon. She sensed that someone was in trouble out here, and helping people out of trouble was her specialty. But for once she was plumb out of ideas as to what to do.

Her boots slipped on the glassy rocks and she slid several feet, landing with her back against the sharp edge of a cracked boulder. The horse skidded along behind her. "Sorry," she said to the animal as she scrambled back to her feet, ignoring the pain where the jagged rock had bruised her ribs. She took another look around. The world was utterly white. In just a few short minutes the snow blanket under her feet had become over an inch thick. Soon it would be blowing into immense drifts up on the plains.

She leaned back against the rocks. Her fists tightened in frustration as she tried to decide what to do. After all, she didn't know for sure that the animal's owner was in the canyon. The horse may have run away and left its rider miles from here. And with the progress of the storm, she and Susannah would be lucky to find their own way back to the ranch. To stay out here any longer would risk both their lives. Reluctantly she turned around once again and started up the cliff.

She almost fell on top of him. The horse pulled her to the left and she stumbled down a crevice, catching herself just before she slid right into him. Molly's first thought was that he was dead. His body was twisted in an unnatural heap and his skin was totally white.

"Molly, are you hurt?" Susannah was climbing down toward her. She sounded terrified.

"I'm fine. But there's someone here. He's hurt...or worse."

The storm seemed to abate for just a minute as the two sisters stared down at the frozen man.

"It's that stranger—the one we saw in town yesterday. The gentleman," Susannah said.

Molly gave a snort of disgust. "Maybe he *is* a gentleman if he's blamed fool enough to try to cross Copper Canyon in this kind of weather."

"What are we going to do?" Susannah asked, her eyes wide.

"We've got to get him up on his horse so we can take him back to the ranch."

"We can't lift a big man like that," Susannah protested.

"It's either that or he dies. Do you want that on your conscience?"

Susannah was silent, but she bent to help as Molly tugged at the man's boots, trying to straighten out his body.

"You take the legs and I'll take the shoulders—they're heavier," Molly ordered. Susannah was taller than Molly, but there was no question about who had the greater strength. They maneuvered the horse so that it was slightly below them on the cliff, leaving less distance for them to lift their burden. "On the count of three. Use all your strength, now," Molly urged. "You can do it, Susie girl. One, two, *three!*"

They half lifted, half rolled the inert form over onto the saddle. Thankfully, the horse seemed too cold to protest and stood stock-still.

"We did it!" Susannah cried in triumph.

"Good job, sis," Molly said, her entire chest filling with relief. Now all they had to do was find their way back home through a blinding snowstorm. "You lead the horse up and I'll hold him on the back. We'll tie him down when we get back on top."

They struggled, pushing and pulling the reluctant mount up the rocks and onto level ground. Both girls were wheezing with the effort by the time they were at the top, and they threw their arms around each other in a victory embrace. "We made it," Susannah gasped.

Molly was more reserved. "We can't rest now. We've got to get started home." She pulled a rope from her own horse and began to tie it around the inert man. There was no movement from him.

"You don't suppose he's dead, do you?" Susannah asked warily.

Molly brushed the snow from her face so that she could see the knots she was tying. "After all this trouble," she said grimly, "he wouldn't *dare* be dead."

For several hours after they arrived home it looked as if the stranger they had rescued might indeed dare to die. His skin was completely cold to the touch, and his breathing was so shallow that at times it seemed to disappear altogether.

An anxious Mary Beth had greeted them at the big oak door of the ranch house, exclaiming over their tardiness in arriving through the storm. When they told her of the man, still tied to his horse out front, she ran to the kitchen to get Smokey. The bewhiskered old man was a roundup cook who had stayed on one spring years ago and had become a fixture at Lucky Stars.

"Where will we put him, Miss Molly?" Smokey asked as he helped her drag the stranger into the house.

"We'll take him up to Papa's room," she answered after the briefest pause.

Susannah and Mary Beth exchanged a look. Since their father's death the previous winter, his room had been unoccupied. When Susannah had once suggested that she would like to move there from her tiny corner room, Molly had answered her with a withering look and had gone upstairs to lock the door. It hadn't been opened since.

Together the four of them carried the half-frozen man up the curving stairs and across the hall, then waited while Molly opened the door to the spacious bedroom. It was just as it had been when their father lived—his stand of pipes on the dresser, his old felt hat hanging from one corner of the clothes tree. But a groan from the unconscious man kept them from dwelling on the past.

"I've never seen skin so white," Mary Beth said in a hushed voice as they laid him out on top of the high poster bed.

"Bring some coal oil, Smokey," Molly directed. "We'll have to rub it on him."

Susannah and Mary Beth stared at her. "All over him?" Susannah asked.

"You girls ain't rubbing no 'all over' on any shiftless cowboy," Smokey said indignantly. "If he needs rubbing, I guess I'll be the one to do it."

Molly paused and looked up and down the stranger's lean body. "I guess we could leave that part to you," she told the old man. "But mind you're gentle about it, or you'll rub that frozen skin right off him."

Smokey gave a little grunt. "I reckon I've unfroze my share of fingers and toes and ears in my time," he muttered. "Now, you three can just skedaddle on downstairs."

Molly set Mary Beth and Susannah to fixing supper and some hot soup for when their patient regained his senses, then she went back up to the bedroom with the coal oil. She hesitated at the door. Smokey had stripped off the stranger's clothes, leaving his lower half covered by a blanket. She'd never seen a man's naked chest close up. Papa had always said that any hand showing up around the big house without a shirt would be turned off the place. He'd guarded his daughters' sensibilities as if they'd been princesses in a European castle rather than redblooded girls on a Wyoming cattle ranch.

She averted her eyes from the bed and held out the can of oil. "Are you sure you don't need any help?" she asked.

Smokey walked over and gave her cheek a little pat. "You go down and get something warm into your gullet, missy. Let me worry about him."

"Do you think he'll be all right?"

Smokey shrugged. "He looks pretty froze. But we'll do the best we can for him."

"I'll come back up in a little bit and sit with him, so you can have your supper."

"Take your time. He's not going anywhere."

But Molly found she could not rest easy downstairs without knowing about the stranger's progress. After gulping a few bites of stew, she said, "Mary Beth, you do the washing up tonight so Smokey can help out upstairs. And Susannah, bring some more firewood up to his room. We'll need to keep it warm in there all night long."

Susannah's lower lip came out slightly. "I can hardly move, Molly."

Molly felt much the same way herself. The struggle at the canyon and then battling the fury of the storm all the way home had taken its toll. But she pushed herself up from the table and said, "You can haul the wood or wash the dishes. You two work it out between yourselves, just so it gets done." She stalked across the dining room to the front entryway and the graceful curved stairway that had been her papa's pride and joy. No other ranch house in the territory had one like it.

"You have to help, too," Susannah retorted.

"I'll be up with the cowboy."

"I'm not sure that he's a cowboy," Mary Beth corrected shyly. "Parker, he said his name was. Parker Prescott."

"Kind of a gentlemanly sounding name, don't you think?" Susannah added.

"Gentleman or not, he won't be anything but a corpse unless we keep him warm," Molly said.

Susannah's smile dimmed. "I'll bring up the wood," she said.

And Mary Beth added, "I'll bring some, too."

By midnight the man's skin had turned red. He still hadn't regained consciousness. Molly had sent Smokey to bed, but she was determined to sit by their patient's side through the night. She didn't know whether Mr. Parker Prescott was a gentleman, but he *was* a human being. And if he was going to die, she wasn't about to let him do it alone.

She'd sat with her father through two weeks of restless nights before the pneumonia had taken him last year. And she'd had her share of sleepless nights ever since. Sometimes, usually at times like this in the darkest early-morning hours, the responsibility of it all would overwhelm her. Everything depended on her— the ranch, her sisters, even Smokey and poor Beatrice, both of whom were too old to find a place at any other spread. And now this stranger's fate had ended up in her hands, as well.

She sighed and walked over to the bed to examine him. Against the snowy white of the pillow his hair was a dark chestnut color—thick and wavy. He had the chiseled features of an Eastern blue blood, but the upper part of his body, which was not covered by the blanket, was as strong and well muscled as the loggers who came through town on their way to the north woods. She watched the gentle rise and fall of his chest for a few moments. His breathing appeared normal once again. And his skin tone was looking better. She reached out to lift one of his hands. Fingers were often the hardest hit by frostbite. But he'd been wearing thick leather gloves, and she could see no sign of the deadly white spots that would indicate frozen skin.

She held his hand for a long moment, wondering at her own fascination. She'd certainly bandaged enough banged-up knuckles and sprains among the cowpokes. But this stranger's hand didn't look like those of the cowboys she'd nursed. His skin was clean and soft, the fingers long. There were, however, calluses on his palm. He'd not been entirely idle, this gentleman of theirs.

With a little grimace she put his hand back. She reckoned the rest of the household was asleep by now, but she wasn't about to have someone come in and see her musing over some stranger's hand. She went back and sat in the rocking chair next to the fire. The important thing was that it appeared Mr. Prescott was going to recover. Which meant that soon he could ride on out of here and things would be back to normal.

"Oh, my!" Mary Beth's voice from the doorway woke Molly from her doze. Through the shutter slats she could see that it was daylight, though the storm still raged. She sat up and rubbed her eyes, then glanced over at the bed.

She saw at once the cause of Mary Beth's exclamation. During the night the man had twisted the blanket around himself in such a way that only the barest portion of his naked body was concealed from view. Fortunately that portion included his most private parts, but it was still a shocking sight. One long, hairy leg was exposed to view clear up to his backside. Molly felt a bit queer in her midsection. She jumped up and walked over to the bed, intent on protecting her sister from seeing anything more.

"Oh, my!" Susannah's exclamation came like an echo behind Mary Beth. Both girls stepped into the room and stood staring at the bed.

"You two can go on downstairs," Molly snapped. "It's not decent for you to be seeing him like this."

"It's not decent for you, either," Susannah said, sounding more intrigued than shocked. She walked across the room, then made a slow tour around the end of the bed. "He's surely a pretty thing, isn't he?" she said with a low laugh.

"Has he woken up yet?" Mary Beth asked cautiously. She stayed put over by the door.

Molly grasped one end of the blanket, but it was so twisted around him that she couldn't pull it free. "I must have dozed myself," she answered. "But I don't think he has. His color looks good, though."

"More than his color looks good, if you ask me," Susannah said with a little giggle.

"Susannah!" Mary Beth chided.

Molly grabbed a coverlet from its stand and flung it out over the entire bed, burying the patient. "You two ought to be down fixing breakfast," she said again, facing her sisters with her hands on her hips.

"Smokey's fixing it. He said we should come up and help you."

"I don't need any help."

"We'll just watch, then," Susannah said with a wicked grin.

Molly gave a huff and went back to trying to free the twisted blanket, working underneath the coverlet. In exasperation she gave a forceful tug. The patient rolled, causing the blanket to come free in her hands and knocking her off balance. She ended up in a heap on the bed, not two feet from Parker Prescott's wide open brown eyes.

"Hello," he said mildly.

Molly pushed the hair out of her face and scrambled backward, making sure that the coverlet stayed over most of his body.

"Ah . . . hello," she said.

Susannah gave one of her musical laughs. "You're awake!" she said.

Parker turned his head toward the tall blonde standing next to the bed. He blinked a couple of times. "If this is heaven," he said, "then dying was worth the price."

Molly felt an odd mixture of relief, irritation and panic. She was pleased that the stranger had recovered his senses and was not going to die in their midst. But she was not pleased at the way he was eyeing her sister. Charlie Hanks had guarded his three daughters like a shepherd guarding a flock of sheep surrounded by slavering wolves, a comparison that, he always said, was being overly complimentary to the cowboys of Canyon City. When he'd died, Molly had simply taken over the guarding duty, as she had all the others. Now all at once she had one of those very wolves lying naked in her father's bed. What was worse, Susannah's eyes were sparkling with interest as she returned his gaze.

"La, sir," Susannah said, her voice flirtatious, "we simple prairie girls aren't used to such pretty talk."

Parker looked from Susannah over to Mary Beth at the door, then more briefly at Molly, who had hastily pushed herself off the bed and was standing over him with a glower. Finally he turned back to Susannah and shook his head. "I can't believe you girls don't have every eligible cowboy in the territory swarming over this place trying to talk pretty."

"A few have tried," Molly said curtly. "We aren't interested." She glared at him as she folded the freed blanket.

"Speak for yourself, Molly," Susannah retorted. "Mr. Prescott can talk to me all day long if he's a mind."

Parker looked from one woman to the other. It was almost impossible to believe that they were sisters. Susannah was regarding him with that special kind of male-female look that he'd forgotten how much he missed. Her older sister, on the other hand, was watching him as if he were some kind of poisonous lizard.

Making sure that he was decently covered by the quilt, he sat up. He closed his eyes briefly as a wave of dizziness hit him. When it passed, he said, "Perhaps before we go any further one of you would be kind enough to tell me how I came to be here in the first place."

"We rescued you!" Susannah said, beaming. "You were near frozen to death."

"We dragged you out of Copper Canyon in time to save you from that," Molly added, pointing at the window where the snow still whipped against the glass. "What in tarnation were you doing out there in weather like that?"

Parker looked sheepish. "I . . . ah . . . didn't know it was going to storm."

"Haven't you got eyes in your head, man?" Molly asked. "It was building up in the western sky since daybreak yesterday."

"Maybe he's not used to Wyoming weather, Molly," Susannah told her sister in a tone of reproach. Then she turned to Parker. "Anyway, Mr. Prescott, the important thing is that we found you, and you're going to be all right."

"I reckon if you saved my life you better call me Parker, Miss Hanks," he said with another of his just-for-the-ladies smiles.

"And I'm Susannah," she said with a nod.

Suddenly Molly felt invisible. Parker and her sister were looking at each other as if the rest of the room had faded from view. That panicky feeling came back. Susannah was too darn pretty for her own good. And even Molly had to admit that the stranger was the handsomest male who'd come their way in quite some time. His eyes, gleaming now as they locked with Susannah's, were nearly the same rich chestnut color of his hair.

Molly couldn't blame Susannah for her interest. She'd have to act quickly to scare the man off before problems could develop. "The storm should lift by noon, Mr. Prescott," she said loudly. "If you're feeling all right, you can be on your way."

Both Parker and Susannah looked over at her as if surprised to find her still standing there.

"Don't be churlish, Molly," Susannah chided. "We need to give Mr., ah, *Parker*—" she paused to flash him a smile "—time to recover."

Molly's frown deepened. "He's looking pretty darn healthy to me," she said. The coverlet had slipped down again, revealing their guest's well-sculpted chest with its sprinkling of chestnut-colored hair.

"Actually," Parker said slowly, "I was on my way out here to your place when I got lost in the canyon."

"Out here?" Susannah and Mary Beth chimed in unison. Mary Beth had not moved away from the door.

"What for?" Molly asked curtly at the same time.

"I heard you might be hiring." Parker turned to address Molly with his answer. Though he would prefer to continue looking at Susannah's dazzling smile, it was obvious that the oldest sister was the one he would have to deal with on matters of business. Her sisters might talk sweetly and smile at him, but if he wanted work he'd have to convince the unsociable Miss Molly.

Molly looked down at him in disbelief. "Hiring what?"

"Hands. Cowboys," Parker said, meeting her eyes with a steady man-to-man gaze.

"You're a wrangler?" she asked with a scornful laugh.

Damn, but the woman had an abrasive way about her. He kept his voice even. "No, ma'am, I don't reckon I am. But I can ride and I can shoot. When I'm not lying in bed after being half-frozen, I've got a strong back and two strong arms and I'm not afraid to work. I guess that qualifies me just about as well as any of the other men you got working here."

Molly suspected that Parker Prescott already knew that there were no other men working at the Lucky Stars. As he looked up at her with just a hint of challenge in those velvety eyes of his, she suspected he knew exactly how badly she needed an extra rider and an extra pair of strong arms. But she wasn't about to give him the satisfaction of telling him so. And she wasn't about to let him think that just because they needed a man around the place, he was free to come in here and seduce her sister right under her nose.

"Susannah, Mary Beth," she said in a tone that brooked no argument, "you two go downstairs. Mr. Prescott has obviously recovered, and I don't want to see either of you back in this room until he's left it."

"Are you going to let him work for us, Molly?" Susannah asked, ignoring her sister's threatening expression.

"When Mr. Prescott feels well enough to get up and...put some clothes on, he and I will discuss the matter. Now go on, get out of here."

"Your sisters are lovely," Parker observed, watching them leave. He knew at once that he'd said the wrong thing. Molly Hanks had probably had that thrown in her face more than once over the years—the contrast between the younger girls' grace and beauty and her own rather plain appearance and masculine ways. He could try to rectify his error by making up a compliment about Molly herself. But he had the feeling that she would detect the falsehood immediately and scorn him for it. He decided that frankness and honesty were the best approaches to the eldest Hanks sister.

"They're lovely, but I can assure you, I'm not here to corrupt them in any way. I'm just looking for somewhere to work through the winter, then I'll be on my way to California."

Molly had backed up several steps from the bed. Without looking at him, she said reluctantly, "Spring's when we need help the most. Roundup time."

She looked as if she would rather be eating a keg of nails than talking with him, but he sensed that she couldn't afford to let an able-bodied man go. "I'll stay through the spring if you need me," he said. "I have no particular schedule."

"Do you know anything about cattle?" she asked. Her voice took on a slightly wistful note. If her expression hadn't been so forbidding, he would have felt a touch of compassion. As Max McClanahan had said, Molly had had quite a burden thrust on her. She couldn't be more than early twenties, though it was hard to tell for sure behind that stern face and those oversize clothes.

He answered honestly with a shake of his head. "I'm willing to learn."

Molly sighed. "I reckon you already know that we need the help, Mr. Prescott." She turned to leave the room. "You can sleep here through the rest of the storm, then you're to move on out to the bunkhouse."

"Much obliged," he said. "And thank you for saving my hide yesterday."

As she reached the door, she spun around to face him. "Just don't make me regret it, mister. If I find you with your hands on my sisters, I'll personally toss you right back down that canyon and leave you there for buzzard meat."

Parker looked across the room at the girl who stood glaring at him from the doorway. He was tempted for a moment to make some kind of joking reply, as he would have with his own sister. When Amelia had been riled up about one of his childhood antics she had scolded him with the same brave scowl he now saw on Molly Hanks's face. But Amelia had never run a cattle ranch, and she had never cradled a buffalo rifle in her arms the way Molly had back in Canyon City. No, Molly Hanks was not Amelia. And he didn't think she would be teased into a good humor.

"I'll remember that, ma'am," he said, keeping his face serious.

"See that you do," she snapped, then disappeared down the hall.

Chapter Three

For the rest of the day Molly avoided the room where their visitor still rested. At the noon meal Smokey had reported that Prescott had been weak and dizzy when he'd gotten up that morning. Smokey had told him to get a few more hours of sleep. Molly busied herself in her father's office going over the ranch ledgers, hoping that the numbers would somehow have changed from the last time she had looked at them.

Every few minutes she found herself walking over to the window and staring outside. The snow had finally stopped, leaving a rolling landscape of white, dotted here and there by dark green firs. She usually found the first thick snow cover exhilarating, but today it just looked frozen and desolate. She didn't know if her restlessness and her strange mood were due to the bleak financial picture or to the knowledge that a strange man was sleeping in her father's bed.

After losing her place in a column of numbers for the fourth time, she slammed shut her father's big leather account book and let loose with one of his favorite expletives. "Hell's bells!"

"Are you all right, Miss Molly?" Smokey's head peeked cautiously around the office door.

Molly ducked her chin in embarrassment. "Ah...of course. I've just finished up with the books."

Smokey looked reproachful as he entered the room, but made no comment.

"Did you want something, Smokey?"

The old cook nodded. "It's your friend upstairs."

"He's not my friend..." Molly began indignantly, but she stopped as she saw concern on Smokey's face. "What's the matter?"

"I reckon it's the chilblains, settling into his ears. They've swelled up something fierce and turned a color I ain't never seen before."

Molly got up quickly. Frostbite was not a light matter on the prairie. Frozen areas could get putrid within hours. People died of it. Damnation. She'd checked the man's hands. But she hadn't thought about the ears, hadn't noticed them under all that curly hair.

She followed Smokey up the stairs. There was no doctor in Canyon City, and even if there had been, it would have been hard work slogging through the drifts to get word to him. Most of the cowboys hereabouts did their own doctoring. They stitched their gashes with the same needles they used on their saddle leather. Molly had wanted to send for a doctor when her father had taken sick, but he'd refused. He'd lived fine without one, and he vowed he could die just as fine without one.

Susannah was sitting on the bed next to their visitor, her skirt fluffed up around her with at least a foot of petticoat showing plain as day. She held one of Parker Prescott's hands in the two of hers, just as Molly had the previous evening.

"Susannah!" Molly admonished.

Her sister looked unconcerned at the tone of rebuff. Her eyes were worried. "He's gone feverish, Molly. Smokey says it's the chilblains."

Molly finally looked at their guest's face. He was awake and making an attempt to smile, but his eyes were red and his cheeks were flushed. Among the tendrils of hair she could see his swollen ears. They were a mottled dark purple.

"We'll need some glycerine," she said at once, forgetting about Susannah's unseemly position on the bed. "And a feather to apply it." She looked back at Smokey. "And we'll need more blankets."

At her commanding tone Susannah dropped Parker's hand and slid off the side of the bed, Smokey disappeared down the hall and Parker himself sat up, weaving a little as he did so. "I'm sorry to be putting you all to such trouble," he said.

Molly walked over to him and bent for a closer look. Both ears were monstrous, the right a little worse than the left. She should have checked them last night. Heat radiated from his skin. "It'll be more trouble if you die on us, mister," she told him. "So just lie back down there and let us try to get you better."

He moved down under the covers once again and closed his eyes. "I don't intend to die on you, Miss Hanks," he said weakly.

"Now, that's the first sensible thing I've heard you say, Mr. Prescott." She turned to her sister. "Susannah, go make some hot plasters for his chest. We've got to sweat out this fever."

They worked on him straight through the supper hour. His fever rose as they piled on the coverings and by eight o'clock he was out of his head and ranting. He seemed concerned about his horse's leg and then asked for his sister. And finally, with anguish, he called for someone named Claire.

Molly had taken over the position next to him on the bed. She supposed she didn't look any more decorous than Susannah had earlier, but it didn't seem to make much difference now. She gnawed at her fingernails, trying to decide what to do. She'd known of cases where a finger or a toe had gone bad and had had to be cut off. But an ear? The mere thought made her shudder.

Neither Smokey nor her sisters were of much help. Smokey sat in a chair on the other side of the bed and looked mournful. "Nice-looking young feller," he said with a shake of his head. "It's a low-down shame."

"He's not going to die, is he, Molly?" Mary Beth asked for what must have been the twentieth time in two days.

Molly resisted making an angry comment. Mary Beth was the baby of the family and approached life with a bit more trepidation than her two sisters. "We won't let him die, Mary Beth," she answered her sister resignedly, hoping that she was telling the truth. They'd built the fire up to a blaze and shut the hall door, so it was steaming hot in the room. Their patient was drenched in sweat. Molly walked over and wiped his forehead. He snapped his head back and forth underneath the wet cloth.

"I'm not giving you up, Claire," he said almost lucidly. Then he reached up, grasped Molly's wrist with a surprisingly strong grip and moaned, "Noooo."

Was Claire a former sweetheart? she wondered. Or a current one who was awaiting him in California? He had said that he had no schedule, which didn't sound like a man on his way to be reunited with a lover. Either way, it was of no concern to her, Molly told herself.

Smokey got up from his chair and walked over to the bed. "I hate to say this, Miss Molly, but I think we better cut the danged things off."

"Cut what off?" Mary Beth asked, her eyes wide.

"Them ears."

All three girls looked at the sick man with horror.

"Have you ever seen it done, Smokey?" Molly asked.

The cook shook his head. "Heard of it, though. And I've seen 'em chop off plenty of fingers and toes. If we don't do it, the pizen could go right to his head."

"Blood poisoning, you mean."

"Yup. Right to his brain."

He waited, looking at Molly. Susannah and Mary Beth were looking at her, too. Why did it always have to be her decision? "Would you know how to do it, Smokey?" she asked.

"Cut 'em off, stitch 'em up, I reckon."

Smokey's surgical technique obviously left something to be desired. But what if they waited and the *pizen*, as Smokey had said, did travel into his brain? A man could live without ears, she supposed, but she was curiously reluctant to maim the handsome stranger.

"No. We'll wait," she said finally.

Smokey shook his head gravely but didn't say anything. After a few moments he returned to his seat near the door. Another quarter of an hour passed. No one spoke, but Molly knew they all were thinking about her decision, wondering if it would cost Parker Prescott his life.

She wiped sweat from her forehead and felt it under her arms. "It's so hot in here he's like to suffocate," she said irritably.

"But he's got the fever. We've got to keep him warm," Mary Beth protested.

Susannah was dozing in the rocking chair by the fire. She opened her eyes and said sleepily, "Just 'cause he's got himself frostbit doesn't mean we should roast him to death, if you ask me."

Molly straightened from the bed and made another decision. "Open the door, Smokey, and let's get some of these blankets off him."

Smokey looked doubtful. "He could take a fatal chill."

"Well, his skin's hot as a branding iron right now, and he's delirious. I have a feeling he'd feel better if we cooled him down a little."

Smokey opened the door, and a chilly whoosh of air blew into the room. They pulled the stack of covers off him, leaving only the quilt and one blanket. Almost immediately his tossing and moaning subsided. As the room cooled, Molly felt calmer. She put another coat of glycerine over the swollen ears and wiped his face again with the cool cloth. His breathing grew deeper, more even.

After several minutes Molly said in a soft voice, "I think he's fallen asleep." She looked around the room. "Why don't you all go to your rooms and get some rest? I'll sit with him."

"You were up with him last night, Miss Molly," Smokey protested. "I'll stay by him tonight."

Molly shook her head. "I'm not tired. If I need you during the night, I'll knock on your door."

"You can knock on mine, too, Molly," Susannah said in a subdued voice.

Molly looked up at her sharply. Even when their father had been so sick, Susannah had not been willing to allow her beauty sleep to be disturbed.

"I'd not mind sitting up with him," Susannah added. Her eyes regarded the sick man with concern and something more.

"He's breathing easier now," Molly said, motioning toward the bed. "I think I'll be all right with him."

With final glances at the sleeping man, her sisters and Smokey left the room. Molly pulled the rocker close to the bed and sat down. She hoped she'd done the right thing by cooling down the room, she thought groggily as she pushed the chair back and forth. She hoped the fever would break overnight. The old rocker creaked rhythmically.... She hoped she wouldn't have to cut off her patient's ears.... Her head lolled against the chair cushion.... She hoped she had misread the look in Susannah's eyes....

Parker's mouth tasted as if he'd eaten a dead squirrel. His head pounded, and his ears felt as if someone had stuffed them full of cotton. He was still in the bedroom of the Hanks's deceased father, even though the sunshine through the slats of the window meant that the storm had long since ended. He must have been so plumb tired that the fierce Miss Hanks had decided to extend her charity a few more hours. For some reason, he could remember little of the previous day, other than the fact that Molly Hanks had threatened to turn him into buzzard meat if he touched her sisters. He smiled. She had a right tender way about her, that one.

After a moment of debate he decided he would have to move his head. The prospect did not please him, but he had to move some part of his body, and he might as well just start right in where it hurt. Nausea hit him as he turned to one side, but he controlled it as he focused on the woman in the chair beside him. Not the termagant older sister, but Susannah, looking pretty as spring in a bright yellow dress with flounces of lace from the high neck to just above where the tightly fitted bodice showed off her full... Parker blinked twice. He was in a strange place, coming out of some kind of delirium, weak and disoriented, yet he could feel his body reacting to Susannah's female perfection. Perhaps her sister had been right. Perhaps he should be left for buzzard meat.

"You're awake," Susannah exclaimed.

"Have I..." Parker stopped to swallow down the fuzz in his mouth. "Have I slept long?"

"You were out of your head yesterday afternoon and into the night. We didn't know if you were going to make it. Smokey wanted to cut off your ears, but Molly wouldn't let him."

She had jumped up and come to the side of the bed, speaking excitedly. Parker's head throbbed. "Cut off my *ears?*" he asked, not certain he had heard correctly.

"They're frozen," Susannah said with a frown, her excitement decreasing.

He raised a hand to the side of his head and encountered a large, sticky mass that seemed to have no relation to the rest of his body. He looked up at Susannah in dismay.

"Don't touch them or they might fall off," she said quickly, and he pulled his hand away as if he had been burned.

He tried to bring the rest of the room into focus at the same time as he tamped down another wave of sickness. "Have you been beside me all night?" he asked her.

She hesitated a moment. "Molly was helping, too," she said finally.

He smiled. "I owe you a big debt."

She stood and leaned across the bed, putting a cool hand against his forehead. "Last night you were burning up with fever. You seem cool enough now."

He wasn't feeling cool. Her chest pressed gently against his arm as she bent over him. She smelled faintly of lemon. Even still weak from a night of fever he felt a surge of desire. He bit his lip until she pulled back. It might be harder than he had thought to keep his promise to Molly Hanks through the long winter.

She was looking at his ears. It was odd, but he couldn't feel them. He carefully touched first one side, then the other. "You were serious about cutting them off?" he asked.

Susannah nodded. "They've got the chilblains, Smokey says, and the pizens are what made you go out of your head."

"Do you have a mirror?"

"I . . . I don't think you want to see them, Mr. Prescott. They're just about every shade of the rainbow this morning."

Parker grinned. "Sounds pretty. But didn't we agree that you're to call me Parker?"

Susannah nodded. "Molly might have something to say about it, though. She gets nervous when we start getting too familiar with anyone wearing pants—except for her, of course," she added with a giggle.

"Well, at least you can call me Parker when we're by ourselves, Susannah."

"Which isn't going to be often," a blunt voice said from the doorway.

Parker jumped, sending a spiral of pain from the base of his neck up to the top of his head. Molly Hanks stalked across the room and looked down at him. "You look as if you plan on sticking around for the winter after all, Mr. Prescott," she said. Her blunt comment from the door had made him expect to see her upset, but she actually sounded pleased to see that he was recovering.

"Thanks to you and your sister," he said. "I'm beholden to you both."

"Just get yourself healthy enough to help out around here and remember what we talked about yesterday. That's all the thanks I ask."

He started to nod but thought better of it. He wouldn't move his head again unless he had to. "I probably owe you my life," he said. "And I understand that I definitely owe you my ears." Smiling didn't hurt, so he turned the full force of one of his best on Molly. He saw immediately that it had some effect. She might dress tough and talk tough, but he had the feeling that underneath, Molly Hanks was not so very different from her two sisters.

"We'll keep putting on the glycerine," she said, ducking her head to hide the flush that had crept over her face. "But the swelling's gone down some from last night. I think they'll be all right."

Smokey appeared in the doorway. "He's doing better?" he asked in his gravelly voice.

Molly turned around with a smile. "Yes. I think we've got those pizens on the run."

The cook gave a satisfied nod. "You've got a visitor."

"A visitor? Through this snow?"

"Mr. Dickerson. The son."

"Jeremy or Ned?"

Smokey grimaced. "Mr. High-and-Mighty. Jeremy."

Without appearing aware of her actions, Molly smoothed her hair with both hands. "Tell him I'll be down directly," she said.

"I told him to wait in the parlor, but he says he wants to come—"

From behind him an authoritative voice interrupted. "What's going on here, Molly? They told me you're caring for a stranger in your father's room."

The man who pushed past Smokey to enter the room was about Parker's size. He was dressed well in a black pin-striped suit and string tie. His boots were polished and the hat he held in his hand would have set most cowboys back three months' pay.

Molly straightened at his approach. "I don't mean to be rude, Jeremy, but if Smokey asked you to wait downstairs, you should have done so."

Parker felt oddly proud to hear her stand up to him. The man was obviously not used to following orders. Gritting his teeth against the pain in his head, he sat upright in the bed. He didn't want to be flat on his back when he made Jeremy Dickerson's acquaintance.

Dickerson smiled at Molly. Both his straight black hair and black mustache were neatly trimmed. In spite of riding from somewhere through fields of new snow, he had not a hair out of place. "Forgive my eagerness to see you, my dear," he said to her. She did not flush as she had when Parker had smiled at her earlier.

"It's no matter," she muttered.

Dickerson strode over to the bed and stared at Parker, then addressed Molly as if he were some sort of dumb animal. "Where'd he come from? And why have you got him here in Charlie's room?"

Parker couldn't tell if Molly was irritated by the tone of authority. She was not bristling as she had upon occasion with Parker himself. She answered evenly, "He's our new hand, and he's recovering from frost-bite."

Jeremy looked down his nose. "He looks healthy enough to me."

Hoping he wouldn't be sick, Parker leaned forward and extended his hand. "Parker Prescott," he said. "Pleased to make your acquaintance."

Dickerson looked taken aback by Parker's move, but he recovered and halfheartedly shook his hand. Then he turned back to Molly. "I don't like the idea of a stranger staying here in the house with you girls. It's not the same as when your father was under the same roof to protect you."

Now there was a definite bristle in the set of Molly's shoulders. She ignored his comment, but stayed calm as she said, "Why don't we go on downstairs and have some hot coffee, Jeremy?" She started moving toward the door. "I can't believe you came here through all this snow."

"I just wanted to be sure everything was all right...."

Dickerson followed Molly out the door, and Parker said to his back, "Nice to meet you, too."

Susannah giggled and stuck her tongue out at the retreating pair.

"Who was that charming fellow?" Parker asked.

Susannah's expression grew sober. "That charming fellow," she said, "is my future brother-in-law."

Chapter Four

Parker's dark eyebrows shot up. "He's engaged to your sister?"

"Well, not exactly. But he expects to marry her. The Dickerson ranch adjoins ours, and it's something our pa always talked about with Jeremy's pa, Hiram."

Parker sank back into his pillow. He'd been holding himself up with his arms and they were starting to quiver. It was amazing how weak a man could grow in just a couple of days. He couldn't say why the news that Molly Hanks had a serious suitor seemed so astounding, but it did. "We *are* talking about Molly?" he asked Susannah.

"Molly's the one he wants, all right. You see, even though Papa left the Lucky Stars to the three of us, Molly is—how do they say it legally?—*executor* of the property, even if Mary Beth and I get husbands of our own, which isn't likely the way she greets every man coming within a mile of the place with that rifle of hers."

"It's an impressive weapon."

Susannah grinned at him. "Didn't scare you off, though, did it?"

Parker relaxed and enjoyed the sheer pleasure of watching her smile. "It would take something mighty powerful to warn me off a lady as pretty as you, Susannah. Though if your father had been behind the barrel, I might have had to think it twice."

Susannah's expression became thoughtful. "Well, now, there you go. I guess what Molly says is true."

"What's that?"

"That the only things men take seriously are other men. They won't believe a woman is ever a threat."

"I didn't mean—" Parker began in apology, but Susannah interrupted him.

"I can assure you, Parker, if Molly had thought you represented a danger to us, she'd be fully capable of sending a ball spinning right through your middle."

Her smile had faded, and Parker realized that, while she was not as tough as her older sister, there was a little more than spun sugar to Susannah herself.

"I'll keep that in mind," he answered sincerely.

Susannah smiled again. "Not that Molly's ever actually shot anyone, you understand. I just know that she'd do it if the moment came. Molly always does what has to be done, no matter what."

"An admirable quality."

She gave a pretty little shrug. "I guess. But that's enough about Molly." She flounced down on the side of the bed. "You're not too tired, Parker? Do you want me to stay awhile?"

He reached for one of her slender hands. "I'd be honored, Mistress Hanks," he said with exaggerated reverence.

Susannah giggled and gave a little bounce on the bed. "Oh, Parker, it's been gloomy and dull around here since Papa died. I'm so *very* glad you've come."

* * *

By the next day Parker had recovered sufficiently to leave his bed, at least to take care of the most urgent of his personal needs. Once he had regained consciousness, it had at times been agony awaiting the appearance of Smokey so that he could ask for help in using the night jar that sat discreetly tucked under Mr. Hanks's carved washstand. But he'd be darned if he was going to start his stay on the Lucky Stars by involving any of its three owners in such matters.

He'd spent a few moments musing over what he'd do if Smokey rode off somewhere for several hours. Asking Mary Beth was out of the question. She hadn't ventured within five feet of the bed, and mostly watched him as if he had arrived from another planet. Although the few times she did send a shy smile his way, it had been mighty sweet.

He'd have to choose between Molly and Susannah. He reckoned Molly would be downright belligerent about having to deal with such intimacies. On the other hand, Susannah, even though she was what his mother used to call "a decent girl," gave the impression that she would be willing to get that intimate and more, if he led the way. As he lay helpless on his back, he wasn't sure which scared him more.

Fortunately, it never came to the test. He was up and around, still dressed only in an old nightshirt of their father's that Molly had pulled out of the big mahogany wardrobe and given to him without comment.

Susannah poked her head in the door. "You're walking!"

"Like a hundred-year-old man," Parker said with a scowl. "I can't seem to get my strength back."

"You were very ill, Parker. Give yourself a little time." She crossed the room and pulled his arm through one of hers. "Lean on me. We'll take a stroll."

With Susannah supporting him, they slowly walked to the end of the narrow upstairs hall. Parker looked down to watch his unsteady footing as they made their way along the Persian runner that covered the center of the polished wood floor. It was an elegant carpet, darkly patterned, that suited the dark wood of the paneled walls. Parker wished his sister could be here to see this house. It might change her opinion of the Wild West. She'd seen only two homes in her short stay in the Black Hills—his crude log cabin and Mattie Smith's place. Mattie's had been nice enough, but nothing like the Lucky Stars ranch house. And besides, it was a brothel, which meant that poor Amelia had spent most of her visits wondering which direction not to look.

"You have a lovely place, Susannah," he said.

"Papa was proud of his home. Some of the things here have come all the way from the Orient."

"And now it all belongs to you and your sisters?"

Susannah looked reflective. "Even though I grew up here, I always felt as if it belonged more to Papa than to any of us. And now to Molly."

"But you inherited it equally, you said."

"I suppose. I guess we just all assume that Mary Beth and I will leave here some day, whereas Molly won't. Molly will *never* leave the Lucky Stars," she added more firmly.

They had reached the end of the carpeting and started back. Parker would be glad to hit the bed again. A great hired hand he was turning out to be—

he could walk all of fifty feet and then he had to sit down. "Anyway, it's a wonderful place."

"One of the biggest ranch houses in Wyoming Territory," Susannah said with a touch of the pride she had attributed to her father.

"I don't doubt it." He gazed up at the huge carved beams of the vaulted two-story ceiling, then he slipped his arm out of Susannah's to lean on the railing that overlooked the imposing living room. He hoped it appeared that he was examining the impressive architecture of the house, but actually he just wanted to rest a moment. The balustrade would take more of his weight than he was willing to throw on Susannah's slender arm.

As he took in a deep breath, there was a pounding on the front door beneath them. Susannah joined him at the railing and they both peered down as her older sister crossed under them to answer the door.

"Why, Jeremy, what a surprise." Molly did not sound too enthusiastic. "To what do we owe the honor of two visits in two days?"

Jeremy moved a step forward, expecting Molly to usher him into the house. When she didn't move, he was forced to retreat slightly. "I'm always eager to see you, Molly, if that's what you mean. But today I came to be sure that cowboy was out of your father's room."

Molly cocked her head. "Why am I having trouble understanding how that is any of your business, Jeremy?" Her voice had a restrained calmness that Parker had already come to recognize as more dangerous than her explosions of temper.

Evidently Jeremy could also read her mood. He took yet another step back—all the way onto the porch—took off his expensive hat and spoke with a cajoling tone. "Now, Molly, my dear. You know that I care about everything that goes on with you and your sisters here at the ranch. Why, Pa and Ned and I feel as if we owe it to poor Charlie, rest his soul, to watch out for y'all."

When Jeremy Dickerson started in with his *y'alls*, Molly knew that he wanted something. The Dickersons had been Southerners long ago before the move to Wyoming, and Jeremy could pour on the honey when he had a mind to. Molly didn't know why it riled her so, or why she should be upset that he had come to check up on her. It was, in fact, a neighborly thing to do. None of them knew Parker Prescott. He might be a thief or a scoundrel. He could have murdered them all in their beds by now. She gave a little laugh at the absurdity of the idea and stepped back to let Jeremy enter. "Well, as long as you're here, come sit awhile."

Jeremy smiled, evidently pleased that his charm had smoothed Molly's prickly disposition one more time. But then he unwisely returned to his first topic. "Honestly, my dear, I don't like that new man of yours. I can read people, you know, and he's not the sort you want around here."

"You mean I should hire one of the dozens of others I have clamoring on my doorstep?"

"I've offered to lend you workers," he reminded her.

"I don't want to borrow from you, Jeremy. I thought I'd made that clear. I'll run this ranch on my own and I'll have my own help. Hiring Mr. Prescott is just a start."

"I don't like him," Jeremy repeated.

From above them, Parker and Susannah listened in amused silence. Parker leaned over and whispered in her ear, "Your neighbor doesn't like me, Susannah. Should I be devastated?"

She smiled broadly, causing two tiny dimples to appear in her smooth cheeks. "Isn't he an overbearing *prig?*" she whispered back.

"I guess that's as good a word as any."

Susannah leaned her head back and gave Parker a long look. "Let's play a little," she said slyly.

Parker looked puzzled at her suggestion, but she only smiled, pulled his arm off the railing and draped it around her neck. Then she moved close to him. He shifted self-consciously. Parker wasn't sure if Susannah was aware of how her breasts pressed against the thin lawn of his nightshirt, but *he* certainly was.

"You see, Parker," she said loudly. "You're getting so much stronger. I barely have to hold you."

Molly and Jeremy turned their heads in unison to look up to the second-floor balcony. From their position beneath the railing, Parker and Susannah's posture must have looked even more intimate than it felt. "Susannah!" Molly gasped.

Susannah turned her head casually, then gave a wave down to the onlookers. "Oh, hello, Molly... Jeremy. I was just helping Parker take a little walk. Doesn't he look *so much stronger?*"

Her voice dripped. Parker had finally caught on to Susannah's definition of "play" and had trouble restraining a smile. "Good afternoon, Mr. Dickerson," he called down, meeting the neighbor's glaring dark eyes with a calm stare.

"Susannah," Molly said angrily, "if *Mr. Prescott* is that much recovered, I'll send Smokey up directly to see that he gets some clothes on and gets moved out to the bunkhouse.''

Susannah's pretty lips turned down. "You can't put him out there yet, Molly. He's still recovering."

"He can recover outside," she snapped.

Parker, his bout of weakness gone, pulled Susannah away from the edge of the railing. "It's all right," he said to her in a low voice. He leaned over the edge one last time. "Nice to see you again, Mr. Dickerson," he called. Then he guided Susannah toward the master bedroom. "I'm feeling quite good, actually."

Susannah frowned. "Molly's such a stick at times. I'm afraid I've made a muddle of things. She's making you leave because of the show we put on out there."

Parker grinned. "It doesn't matter. It was worth it to see the expression on Dickerson's face when he looked up and saw you in my arms."

She giggled. "It *was* funny. I thought he was going to swallow his tongue. Well, I guess I should leave you alone to get dressed," she concluded reluctantly, and left the room.

The fickle November weather had turned seductive once again. The light breeze felt almost warm as Parker made his way with Smokey out to the Lucky Stars bunkhouse. The snow was slippery and wet under their boots. In the sunlight the drifts were shrinking into hard, icy mounds. A small waterfall of snow melting from the roof cascaded down alongside the door of the Spartan wood bunkhouse. No Persian rugs here. He followed Smokey inside, ducking to avoid the cold drips.

"Home sweet home, lad. It's not as comfortable as up at the house, but I guess you've probably seen worse in your day."

Parker made no reply. Though his parents had spent most of the family money trying to convert the world to their various causes of abolitionism, temperance and so on, the money from his father's bank had been enough that the Prescott family had lived in considerable luxury compared with most of the rest of the country. Except for his few months in the Black Hills, Parker had never awakened in the morning without stepping on a carpet, never had to go out the back of the house in the middle of a January freeze to relieve himself. He'd never gone to sleep in a room without real windows with linen drapes and a real bed with a silk coverlet. "I reckon this will be just fine, Smokey," he said, surveying the barren room. There were five bunk beds lining the walls and a big round table in the center. In one corner of the room was a stack of wood piled next to a rusty iron stove.

"You can light up the stove," Smokey said. "And I'd take the bunk right next to it, if I was you. This thaw's not going to last, and it can get colder'n a whore's heart in here."

Parker grinned at the old man. "Now, just what would you know about whores, Smokey?"

The cook scraped a boot along the dusty wood floor. "I know a thing or two about them, you young whippersnapper. Just because I'm long in the tooth doesn't mean—"

He stopped his sentence dead and stared over Parker's shoulder.

"I see you're making Mr. Prescott comfortable, Smokey," Molly said in a voice that was as frosty as the room.

"Shucks, Miss Molly. You shouldn't sneak up on a body like that. We was having a conversation not fit for a lady's ears."

Parker had the fleeting impression that Molly had set her face in those stern lines in order to keep from laughing, but when she started to speak again he decided he must have been mistaken.

"There's not a conversation that goes on around this ranch that's not fit for my ears, Smokey. I've told you that before."

"Yes, ma'am." Smokey did not seem to take the dressing-down too seriously.

"If you're finished here, I'd like to speak with Mr. Prescott."

Smokey looked from her to Parker, then gave a nod and made his way around her and out the door.

Parker waited for Molly to speak, but she seemed to be uncharacteristically at a loss for words. She looked at the ground, then back up to his face with a sweep of long eyelashes several shades darker than her light brown hair. Her eyes were as blue as her sisters', he noted. More so. Or perhaps it was just the difference in intensity. Finally he said, "You wanted to talk to me?"

She bit her lip. "How are you feeling, Mr. Prescott? I mean . . . ah . . . are you sufficiently recovered to . . ."

"To be cast out into a freezing bunkhouse?" Parker finished for her, amused at what was apparently a rare attack of conscience.

"I just wanted to be sure you wouldn't get sick on us again," she said stiffly.

"I don't think I'd dare risk it, ma'am."

"And why's that, Mr. Prescott?"

"Because, ma'am," he said respectfully, "I might end up staked out for buzzard meat in Copper Canyon."

Molly gave a half smile and the lashes swept down again. "I did mean the warning about my sisters, Mr. Parker."

"I know that, Miss Molly. May I call you that?" He ducked his head a little to catch her eyes, then gave her one of his made-for-charm smiles. "Seeing as how there're three Miss Hankses, it could get confusing around here if we insist on all the formalities."

Molly took in a little gulp of air. She would rather swill the pigs on a ninety-degree day than admit it, but she reckoned that Parker Prescott was just about the handsomest thing she'd ever seen. There'd been a heap of cowboys who'd come and gone at the Lucky Stars since Molly had been old enough to notice, but there'd never been one like him. Of course, Canyon City was hardly the place to find the pick of the crop. But even when she'd traveled to Denver with Papa, where one might expect to find other "gentlemen," as her sisters described them, she'd not seen the like. He was waiting for an answer. What had he just asked her?

"Ah . . . three Miss Hankses. Yes, I see your point. I suppose Miss Molly would be acceptable, Mr. Prescott."

Parker leaned back against the table, crossed his arms and studied her. "So then . . . I guess you'll have to call me Parker. Or else it would be too impertinent of me to call you Miss Molly."

Molly felt as if the entire conversation was out of her control. It was an unaccustomed sensation, and one she was not sure she liked. "Fine. Names aren't of that great importance out here, anyway, Mr.—Parker. I suppose back East you pay more attention to those things."

"I suppose."

"You *are* from the East?"

Parker nodded. "New York."

Molly's eyes widened. "New York City?"

"Mmm," he confirmed with another nod.

She wanted to say, *What in tarnation are you doing in Canyon City, Wyoming, Mr. Parker Prescott?* But the unwritten law of the West was you didn't ask about things that were none of your business. So instead, she said, "Well, I just wanted to see if you were settled in."

"And to see if I was healthy enough to sleep out here in the cold."

Her brief moment of remorse or whatever it had been appeared to be over. "There's a wagonload of wood out there. As soon as you're feeling up to it, I suggest you start chopping."

Parker let his grin break through. This was the real Molly Hanks. He was beginning to consider it a challenge to see how riled he could get her without risking losing his job. It was an unfair contest, really, because he knew that she wouldn't have kept him on at all if she hadn't needed him desperately. "I'll do that, ma'am," he told her.

"So you do feel recovered?" She took a step closer to him. He unfolded his arms and grasped the edge of the table as she reached up to touch one of his ears. The swelling had gone down, but their color was still far from normal. Her hand was surprisingly gentle. She smelled of saddle soap.

Suddenly she seemed to be aware of how close their bodies had become. She backed away with a little stumble and her voice once again lost its power. "If you start to feel dizzy or anything, you let us know."

"Yes, ma'am."

She looked uncertainly from him to the cold stove. "Can you get a fire started in that thing?"

"Yes, ma'am."

The gear he had packed on his horse was already piled in a heap in the middle of one of the bunks. "I'll have Smokey bring you out some warmer bedding," she said.

"That would be very kind." There was uncertainty in her eyes. Parker had the feeling that if he wanted to plead his case, she would change her mind and tell him to come back over to the big house. But as he was considering the possibility, he remembered the reason for his exile, and apparently she did, too.

"I did warn you about my sisters."

"Yes, ma'am."

"I mean...Susannah told me that it was all her fault and that she was just trying to bother Jeremy...." She was still wavering. It was almost as if she was trying to give him an argument to change her mind. But Parker had decided he would not press the issue at the moment. If he talked her into letting him stay up at the house a few more days, then he'd be on the owing side. This way, he had Miss Molly feeling sorry for him, and more than a little guilty. Leave a little on the table, his father always used to say. You never know when you'll need to call in a debt. Parker had come west to avoid working the rest of his life at the family bank, but he supposed that he'd picked up some of his father's negotiating skills somewhere along the line.

"I don't believe Miss Susannah has a very high opinion of your Mr. Dickerson," he said, making no mention of his accommodations.

Molly hesitated for another minute, then sighed. "He's not *my* Mr. Dickerson. He's just a neighbor who is good enough to help us out now and then. Susannah thinks he's a little overbearing at times."

"I think I might learn to agree with her."

She backed up to the door and grabbed the latch behind her. "Mr. Prescott...*Parker*," she began firmly. "When I agreed to your employment, you said you were willing to learn. Perhaps your first lesson should be to remember that you are now a hired hand. You're on this ranch to work. It's not your job to have opinions about our neighbors, or our friends, or my sisters and me, for that matter."

"I'll keep that in mind," he said mildly. "Anything else?"

"No." She looked around the room. "Smokey will bring you out some breakfast in the morning."

"Much obliged."

She gave a brisk nod, then opened the door and left. Parker grinned at her back. The oldest Hanks sister talked a tough game, but she wasn't as hard as she looked. She hadn't come out here to see that he was settled. She'd come because she was worried about him. There'd been genuine concern in her eyes when she'd checked on his ears. Oddly enough, he could still feel the traces of her fingers in his hair.

He pushed himself away from the table and headed for the stove. Wincing at the stiffness in his joints, he knelt beside the woodpile and began to stuff logs into the iron potbelly.

He found a box of matches on top of the stove and lit the fire. The dry wood took immediately, snapping warmth out into the room. Parker began to hum a little tune. It was an interesting discovery. Miss Molly wasn't so tough after all. When she'd opened the door to leave, her hands on the latch had been trembling like a frightened rabbit.

Chapter Five

Parker finished off the last of the flapjacks Smokey had brought out to him, then gulped his coffee. It had already grown cold in its tin cup. He hadn't bothered to stoke up the stove, which had gone out during the night. The mild weather appeared to be holding and the temperature in the bunkhouse was tolerable. In fact, the cold night seemed to have done him some good. His body was almost back to normal, and for the first time since he'd started down into Copper Canyon his head felt clear.

He'd awakened at dawn and unpacked his gear, stowing it neatly in the big, empty cupboard. Then Smokey had shown up with the food, grumbling that he saw no reason why Parker shouldn't just come on up to the house and eat with the rest of them.

"It was different when Mr. Hanks was around. This place was full up back then," he'd said, looking around at the empty bunks. "The cowhands ate at the cookhouse out back. Charlie liked to keep them away from his three treasures, you know." Smokey looked older suddenly as his eyes softened in memory of his boss and friend. He paused for a minute, then continued briskly, "Can't say as I blame him. About the hands, I mean. Some of them galoots I wouldn't invite to my privy, much less my dinner table.''

He'd stayed to reminisce a few more minutes about "those days" before finally moving stiffly out the door, shaking his shaggy gray head. Parker had the feeling that Smokey, as much as he cared for his old boss's "three treasures," had no more belief than the townsfolk that three young women could run the Lucky Stars. Parker didn't share his pessimism. Growing up surrounded by female suffragists and temperance crusaders, he knew a woman could be as bright and as strong and as stubborn as a man. Hell, one look at Molly Hanks should be proof enough of that. But it didn't seem as if anyone was willing to give her a chance.

He pushed aside the breakfast dishes and stood. He'd do what he could to help, at least through spring, though he wasn't at all sure just how much help he would be. He'd made it clear to Molly that he wasn't an experienced cowhand, but he hadn't dared tell her the whole truth—that he'd never so much as been near a cow. A *steer*. Whatever the hell they called them out here. With a sigh he reached over to the bunk and snatched up his hat. He supposed she'd find out soon enough.

Molly knew that she had not been in the best of tempers at breakfast that morning. She'd snapped at Susannah and even had a harsh word for Mary Beth when both her younger sisters had argued that their new hired hand should be invited to take meals with them in the house.

"It's downright silly to try to have a mess for one cowboy," Susannah had said with a slight pout.

And Molly had to admit that her sister had a point. But she just wasn't ready to sit down at a table with Parker Prescott. For one thing, she didn't trust the way he looked at Susannah, his brown eyes lit and dancing. And then there were the odd sensations Molly herself had been having. Scary feelings, like a sudden chilly wind in a mountain pass. She'd had one yesterday when she'd seen Parker's arms around her sister up on the balcony. And again last night, after weaving her fingers through the soft waves of his hair. She'd lain awake for what had seemed like hours last night trying to figure out what was wrong with her. Which undoubtedly had not helped her crankiness this morning.

The meal had ended without resolving the issue. Molly supposed that eventually she'd invite Parker to eat with them, but she'd like to feel a little more in control of things before she did. Part of the problem was the unavoidable intimacy of their first few meetings. She'd scarcely seen the man dressed, for pity's sake. It would undoubtedly be easier once their roles as boss and hired hand were firmly established.

She gave a last swipe to the breakfast platter and hung the dish towel on the rack. The sooner the better, she reckoned. Of course, if Parker was still feeling poorly, she couldn't put him to work yet. But if he was recovered enough, she might as well get him started. It was a nice warm morning. They could get a lot done. And they could establish once and for all just exactly who was the boss.

Parker could tell that his bout with frostbite and fever had taken a toll. Back in the Black Hills, when he'd been at his most enthusiastic about the mine, he'd worked for sixteen hours or more without a break, well into the late-summer twilight. But right now he felt much as he had when he'd been beaten up by Big Jim Driscoll's thugs after Claire's death. Every muscle was screaming.

He and Smokey had spent most of the morning baling, with Molly appearing every now and then to check up on them and add one more chore to their list. At noon Smokey had left to get dinner started, leaving Parker glumly eyeing the endless mound of hay left to bale. According to his new boss lady, after finishing with the hay, he was to shore up the timbers around the pigpen, then repair the chute at the end of the corral, put a new set of hinges on the bunkhouse door, clean the stable...what else? Parker plunged his baling fork into the ground and leaned backward, stretching out the muscles of his long back.

"Getting tired, cowboy?" Molly asked from behind him.

He turned around in annoyance. One of these days he was going to figure out how to hear her coming. "You part Indian or something?" he asked her.

She frowned. "No. Why?"

"'Cause you sure do know how to sneak up on a person."

"That's what you get for daydreaming on the job. I suppose you were pining away for whatever fancy pen-and-paper job you used to do back in New York City."

"I worked in a bank."

Molly gave a little laugh of triumph. "I suspected as much. Kind of hard to build up a sweat adding up numbers, isn't it?"

She was wearing her typical oversize pants, but thanks to the warmth of the day she had discarded her ever-present baggy jacket and was wearing a blouse that looked almost feminine. Certainly the curves molded by the silky fabric looked feminine. She wasn't as amply built as either of her sisters, but everything was most definitely in the right place.

Parker gave himself a shake. In Deadwood one night last spring when he'd been discouraged about his mine and homesick for his family back in New York, he'd sought solace at Mattie Smith's tidy main street brothel. There he'd met Claire Devereaux, an almost ethereal beauty who had grown up as an orphan when her parents drowned on the family's passage from France. She'd shared her hopes and dreams with Parker along with her perfect body, and he'd fallen irrevocably in love. When Claire had died in the dreadful smallpox epidemic that swept through Deadwood last fall, he'd thought it would be months—years, maybe—before he'd ever want a woman again. But it appeared that the body had a way of continuing to work even when the heart inside it was dead.

"I've built up a sweat or two in my day, Miss Molly," he answered her quietly.

Something had flickered behind his eyes that made Molly pause. Her head was telling her that she would never get the upper hand with Parker Prescott unless she stayed on the attack, but her resolve kept weakening. She hated to think that she was as silly as Susannah and Mary Beth, dazzled by his easy charm and New York manners. "Well, you'll sweat plenty while you're working here," she said finally. "But I suppose it wouldn't hurt to go easy to start. Three days ago we didn't even know if you were going to live through the night."

"I'm ready to earn my keep." He pulled up the fork and stabbed at a pile of hay.

Molly watched him work for a minute. Who'd have thought a tenderfoot Easterner could have shoulders like that? She backed away. "No, really, Mr. Prescott. You can stop now and come in for dinner."

"Come in?"

She bit her lip. She'd set out this morning determined to establish her authority over her new hired hand. Instead, she felt even more tongue-tied than she had in the bunkhouse with him last night. "Yes, come in. Inside. We don't have time to be settin' up separate dining for just one lone cowboy," she said, echoing Susannah's arguments of the morning.

Parker turned toward her, the forkful of hay stopped in midair. "I'd be honored to join you and your sisters, Miss Molly, but only if you'll call me Parker."

She nodded.

"Fine. I'll just wash up, then, and change my shirt."

"No need for formalities at our table, Mr. Pres...Parker. We all know what a barn smells like."

Parker grinned at her. "So do I, but it doesn't mean I have to smell like one myself. There're barn smells and there are man smells, Miss Molly. You might enjoy learning the difference one of these days."

He threw the hay, fork and all, over onto the pile, then tipped his hat and walked away. Molly watched him head toward the bunkhouse, her cheeks flaming with a blush for the first time in her life.

* * *

After the first few moments it felt entirely natural to have Parker sitting at the big Lucky Stars dining-room table. Not long after Charlie Hanks's death, Smokey had taken to joining the girls there. Parker sat opposite him, next to Susannah, while Molly took the hostess position at the end. No one sat in their father's old place opposite her.

Their new hand's presence had enlivened the meal. Molly couldn't remember when the conversation had been so spirited, the laughter so frequent. Certainly not since Papa died. Parker seemed to know a lot about many things. He'd traveled all the way to Paris and had studied for a year at Harvard University before he'd become restless and returned to work at a bank in New York City. He was just a year older than Molly herself, but he'd seen and done wondrous things that she couldn't imagine doing in an entire lifetime.

Of course, it might be that he was showing off a bit for Susannah. His conversation had been directed her way often enough during the meal. Molly studied the pair as he leaned his dark head toward Susannah's blond one to catch something her sister was saying. Susannah was wearing a simple blue gingham gown today that made her eyes the deep blue of an autumn sky. The two made an attractive couple. Molly wondered if she should relax her guard a bit and see if anything developed between them. Susannah and Mary Beth had to find husbands at some point, and, goodness knows, there weren't many candidates to choose from around Canyon City. As Molly drummed absently with her spoon on the table, Susannah gave one of her magical little laughs, bringing a flare of response from Parker's bright eyes. It was an interesting thought . . . her sister and a Harvard man.

Suddenly he was addressing her. "So do you agree, Miss Molly?"

"I . . . I'm sorry. I guess I was daydreaming."

"Dangerous practice," Parker said gravely. A hint of a smile twitched his full lips. "You never know what kind of varmint might sneak up on you when you're daydreaming."

Molly gave a reluctant smile as Mary Beth explained, "Smokey was saying that with the weather this mild, the cattle should last until Christmas without extra food. Parker asked if you agreed."

Parker's gaze had moved back to Susannah. Molly took a deep breath. "Yes, I agree. And we'd better be right, because if we have a hard winter, we're going to lose some animals. We don't have too much supplementary feed left."

Without looking back at her, Parker said, "You've forgotten about the thousand bales Smokey and I put up this morning."

Smokey gave a great laugh that rumbled up from his belly to his beard. "It just *felt* like a thousand, lad. But you did a good job for your first day."

"You shouldn't make him work so hard yet, Molly," Susannah objected.

"He was dreadfully sick, remember?" Mary Beth added.

Parker looked from one sister to another. He really did feel fully recovered. After their leisurely dinner he was ready to get back to work, but he had the feeling that it was in his best interests not to take sides in a discussion among the three girls, even when he was the topic.

"I'm not *making* him work," Molly said. "I'm *paying* him to work. He's the one who wanted the job."

Susannah refused to give in. "You could at least let him ease into it a little. He's been working since dawn. That's enough for his first day. Why don't you let me take him out on a tour of the ranch?"

When she'd come in from talking with Parker before lunch, Molly had had exactly the same idea herself. Except that she'd thought *she* would be the one to show their new man around. An easy ride around the spread would allow Parker a little more time to rest up, and she had found the thought of spending an afternoon with him pleasantly challenging. But she'd seen the instant enthusiasm in his face at Susannah's suggestion, and she was sure it stemmed from the company not the ride. What male under the age of senility would not want to go riding with Susannah?

There was no trace left of the smile that had lit her face after Parker's teasing. "All right. He can take Midnight."

"Is something wrong with my horse?"

"Her legs swelled up after we pulled her out of the canyon. Nothing serious."

"I should take a look at her." When he'd had to leave Diamond in Canyon City, he'd hoped to be able to trade back for her some day. The big mare had been with him since he'd first arrived out West, and he had grown used to her company.

"Help yourself. But you'd do better on Midnight for your ride."

Parker noted that her voice sounded stiffer than usual. "Are you sure you won't be wanting to use Midnight yourself today?"

Molly pushed herself back from the table and stood. "Yes, I'm sure. Unlike some people, I need to stay around here and get some work done. If you'll excuse me..."

Then she turned and left the table, leaving the four staring after her.

"Maybe we shouldn't go," Parker said after a moment.

"Oh, pooh," Susannah scoffed. "Don't mind Molly. She's always grouchy."

"It'll be all right, Parker," Mary Beth said gently.

And Smokey added his assurance. "You go on ahead, boy. The work'll keep till tomorrow."

"I don't want Miss Molly to think I'm a shirker."

Susannah stood and grabbed his arm. "She won't think anything of the kind. It's just that Molly doesn't know what it means to have fun."

Parker followed docilely along as Susannah pulled him out of the dining room. For a moment he felt a pang of sympathy for the oldest Hanks sister. She was only a year older than Susannah, five years older than Mary Beth. He thought of his years growing up with Amelia. They were just a year apart, like Susannah and Molly. Often it had been just the two of them when their parents were off on one of their crusades. He'd protected Amelia, as Molly seemed to protect her sisters. But in return, Amelia had mothered him. They'd played, learned, fought, made up—experienced life together. His mind was still on the question as he and Susannah saddled up for their ride. Whose fault was it that Molly had grown up not knowing how to have fun?

* * *

Except where it had drifted up, the snow was almost gone. Obviously at this time of year, the warm weather wouldn't last. But as they rode around the periphery of the Lucky Stars, Susannah pointing out landmarks along the way, the day had the feeling of spring.

"Isn't it glorious?" Susannah shouted, flinging out her arms. And with Susannah in her black riding outfit and hat, her blond hair streaming out behind her, Parker decided that more than the weather was glorious.

They dismounted alongside a stream to let the horses drink and rest a spell. "This is called Cougar Creek," she told Parker. "But the most dangerous critters you ever see along here are the fat old coons that come down to wash up their supper."

They left their horses and started walking slowly downstream. "Do they really do that?"

"Sure they do. You really are a tenderfoot, aren't you? Haven't you ever seen a raccoon at a creek?"

Parker shook his head, then grinned at a sudden memory. "Back in Deadwood my sister put a berry pie out to cool in the creek by my cabin and a raccoon came along and ate the whole thing."

"Well, of course it did. What raccoon would pass up a fresh berry pie? Your sister must be as much of a tenderfoot as you."

"My sister's an Eastern lady. I don't think she'd ever fit in entirely out here. She's back in New York City now, with her new husband."

Susannah's face grew wistful. "I bet she has elegant clothes and talks fine."

"She can talk fine when she wants to, I guess. But she's not any more elegant than you or Mary Beth. I couldn't believe it when I saw the two of you standing in the street in Canyon City."

The ground was too wet to sit down, so they stopped and leaned their backs against twin birch trees whose branches were bare except for an occasional tenacious yellow leaf. Susannah looked up at the sky. "That's your Eastern charm talking, Parker Prescott. There's no way Mary Beth and I can compare to the ladies back in New York."

Parker recognized that the conversation was drifting from getting acquainted to flirtation, but he was enjoying himself too much to worry about it. He had no intention of letting it go too far, and Molly and her buffalo gun were safely back at the house, so what did it matter?

"I swear to you, Susannah," he said. "In all of New York, in all of Boston, even in Paris and London, I've never seen any girl prettier than you." He hadn't mentioned Deadwood. It was a beautiful fall afternoon and he was flirting with a lovely girl. It was not the moment to think of Deadwood or Claire.

Susannah pushed away from the tree with a little twirl and spun her way over to Parker. "Molly says I shouldn't believe it when men start to talk fancy, but I think I will anyway."

She nearly spun right into him and he reached out his arms to steady her. "Molly may be right, Susannah."

"Fiddle. I don't care if she is. I intend to enjoy listening to your fancy talk, Parker. I've never had the chance before—first there was Papa hovering over me, and now Molly. But I'm too old to have a nursemaid, and it's about time Molly understood that."

His hands were still gripping her upper arms and her flushed face was just inches from his. Parker took in a slow breath. Flirtation was one thing, proximity was another. He turned her around and placed her gently up against the tree, then took a long step back. "I'm sure Molly just wants to protect you. I feel that way about my sister. I worry about her. It's hard to stop worrying just because you've both grown up."

Susannah's lower lip stuck out a little, but instead of making her look petulant, it merely served to call attention to the ripeness of her mouth. "Sometimes I think she's jealous of us."

"Jealous?"

"Of me and Mary Beth, because we're...you know...the cowboys all say that we're the pretty ones."

Parker frowned. "But it seems as if your sister doesn't care about being pretty—doesn't even *want* to be."

Susannah looked at him as if he were a slow-witted child. "There's no such thing as a girl who doesn't want to feel pretty, at least sometimes, deep down."

Coming from Susannah, the sudden nugget of wisdom surprised Parker. In a different way, he realized he was being as prejudiced as the cowboys in town. He'd already categorized Molly as the smart one, Susannah as the pretty one. His mother would be ashamed of him. Hadn't she always taught him that each human being was made up of far too many layers to be put into a category?

"Well, maybe one of these days we can do something to make Molly feel pretty," he said lightly.

Susannah's serious moment was gone. She giggled and said, "I don't know how. If you try some of your sweet talk on her, she's like to lay you out flat."

"I wouldn't be able to let her get away with that, I'm afraid."

Susannah considered him for a moment, rocking back and forth against the tree trunk. "I think you'd do best to stick with me, Parker. You and Molly might really get into it one of these days."

"We might get into it if I stick with you, Susannah. Molly's warned me off you and Mary Beth. I'm surprised she agreed to let us ride alone together today."

Susannah gave a huff. "There! You see what I mean. How does she expect us to ever get a...I mean, get acquainted with any gentlemen...if she keeps them all away with threats?"

"Maybe that's something you should ask her."

He hadn't meant to say it quite like that. He'd resolved not to take sides between the sisters. Of course, he'd also resolved to keep his hands off Susannah, and that was proving far more difficult than he had expected. As she danced and squirmed against the tree trunk, not more than a yard from him, his feet were ready to take a step closer of their own volition. The palms of his hands itched to close around her silky hair. He had to force himself not to move.

"Well, maybe I just will," Susannah said, a frown marring the smooth skin of her forehead. "Maybe I will ask my sister exactly that."

While taking care to avoid the scattered patches of melting snow, Susannah and Parker raced their horses over the last long stretch of prairie toward the ranch house. The speed felt good. Parker laughed as the wind hit his face and his muscles moved in harmony with Molly's fine mount. He might be a novice at most things around the ranch, but he could ride. It had been one of the few activities his family had engaged in together back in the rolling countryside of upstate New York. It had been a while since he'd ridden just for the joy of it, and at the moment it seemed exactly the remedy he needed to take his mind off Susannah's unconscious invitation back by the stream.

"I think you should tell Molly that you're too sick to work more than half days," she shouted to him as they slowed their horses at the outer gate. "Then we could ride together every afternoon. There are still some more places I could show you. More private places."

Parker gave her a sideways glance. He had *thought* her invitation had been unconscious. But Susannah, though inexperienced, seemed to be one of those women who just had an instinct for this kind of thing. Whereas Molly turned shy and silent when things turned personal, Susannah reveled in it. Perhaps her sister's warnings were well-founded. A young woman as ready for loving as Susannah could get into a heap of trouble mighty fast.

"I'd love to ride out with you again, Miss Susannah, but I've got to show your sister that I can earn my wages around here."

"Now you've gone all formal on me again, Parker."

"I don't mean to. But you yourself agreed that we'd need to be more formal when other folks were around." He nodded toward the other end of the corral where Molly, Mary Beth and Smokey were standing with Jeremy Dickerson and three other men Parker didn't know.

"I wonder what's going on?" Susannah asked.

"We'd best find out."

They turned their horses around the corner of the rail. As they approached the group, Parker saw that they were standing around a pretty, light brown calf with a moon face.

"It's about time you two got back," Molly called, her voice harsh. Susannah made a face.

"Is something wrong?" Parker asked, jumping lightly from Midnight's back. The other two Dickersons were easy to recognize. The father and brother had Jeremy's same slick black hair and prominent nose. The other stranger was wearing a star on his rawhide vest.

All four men glanced at him with varying degrees of indifference, then the man with the badge spoke to Molly. "This little feller came wandering practically up to the Dickersons' front door this morning, Miz Hanks. It's not branded." His eyes were reproachful.

None of the shyness Molly had shown with Parker was in evidence as she faced the sheriff. "You know darn well, Sam Benton, that I couldn't round up my heifers for branding this fall because there wasn't a single blasted cowpoke west of the Mississippi who would hire on to help me."

"You can't keep track of cattle without branding," the sheriff said with a shake of his head.

"Well, what in tarnation was it doing all the way over at the Lazy D?"

The older Dickerson took a step toward Molly and put his arm across her shoulders. "Cattle wander, Molly. You know that. You've got to get yours marked up. If the weather holds, we'll come on over and help you out."

Molly hesitated. Parker had the feeling that she was more than a little reluctant to accept help from the Dickersons, even though it appeared that the old man was just trying to be neighborly.

So far none of the visitors had acknowledged Parker's presence. "How many men does it take?" he asked, not afraid to show his ignorance. There was no point in pretending to be something he wasn't.

All the heads turned toward him at once. "Who's that?" the older Dickerson asked Molly.

Parker stuck out his hand. "Parker Prescott. You're Hiram Dickerson, I presume."

After a minute's hesitation Hiram shook his hand. Then Parker offered it to the younger Dickerson brother, who accepted it more readily than his father. "Ned?" he confirmed with a smile and a nod. Finally he turned to the lawman. "Jeremy and I have already met, but I haven't had the pleasure, Sheriff."

Sheriff Benton was a big man, but middle age had shrunk his shoulders and increased his girth, making him a less formidable sight than he had been in his prime. He drew back as Parker took a step toward him and extended his hand. But finally he, too, shook it. Parker stepped back and surveyed the group. "So now that we're all acquainted, let's get back to the problem here. How many men does it take to do this branding procedure?"

They were looking at him as if he were some kind of unknown species, and Molly seemed to be enjoying their discomfiture. She laughed out loud. "Parker is our new hand," she told the group.

"It doesn't sound like you know much about wrangling, young man," the older Dickerson observed.

"I believe Mr. Prescott specializes more in the ladies than he does in cattle," Jeremy said with a sneer.

Parker met Jeremy's sharp eyes. So it was to be open battle. Right from the start. Well, that was all right with Parker. It never hurt to know where you stood with someone. He turned away from Jeremy and addressed his calm answer to the elder Dickerson. "I know nothing about wrangling, sir. But I've told Miss Molly here that I'll do my best to learn."

Jeremy gave a snort. "It's not exactly like dealing a deck of cards. This calf's almost four hundred pounds. You think you could throw her down and burn a brand on her?"

Parker gave Jeremy a quick up-and-down glance. Though the two were of similar height, Jeremy had a more slender build. In his three-piece suit and string tie he looked much less rugged than Parker in his worn Levi's and rough linen shirt. "I'd wager I could pull her down just about as quick as you could, Jeremy, my friend," he answered with a smile.

Jeremy did not smile back. He turned to Molly. "Don't be a stubborn fool, Molly. The snow will be blowing back in before long and then there'll be nothing we can do. Next spring you'll have a rangeful of year-old heifers wandering around with no identification."

"I'm hoping to have an early spring roundup," she said defensively.

"With what help? Cowboy Joe, here?" he asked with a dismissive nod toward Parker.

"If I offer enough money, I can get hands."

"And where do you get the money?"

It appeared that everyone but Jeremy could see that Molly was getting angrier every time he opened his mouth. Parker rocked back on his boot heels and waited for the explosion. He wasn't disappointed.

"That is none of your damn business, Mr. Dickerson."

"I'm just trying to—"

"And furthermore, the next time you come around here trying to tell me how to run my ranch, I'll take that fancy hat of yours and cram it down your throat."

Susannah and Mary Beth were watching their sister with their mouths open. Smokey was noncommittal, but there was a twinkle in his gray eyes.

Ned Dickerson tried to soothe her down. "There's no need to get riled, Molly. Jeremy is only concerned about your welfare. Yours and Miss Susannah's and Miss Mary Beth's." As he said the last name he darted a quick glance over at the youngest sister, who immediately averted her eyes.

Molly turned to his father. "Mr. Dickerson, can you imagine coming in here when my father was alive and asking him about how he was managing things and how he was going to get the money to run his operation?"

The older man shook his head. "No, but Charlie'd had years of experience and, besides, he was . . ."

"A man," Molly supplied.

"Well, now, child, there *is* a difference." He tried to give the observation a touch of humor by smiling and reaching out to give a little pull at her chin.

Molly's temper was cooling, and her answer held a tone of resignation. "That's the problem, Mr. Dickerson. I'm not a child. And I don't want to be treated like one." She turned to the sheriff. "Thank you for bringing back the calf, Sheriff. Now, if you'll excuse us, we still have some work to attend to before dark."

Chapter Six

The visitors had left without further suggestions as to how Molly should run the Lucky Stars. But no one had gone back to work. When Parker had asked her what she wanted him to do, she'd told him that they would start in again in the morning. She'd gone in to help Smokey with supper, leaving Parker and Susannah to tend to their horses. Mary Beth had disappeared somewhere about the time the Dickersons rode off and didn't show up again until after the rest of them had already sat down to supper.

There was a subdued mood at the table that evening, and Parker surmised that Susannah had decided to put off any confrontation with Molly for a later date. She was as decorous as a schoolmarm in the few comments she addressed to him. There was not a hint of the flirtatious tone she'd used during their ride together. Molly herself had little to say to anyone. The meeting with the Dickersons and the sheriff seemed to have sapped her strength.

Parker volunteered to help Smokey clean up the dishes following the meal. When they'd finished, he asked the cook if he'd be interested in a game of chess.

"Too dadblamed many rules in that game." Smokey had refused with a smile. "Besides, at my age, I need my beauty sleep." With a wink he headed off toward his room at the back of the house. Parker looked around the empty dining room, somewhat at a loss as to what to do next. None of the sisters was anywhere in sight. He didn't feel much like heading out to the cold, empty bunkhouse, but it didn't look as if there would be any after-supper socializing in the parlor, either. He'd been invited to take his meals at the big house, but was he welcome to stick around once he'd been fed?

Finally he decided he'd better not stay without an invitation and, reluctantly, he crossed the big hall and went out the door.

Molly's voice came out of the darkness. "Thanks for helping Smokey out with the cleanup. I wasn't much up to it tonight."

She hardly sounded like the same woman who had roundly dressed down the Dickersons out in the yard just a few hours ago. As his eyes grew accustomed to the dark, he could see that she was sitting on the porch steps. Her oversize coat was hunched around her shoulders, making her look small and vulnerable, not at all the way she appeared when she was striding around the ranch giving orders.

Parker hesitated a moment. "Would you like some company?" he asked finally.

She cranked her head around and looked up at him. "Mmm."

He took her answer as affirmative and sat down alongside her. "It's starting to chill up again," he said, picking a safe topic.

"Well, it is November after all."

They sat in silence for several moments.

"I enjoyed seeing the ranch today. You have quite a place here, Miss Molly."

"You know what, Parker?" she said suddenly, cocking her head. "Let's just make it plain Molly. Miss Molly sounds like some kind of barn dance."

Parker grinned. "Just plain Molly it is, then."

"That's me, all right," she said under her breath.

She sounded dispirited. Parker thought back to his conversation with Susannah that afternoon. "You're not, you know," he said softly.

"Not what?"

"Plain."

She ducked her head in embarrassment. "Spare me your fancy New York flattery, Parker. I'm not like my sisters. I don't need that kind of attention."

The moonlight softened her features, blended the lines that were etched in her sun-weathered face. She *was* beautiful, he realized with a start. Not peaches-and-cream perfection, but a kind of beauty that would last a lifetime. When Molly Hanks was ninety years old her face would still have the strength and character he was looking at this minute. Her blue eyes would shine with the same intensity. He shook his head, keeping his eyes on her. "It's not New York flattery, Molly. You're a beautiful woman, every bit as beautiful as your sisters."

She just shook her head and looked away. "Blarney, my mother used to call it."

"Your mother?" Max McClanahan had told Parker that Mrs. Hanks had died when Mary Beth was born.

"I was only five when she died, but I can still remember some of the phrases she used to say. I have a picture of her in my mind with a dish towel wrapped around her tiny waist, waving a soup ladle at my father and saying, 'That's enough of your blarney, Charlie Hanks.'" She gave a sad smile. "My mother was from the old sod—Irish."

He was intrigued by this new, reflective side of his boss lady, but he had the feeling that if he tried to take advantage of it to get to know her better, she'd skitter back into the shell that she wore around herself most of the time. He kept his voice light and teasing. "Irish. So that's where the temper comes from."

She chuckled. "My father used to say that I was most like her of the three of us. But I remember her as being an absolute angel. I don't think my temper comes from her, though maybe it's the Irish blood inside me."

"Wherever it came from, it's healthy enough, if today was any indication."

She sighed. "I do occasionally have a tendency to fly off a bit, which I sometimes regret. But today I believe my anger was justified. The nerve of that man asking me where I'd get money to hire a crew!" Her face set in tight lines at the memory.

Parker studied her curiously. "I thought... that is, Susannah told me that you and Jeremy were almost engaged to be married."

"So he'd like to think. But it's the ranch he wants, not me."

Parker frowned. "Now, why would you say that?"

Molly turned so that she was facing him and leaned her back against a wooden column. "I think the answer to that's obvious, Mr. Prescott, or are you going to try some more of your New York blarney on me?"

The pensive, vulnerable young woman he'd briefly glimpsed was gone and boss lady Molly was back. She pushed herself up against the wood column, setting her shoulders straighter. She still didn't fill out the big coat, but she didn't look like a lost little girl anymore, either. Parker felt a surge of irritation. Hell, if the woman didn't want to believe that she was attractive, what difference did it make to him?

He decided to change the subject altogether. "So what are you going to do about the unmarked cows?"

Molly burst out laughing. "Calves, Parker. Or cattle, dogies, beeves, or heifers if they're a year old. A cow is something you get milk from."

He grinned at her. "Then why am I going to learn to be a cow-boy?"

She pursed her lips in thought. "Well, that's a good question."

Just now, when her face was animated—quicksilver changes from a smile to puzzlement and back to a smile—he'd defy anyone to consider Miss Molly Hanks plain. But he'd already made the mistake of opening his mouth on that subject tonight. He tucked away a resolution to find the chance to bring up the matter again on another occasion. "I guess it's not important what I call myself as long as I do the job, right?" he asked her.

"You can call yourself a bloody opera star for all I care, Mr. Prescott, as long as you do the job," she said with a firm nod.

"I have heard that cowboys sing to their cows... cattle."

Molly looked amused. "You can give it a try, if you want. I've found that hard riding and good roping are a bit more to the point."

"The riding I think I can handle. You'll have to teach me the roping."

"Have you ever roped before?"

"I can tie knots."

He'd meant the answer to be amusing, but it seemed to depress her. She pulled her coat more tightly around her. "You're right. The chill's starting again. I think I'll go inside."

Parker stood and held out a hand to help her up. She hesitated a moment, then took it and let him pull her to her feet. "And I," he said, his eyes twinkling, "will head out yonder to that nice warm bunkhouse."

He was still holding on to her hand. "You *are* feeling all right?" she asked uncertainly. "Do you want me to check on your ears?"

He shook his head and finally relinquished her hand. "No, thank you. I'm just fine. I'm going to tuck into my cozy bunk and let myself dream about the look on Jeremy Dickerson's face when you were lighting into him today."

"You don't like him very much, do you?"

"No, ma'am."

"Well, he's our neighbor, and I suppose after all he's just trying to help. I hope you'll remember that."

"Yes, ma'am."

She waited for him to say something more. When he continued to be silent, she gave a brisk nod. "We'll see you here at the house for breakfast, Parker."

"I'll be looking forward to it," he said, then turned away from her and clattered down the steps.

Molly awoke with a start. Horrified, she jumped from the bed. Her bare feet hit the icy cold floor, and the frigid air of the room filled her lungs. Her sisters each had small fireplaces in their bedrooms and in the winter went to sleep each night with fires, carefully banked for the night. But Molly's father had scorned such luxury, and Molly had followed his example. Today she probably wouldn't have noticed if she had awakened on top of an ice floe. It was well after dawn—the late dawn of November. She couldn't remember ever sleeping so late in her life. But lately she'd been immensely tired. She'd missed out on her sleep those nights of nursing Parker. And since then she'd slept restlessly. She'd had strange dreams about giant ears in wavy brown hair and velvety eyes watching her, then flaring suddenly with a heat she'd never actually seen, only imagined.

Last night after her discussion with Parker on the steps, she'd been particularly restless. She'd drifted from thoughts of him and his blarney to memories of the Dickersons' visit. She'd fretted, as she had so often these past months, about the ranch and what was to become of it. Her neighbors had been right, of course. She couldn't expect to keep a ranch going if her cattle were running around unmarked over half the territory.

She climbed into her pants and shirt and swiped at her hair with her mother's silver comb. Most of her mother's things had been given over the years to Susannah and Mary Beth. The filigree comb-and-brush set was the one thing she'd insisted on keeping for herself. Her mother's hair had been brown, the exact color of Molly's, her father used to tell her.

She sped down the stairway and into the empty dining room. A plate of johnnycakes and bacon had been left at her place. She walked around the table and picked up a cake. It was cold and hard. Criminy, what time was it, anyway?

Throwing the cake back down on the plate, she ran across the room to the hall and out the front door. Smokey and Parker were out at the barn, working at the baling they had started yesterday. Susannah was watching them, perched on a fence rail. Parker smiled up at her as she laughed at something he had just said. Her eyes were on his shoulders, just as Molly's had been the previous day.

Molly slowed to a stop. There was no point in tearing over there like a little girl let out for play. She was the boss of this outfit now. No matter if her authority at the moment extended only over an old man and a greenhorn Easterner.

"Good morning," she called, making her voice as booming as possible. She walked toward the barn with long, mannish strides.

Smokey turned his head toward her. "Land's sake, lass. I thought you'd up and died."

Molly met his eyes sternly. "I had some thinking to do. Good morning, Parker, Susannah," she finished with a curt nod to each.

Smokey's grin died. "Are you all right?"

"I'm fine. But I'm going to need some help today."

Susannah started to climb over the top of the railing. *She* didn't look as if she'd lost any sleep recently, Molly noted. Her cheeks were blooming and she looked as fresh as a basket of spring flowers.

"What did you have in mind, Molly?" Parker asked over his shoulder as he stepped over to give Susannah an entirely unnecessary boost down to the ground.

"I kept thinking about that calf yesterday—about how in blazes it ended up all the way over to Dickersons'. Calves usually stay pretty close to their mamas the first year,'' she explained to him.

"Maybe it was the storm," he suggested.

She nodded but looked unconvinced. "Anyway, I want to head over to Cougar Creek and check things out."

"Parker and I were there yesterday." Susannah spoke for the first time.

"All the way down to the hollow? Did you see much of the herd?"

"We didn't ride all the way to the hollow, but, come to think of it, we *didn't* see any animals, not a one. That's odd."

"It certainly is," Molly said grimly.

Smokey's weathered face was crumpled with concern. He explained to Parker. "When we knew we couldn't do a roundup, we tried to box up the calves and their mamas in a little valley where they could winter. Hoped it would keep them from wandering too far."

"But they didn't stay there?" Parker asked. Copying Smokey, he stashed his rake behind the hay wagon.

"Maybe something spooked them," Susannah suggested with a shrug.

Molly looked around the group, her face tense. She looked at the overcast western sky. "Maybe. Anyway, I want to get out there and see for myself before the cold weather hits us again. We'll all go." She looked around the yard. "Where's Mary Beth?"

Smokey and Parker looked blank. The youngest sister was normally so quiet, it always seemed to come as a surprise to find that she wasn't around, hanging back somewhere in the corner. "She and I cleaned up the breakfast," Susannah said, "then I came out here and she headed out back. I thought she was just going out to the... to take care of business. Maybe she went back up to her room.''

"I didn't see any sign of her when I got up," Molly said, her voice a mixture of annoyance and concern.

"Does she ride off on her own?" Parker asked.

"Not usually."

"Not Mary Beth," Susannah confirmed.

Molly gave a deep sigh. "Well, we'll have to look—"

Before she could finish her statement the front door to the big house opened and Mary Beth poked her head out, looking around.

Molly called to her. "Where have you been?"

Mary Beth shook her head and cupped her hand to her ear.

"Never mind." Molly made a motion with her hand and shouted more loudly, "Come on. We're riding out—to the cattle."

The younger sister nodded and yelled back. "Let me change clothes. I'll be out in a minute."

Molly and Susannah exchanged a look. There'd been something odd about Mary Beth lately, but Molly didn't have time to think about it now. She had to get out on the range. A wind was whipping up from the northwest again, and, unless she missed her guess, they were about to step back into winter.

Parker stood up in his stirrups and watched in frustration as another big steer headed off in the opposite direction from the herd. Back in New York he'd ridden on fox hunts and steeplechases. He'd led his mount up and down slippery cliffs in the Black Hills. He'd raced the wind across the Wyoming prairie. But he'd be darned if he could get the hang of weaving in and out among these lumbering beasts. They seemed to move without any sense or order, no matter what he did. It didn't help any that Susannah and little Mary Beth seemed to be able to move them along easily like seasoned cowhands. He hoped he could blame part of his ineptitude on the clumsy horse he'd been given in Canyon City. As soon as his boss lady would agree to give him a free moment, he intended to ride into town and get Diamond back.

They'd found a good portion of the Lucky Stars herd scattered across three hills on the far side of Cougar Creek, the portion of the ranch that adjoined the Dickersons' Lazy D. They hadn't been able to identify the mama of the little moon-faced calf the sheriff had brought back, and when the animal had begun a woeful bellowing, Molly had decided that they would take it back to the ranch with them and feed it in the barn until spring.

But in the meantime, she wanted to move as many of the animals as she could toward the box hollow on the other side of the stream. It had been a dry fall and there was little water flowing, but what was there was icy, and the cattle were not eager to plunge in. They'd worked all afternoon zigzagging back and forth, rounding up strays, tugging the occasional rebel into line with a quick lasso. Parker had lassoed nothing but air all day, and he'd given up trying.

He was frustrated and tired, still feeling the effects of his illness, and several times had almost reached the point where he was ready to tell Molly exactly what she could do with her *cows* and ride off the place. But then he'd watch her for a while, straight and sure in the saddle, her face set in the determined lines he was beginning to know. She rode harder than any two of the rest of them. And when the others stopped for a breather, she rode even harder. And he would give it all another try.

Molly rode up alongside him and deftly turned the animal he'd lost back in the right direction. "Just ride right at them and ease them along, Parker," she hollered. "They won't turn around and bite you."

She *was* starting to get on his nerves.

"I'm not afraid they'll bite me," he yelled back at her. "I'm doing the best I can with the brutes, but they just don't seem to get the idea that I'm the boss here."

From the other side of the stream Smokey laughed and hollered, "Treat them like women, Parker. Easy, but with a firm hand. They'll listen to you."

Without a smile, Molly lowered her voice and said, "If you don't think you can handle the job, I won't hold you to your promise to stay."

Parker tightened his hands on his reins and gulped down a flash of anger. "It's my first day, boss lady. I told you I'd have to learn."

Susannah came riding up to them, stopping her horse expertly just next to Parker's. "Stop badgering him, Molly. He's doing fine for just starting out. And besides, we've all worked too long. Let's head back."

Parker wasn't sure he liked having Susannah come to his defense. He could fight his own battles with her sister. But it did smooth his feathers a bit when she leaned over, put a gloved hand on his knee and said in her melodious voice, "You ride beautifully, Parker. We'll make a cowboy out of you yet."

"We'll get this last batch across, then call it a day," Molly said. Her eyes were on Susannah's hand where it still rested on Parker's leg.

"Whoopee!" Susannah hollered, then spurred her horse forward into the icy water. Parker watched as she skillfully sidled her mount near the moving cattle and hurried them across. He looked down the valley to where Mary Beth was using her mount to pen in the animals they had already moved. Though Molly was obviously the workhorse of the family, he was discovering that there was more than froth to the two confections he had first seen on the street back in Canyon City. All three sisters were fighters. He plunged once again into the creek, making the sudden resolve that he would stay and help them with that fight, no matter how many taunts Molly decided to throw his way.

"I can't sneak out to see you so often, Ned. I think Molly's starting to notice." There were two great teardrops in Mary Beth's blue eyes. Ned Dickerson reached out a finger to collect them as they spilled over her lower lids.

"I don't like having you do it, either, Bethy. Let me talk to your sister and tell her the truth."

They were seated on a blanket in the little copse of trees that had served as their hideaway morning and evening for the past two months. Mary Beth would slip away in the morning confusion just after breakfast and again just before dinner. Before the weather had grown too cold, Ned had urged her to meet him at night after everyone was asleep, but she had refused. The few stolen moments were all her conscience would allow. So far.

She shifted in his arms and shook her head sadly. "You know we can't do that. Molly made a promise to my father that she wouldn't let any man come near me until I was over eighteen."

"You're seventeen now," he argued.

"Susannah's nearly twenty-one, and Molly still watches over her like a hawk."

"My ma was married and already had Jeremy by the time she was seventeen."

"My mama, too," Mary Beth agreed glumly.

"I can't stand not to see you."

Mary Beth began to cry in earnest as his mouth closed over hers. Her tears mingled with the heated moisture of their lips and tongues as they sought comfort in the only physical release they had so far allowed themselves.

"I want to marry you, Mary Beth," Ned said fiercely after a few moments. He didn't possess his brother's authoritative air, but he had a soft-spoken self-confidence that had won Mary Beth's heart from the first time she had been alone with him, the afternoon of her father's funeral. She'd climbed up into the loft in the barn, seeking some peace from the houseful of guests and sympathy. Ned had followed her there, and had kissed her that very first day. A shy, comforting kiss that had done more than any of the mourners' kind words to ease the ache in her heart.

Her tears dried in her throat, replaced by the shallow breathing of arousal. "And I want to marry you, but I know what her answer would be. We have to wait at least until my birthday next spring."

Ned looked around at the trees swaying around them. The sun had disappeared over the horizon and it was growing cold. "We won't even be able to meet out here soon. With the blizzard last week, I thought I wouldn't even see you again until spring."

"We'll find some way."

"But you won't let me talk to her."

She put her small hands on each side of his face and gave him a hard kiss. "Not yet. She was so upset with your brother yesterday."

"I think we could all tell that," he said dryly. "But, darling, Jeremy was right, you know. You can't have unmarked cattle wandering around. And you can't run a ranch without hands. She should just let us help her."

Mary Beth had stiffened when he had started to criticize her sister, but when he finished she leaned back against him. "I know. It's just that your brother's so... overbearing sometimes. I think she's afraid if she lets him start doing things for her, he'll just move in and take over the place."

Ned was silent for a moment. "Jeremy thinks the Lucky Stars will be his one day, anyway." At Mary Beth's look, he added quickly. "I mean ... he intends to marry Molly."

"It would be perfect, in a way. Molly certainly couldn't keep us apart if she were married to your brother. But I'm not at all sure Molly wants to be Jeremy's wife."

"It's what our fathers have always talked about."

Mary Beth looked wistful. "Too bad it wasn't us they talked about."

"It doesn't matter. We'll be together, no matter what."

"I believe you, my love." Reluctantly she got to her feet, their few stolen moments over. "But as for Molly and your brother, I wouldn't lay down any bets just yet."

Chapter Seven

Mary Beth had come dashing in to supper at the last minute once again, avoiding questions in the rush to get everyone served with the steaming plates of chicken and dumplings that Smokey had left cooking in his battered Dutch oven all day long. The Lucky Stars kitchen had the latest in modern equipment, but sometimes Smokey preferred using his old cookwagon methods.

After the hard day of riding, everyone was hungry, and the large portions disappeared quickly. Parker, whose appetite had finally returned in full force after his illness, went to the kitchen to serve himself a healthy second helping, and he would have gone for a third if he hadn't heard his mother's voice echoing in his head, admonishing him to mind his manners.

The tension of the impromptu roundup had dissipated with the comfortingly heavy food and the relaxing effects of a bottle of red wine that Molly had taken out of her father's cabinet. "We've earned some of this today," she'd said with a smile.

Parker had sworn off hard liquor after the night he'd been beaten up by thugs hired by Big Jim, the crooked saloon owner back in Deadwood who'd almost ruined him, but he decided that a glass of wine wouldn't hurt him. It felt good to be sitting around a polished table set with real linen and crystal. For a moment he imagined himself back home with his father and mother in earnest discussion over the latest social outrage that they had set out to remedy through some organization or other. Sometimes some of their reformer friends would join them. He and Amelia had almost always been permitted to join the adults at the table, even when they were little, and he'd grown to enjoy the leisurely sessions of stimulating conversation.

There was little conversation at the Lucky Stars table, but he stretched his long legs out and relaxed anyway. It was enough to be eating good food and drinking fine wine, surrounded by three lovely women, each of whom was beginning to grow on him in her own different way.

He had gotten to know Mary Beth the least. When he addressed her, she always answered promptly, intelligently, her shy smile quick to come and go, like changing leaf patterns on a windy day. She had an air of secrecy about her that intrigued him, and she was such a winsome thing—shorter, smaller than her sisters, though nicely rounded with a moon face and huge eyes, a little like the pretty orphan calf they had brought back with them this afternoon.

Then there was Susannah. Though all three sisters were comely, Susannah was the one who fired his blood. He hadn't decided yet exactly how he would handle the almost instant attraction that had sprung up between them. She had made it obvious that she felt it, too. The sense of it had been with him all day as he'd watched her slender, willowy grace and skill

with her horse. She'd been the best rider in the group
by far, yet never lost her femininity for an instant,
unlike Molly, who at times had been actually down on
the ground with reluctant calves, pushing and pulling
them, shouting at them, covered in dirt, her baggy
clothes getting wetter and wetter from the cold stream.
By the end of the day she'd looked like a scarecrow
built of mud.

"So, are we going back out to the hollow tomorrow?" Susannah asked her sister.

Molly nodded as she sipped her wine. "We'll get the
rest of that group across with the others. Do you think
we could fence them in there, Smokey?"

The old cook shook his head. "There won't be time
before the snows come. They should stay put. There's
plenty of prime grazing. It'll just be bad luck if they
wander off again."

"We don't need any more bad luck," Molly said
fervently.

"Maybe we ought to ride over there every couple
days and see that they're staying together," Parker
suggested.

Susannah gave an enthusiastic nod. "Parker and I
can ride over and check on them."

Molly tilted back her head and gave her sister a long
look. "I'm not sure you and Parker riding off alone
is such a good idea. No offense, Parker. It's just that
it's better if we keep things a little controlled around
here."

Susannah slapped her hand on the table, almost
upsetting her wineglass. Parker reached across her to
steady it. He wished he could steady her, as well. He
had the feeling that Susannah was about to claim her
independence, as she had told him she would.

"Now, Molly," she said, her voice only a little out of its normal range, "it's about time we all recognized that you and I are grown women. Of course, when Papa was here, I recognized that he had a certain authority over me, but with him gone..."

Molly's blue eyes narrowed. "With Papa gone, I'm the head of the household," she said quietly.

"Granted. You're the head of the household... but you're not the head of *me*. You're only a year older than I am, and we're both adults now. It's not right anymore for you to be telling me where I can go and who I can see. Or who I can ride with."

Parker watched as Molly took a slow, deep breath. She was smart enough, he saw, not to reject her sister's arguments out of hand. Susannah had a point. Most women her age were married by now with daughters of their own to raise.

"All right," she said finally. "Ride with whom you please. But it won't be with my hired hand. I may not have authority over you anymore, Susannah, but I sure as shooting have it over him." She stabbed a finger in Parker's direction, then pushed back her chair.

The rest of the table watched as she turned without another word and left the room. The benevolent mood had disappeared. "Don't take what Molly says too much to heart, Parker," Susannah said after a moment. "She'll come around. If we want to go riding, we'll just go."

Parker didn't argue. But there'd been something in Molly's eyes just now that had confused him. Before when she'd warned him off her sisters, she had looked like a mama bear protecting her cubs. But this time it had been different. If he didn't know better, he'd swear that the look in her eyes had been jealousy.

*　*　*

It seemed to Molly that Susannah was going out of her way to establish a foothold on her newly proclaimed independence. She had skipped breakfast the next morning and had come down just in time to head out to Cougar Creek once again with the rest of them. But instead of the buckskin riding outfit she normally wore out on the range, she was wearing a blue velveteen habit that their father had bought for her on a trip to Denver, saying that it was a perfect match for her sky blue eyes. In the past, Molly would have ordered her back to her room to change, scolding her for her impracticality. But after the confrontation last night, she decided to stay quiet. Nor did she say a word all morning long as Susannah blatantly teased and flirted with Parker, never quite to the point of abandoning their work, but enough so that it was noticeable to all the rest that there was much more on her mind than herding cattle.

To Parker's credit, he never seemed to lose focus on his work. He met Susannah's advances with his usual charm and courtesy, but he did not respond in kind. He rode hard and seemed to become more adept at maneuvering the tricky animals with each passing hour. By midday, when they stopped to rest and eat a quick meal of cold meat pies, Molly found herself marveling at how quickly he had started to look like a seasoned cowpoke. Her admiration warred with the irritation that flared every time she saw him turning that ready smile on her sister. It was no less irritating to realize that Parker, himself, had little blame in the byplay. Today it was definitely Susannah who was being forward. And Molly knew that their argument last night was a large part of the reason for her behavior.

The ominous clouds were gone today. If they had held a storm, it had blown off to the south. But it was definitely colder. They all were blowing on their reddened hands during lunch and didn't linger to talk once the food was finished.

"There are four or five more over in that gully," Molly told the group as they mounted up once again. "That appears to be the last of them around here, anyway. Tomorrow Parker and I will ride out here to see if we can spot any others."

Parker swung into his saddle, a half smile on his face. He was feeling a small flush of triumph today. For most of his life, learning new things had come easily to him, and it had frustrated him yesterday when he seemed to be having such a difficult time figuring out something as simple as cow herding. But today he'd finally begun to get the idea. Even on the lousy horse he'd been traded, he was learning how to make just the right cuts and turns to keep the dogies rolling.

And then there was his unasked-for role in the drama between the two older Hanks sisters. Susannah was asserting herself, proclaiming herself a woman, for perhaps the first time. And Parker, while he was careful to do nothing that his boss lady could possibly criticize, was secretly tickled to see her discomfiture. He had grown to genuinely like all three young women, but Molly did tend to be somewhat of a bully where her sisters were concerned. Parker figured that if Susannah wanted to use him to teach her sister a lesson, he wouldn't make any objection. As Susannah had said, it was something that needed to be done if either of the two younger girls was ever going to have a chance for a life on her own. Why, Molly had

Mary Beth so cowed that the poor girl probably wouldn't dare look twice at a male. And it just wasn't fair.

It wasn't as if Parker didn't see Molly's side of it. He remembered when Amelia had first admitted to him that she'd kissed a young beau. He'd wanted to tear the boy's head off.

Keeping his smile banked, he rode over to Molly. "If we're finishing up early today, I'd like to ride into town and reclaim my horse from the livery. I'm afraid I didn't make a very good bargain with this one."

Susannah, who had been a few yards behind him, suddenly spurred her horse forward. "I need to go to town, too," she told her sister.

Molly looked skeptical. "What for?"

"Supplies," she answered vaguely. "We need some soap and blueing for the wash."

Molly let out a laugh of disbelief. "Since when have you been so interested in the laundry, Susannah?"

"We can pick up whatever you need," Parker said mildly.

Molly looked from her hired hand to her sister. Just last night she'd sworn they wouldn't ride out alone together again. This was definitely a test of wills, and, after two days of pushing cattle, she didn't much feel up to it. But then, there were lots of days she didn't feel up to things and she managed to get through them. She set her chin and answered, "We could all use a break. We'll call off work for the rest of the day and go in together."

Smokey and Mary Beth had been herding along a frisky heifer who had wanted to head everywhere but the box hollow. They had finally got the critter situated and were riding back up the creek, laughing over a shared joke.

"Go where together?" Smokey asked.

"Into town."

"Sounds good. I wouldn't mind stopping for a shot of Clem's red-eye to chase down that wine we had last night. I'm getting too old for the grapes, I think."

"I don't see how whiskey is going to be any better than wine," Molly observed.

"That's 'cause you're lacking in experience, Molly lass. The grapes'll give you a headache, whereas a shot of real liquor in the gut just gets the blood running through your veins."

Molly shook her head, but she was smiling. Nothing Smokey said ever seemed to rile her. "So we'll ride on back, clean up and then head into town. We can all have supper at the Grand tonight."

"I think I'll just stay home, Molly," Mary Beth said hesitantly.

Molly looked at her sharply. "Why? Are you feeling poorly?"

"No, I'm fine, just a little tired. And I'd like to catch up on the cleaning."

Molly studied her for a moment. One sister rebelling was enough to handle. She would hate to think that Mary Beth had the same intentions. But her youngest sister looked anything but rebellious. She had her typical shy expression, a little like a puppy dog waiting to see if it was deserving of a scratch behind the ears. And Mary Beth did look a little peaked. There were circles under her eyes. "All right. You can stay home. But forget the cleaning, and don't wait up for us. Get to bed early."

Mary Beth looked relieved. "I will."

* * *

The laconic Mr. Fister at the livery had traded Diamond back without so much as a murmur. People sure were different out West, Parker noted. In New York City he'd have had to pay a hefty sum for the deal. It felt good to be with his own horse again. Diamond had been his first purchase when he'd reached the Black Hills, and she had served him faithfully ever since, until she'd hit the hole out on the prairie.

It hadn't taken as long as he'd thought to finish up his horse trading, so he had some time before he was to meet Molly and Susannah over at the hotel. Smokey had gone off to the Grizzly Bear Saloon for his shot of whiskey.

He walked along the main street, leading Diamond and trying to decide what to do. He could go shopping over at the general store. If he'd been back in New York, along about now he'd be thinking about buying some fancy little furbelow for a girl who had caught his eye. But if he bought something for Susannah, he'd feel obliged to find something for her two sisters, and somehow he just couldn't imagine that Molly would particularly appreciate a fancy furbelow.

He stepped back as a buckboard clattered past him, sending a cloud of dust up into his face. As he wiped grit out of his eye he caught sight of the bathhouse sign across the street. Now, there was a sensible idea— he'd pay a visit to the irrepressible Miz McClanahan and clean the range dust off his body at the same time.

The man who had helped him on his first visit was not around this time. Instead, Max McClanahan herself was sitting in the old rocker by the front door. She greeted him heartily.

"Hey there, pilgrim. I hear you almost got your ears froze off over to Copper Canyon the other day."

"You heard right, Max. I guess I'm just as much of a pilgrim as you claimed."

She pushed her bulky frame out of the chair, leaving it rocking wildly in her wake. "Hope you didn't freeze up any other important parts." She winked at him. "That would be what I call a real tragedy."

Parker grinned. "Everything's still in working order as far as I can tell."

"Glad to hear it." She pulled towels and soap out of a cabinet and handed them to him. "You can go in the small room or wait a minute for the big one. There's . . . ah . . . someone occupying it at the moment." Her glance at the curtained doorway was oddly bashful.

"Tub size the same?"

"Oh, sure. And the boiler, too. There's plenty of hot water in either place."

"Well, I reckon I don't need a ballroom to take a bath in," he said, heading for the doorway to the right of the one he had used on his first visit.

"You be sure to call if I can help you with anything," Max teased in her booming voice.

Parker was about to duck under the rough cotton drape when the curtain to the bigger room was pulled open. On the other side stood Smokey, dressed only in red long underwear. His feet were bare and his gray hair was dripping.

"Max, I thought you were coming . . ." He stopped when he saw Parker. "Whoa, tenderfoot. What're you doing here?"

"Same thing you are, I'd suppose. I'm going to scrub the smell of cattle off my hide."

Smokey grinned at Max. "I did stink some when I came in today, didn't I, Maxie?"

She wrinkled her nose. "You smelled pretty much like you always do, you old goat."

Smokey walked across the room and, to Parker's amazement, gave Max a smacking kiss on the lips. "I tell you, Parker, this gal likes me—smelly or not."

Max pushed him away indignantly, but her plump cheeks had turned bright pink. "You've been out on the range too long, old timer."

Parker laughed at their banter. He wondered if Max, unlike the teasing offer she had made to him, actually did "help" Smokey out with his bath. And just how far that might have taken them. They were an unlikely duo, but, then again, who was to say what made two people come together. With him and Claire it had been an instant, painfully fierce attraction that had not let up until the day she died—not even then.

"Don't mind me, folks," Parker told them, pulling back the curtain to the bathroom. "I'll just take my bath and be on my way."

"We're supposed to meet Molly at the hotel," Smokey reminded him.

"I know. I'll be there on time."

Smokey's wet beard curled in a shy grin as he turned toward Max and asked, "I don't suppose you'd want to join us for some supper, Maxie?"

She looked pleased at the invitation, but her voice was gruff. "I guess if the pilgrim's going to be there, I might consider it. At least I'd have one good-lookin' feller to ease my tired eyes."

Smokey looked equally pleased with her answer. "That's settled, then. Go on in and get yourself cleaned up, Parker. We're taking the ladies to dine."

* * *

Molly's father had never entirely approved of Max McClanahan, but that hadn't stopped Molly from being fascinated by the the strident, plainspoken woman. One day when Molly was twelve, she'd run away from school in tears after a group of boys had called her the ugly Hanks sister. She'd never been envious of her sisters' dainty ways and pretty blond hair, but the teasing had cut into a place deep inside her that up to that moment she hadn't even known existed. It had been Max McClanahan who had found her that day, had taken her home and given her lemonade and cookies, and had talked to her for two hours about all the good and powerful gifts a woman had to give to this world, the very least of which was how she looked.

Molly had listened and pondered, and not long after that she'd taken to wearing men's clothing. She'd told her family that the garb was simply more practical for working on the ranch, but in her heart she'd known the change had been her way of stating that she did not have to compete with her sisters' beauty—and that she did not even intend to try. Her father had been at a loss on how to change her mind. They'd had a cook at the time named Mrs. Barter who'd been horrified by the situation and had tried to force Molly to wear the frilly dresses her father continued to bring home to her. But eventually Mrs. Barter had been called back East to live with her ailing sister. Instead of hiring someone new, Smokey had gradually assumed her duties and had never once commented on Molly's style of dressing. Finally everyone had simply come to accept the situation. And whenever Max saw the Hankses, she'd make it a special point to single out Molly for some earnest woman-to-woman talk.

Neither Molly nor Susannah seemed surprised that Max had accompanied the men to the hotel. Evidently whatever the relationship between Smokey and the bathhouse owner, it had been simmering for some time. Molly seemed genuinely happy to see Max as the older woman engulfed her in a hug.

The two days of hard work had given the Lucky Stars crew healthy appetites and, without asking, Molly ordered steaks for everyone. Parker handed his menu back to the waiter in amusement. It was the first time since he'd been out of knee breeches that a woman had ordered his food for him.

"So, Molly," Max boomed. "Parker tells me you saved this butchering old cook here from cutting off his ears over a little case of frostbite."

Molly leaned back in the chair, relaxed, a rare smile smoothing out the tension in her face. "It wasn't a little case, Max. They were a sight to see."

"Can't tell under all that shaggy hair. Show me them ears, boy," Max ordered.

Parker grinned and pulled the hair up on both sides of his head. "They're a little purple yet, but I'm kind of getting to like the color myself."

"He was very lucky," Susannah said fervently. "He could have died."

She and Parker exchanged smiles that were so tangible, it was almost as if they had touched hands across the table. Max watched the exchange with interest, noting that Molly's own smile had faded a little.

"So. What's this I hear about Lucky Stars cattle wandering around all over the place?"

"Tarnation, woman," Smokey put in. "Is there anything you don't hear about? You must spend half your time kneeling down with your ear to the ground."

Max flicked him a good-natured glance, the look of friends who no longer need to pay attention to the courtesies of conventional conversation. Then she continued to Molly. "The Dickerson brothers were over at the Grizzly mouthing off about how you're bringing rack and ruin down on what was the finest spread in the region."

"The Dickerson brothers can go jump off a cliff," Molly retorted. "It's not unusual for a ranch to suffer some setbacks when the owner dies. We'll get back on our feet. We just need time."

"I'll tell you one thing," Smokey said with an admiring look at his boss. "No matter how tough things get, this little filly is not giving up on her ranch. She'll see herself planted in the ground next to her pa before she does."

"Sometimes a little determination is all it takes," Max declared with approval.

"And sometimes it takes a bit of money to go along with it," Molly muttered under her breath. But by then the steaks had arrived and there was a general lull in the conversation while everyone began eating.

After they filled up on the well-done beef, boiled potatoes and onions, talk turned light, even a little silly at times. Parker made them laugh with tales of his adventures when he had first come West, a raw novice who couldn't so much as skin a rabbit for a meal. He'd lived on jerky and cold biscuits for the first month until he'd finally gotten the hang of cooking over an open fire. His first attempt at roasting a duck he'd shot had left nothing but a few charred bones, burned beyond recognition.

"I knew you were a pilgrim the minute I laid eyes on you," Max said, laughing and wiping her eyes. Then she winked at him and he smiled back at her in a secret conspiracy that said neither of them would reveal he'd been buck naked when she first saw him.

No one seemed eager to leave the table, but finally, after finishing their cups of the Grand's potent coffee, Max yawned and said, "Unless I get a better offer, I'm heading for my bed."

Parker held Susannah's chair as they all got up to leave the nearly empty dining room. As they walked through the archway into the tiny hotel lobby, they saw a crowd gathered outside on the sidewalk.

"I wonder what's going on?" Susannah said, pulling Parker along with her out the front door.

It had to be close to eight o'clock, a time when the street would be empty most evenings except over in front of the Grizzly Bear, but tonight it seemed there were people everywhere. Sheriff Benton stood teetering on the edge of a horse trough and appeared to be trying to get the attention of the crowd.

Molly made her way over in his direction. Jeremy Dickerson and his father were standing just behind him. "What is it, Sheriff?" she asked.

He looked down at her, seeming annoyed by the interruption. "There's been a killing, Miss Hanks. Nothing you ladies should be involved in. Why don't you ride on back to your ranch?"

"A killing?"

Jeremy took a step toward her. "A murder. One of our hands, Johnny the Oyster, has been found dead in the alley behind the Grizzly, shot in the back."

"Good Lord," Molly said, clutching her throat. Susannah, Parker and Smokey had come up behind her.

"Do you know who did it?" Smokey asked the sheriff.

Again Jeremy answered for him. "It was Ole Pedersson."

Smokey pushed forward. "Ole wouldn't hurt a horsefly, much less kill someone. And anyway, his brain is too pickled in liquor to be able to shoot a man. Hell, he doesn't even have a gun."

"He was seen leaving the alley, and he's fled out of town on Jack Whittaker's horse."

Smokey shook his head sadly. "Something must have scared him pretty badly to make him do that. But I can't believe he's your killer."

Sheriff Benton took his revolver from its holster and fired a shot in the air. The crowd became suddenly quiet. "All right, folks, it's getting late, and a murderer is getting away," he yelled. "Everyone who went with the posse last year when we pursued the Farrow brothers is hereby deputized to go along again. Do we have everyone?"

The older Dickerson said, "Ned didn't come in with us tonight. I don't know where's he's gotten off to."

"We'll have to go without him," the sheriff said. "Anyone else missing?"

Like other towns in the Wyoming territory, Canyon City relied on a system of vigilante justice to deal with its miscreants. The sheriff's sweeping deputization had no foundation in the law, but it eased consciences now and then. When a posse was needed, it was expected that each of the ranches would send a man or two. Molly's father had ridden out on several occasions.

"You'll need someone from the Lucky Stars," Molly said in a loud voice.

Sheriff Benton looked from her to Smokey, then briefly at Parker. "That's all right, Miss Hanks. We all know that Charlie's gone. We won't hold you to any obligation until you have a man out on the place again."

"We'll do our part," Molly said firmly.

Benton's eyes went back to Parker. "We don't like to take strangers along...."

She took a step closer and puffed out her chest a little as she looked him straight in the eyes and said, "I don't reckon I'm a stranger, am I, Sheriff?"

Chapter Eight

Jeremy stepped to her side and took hold of her upper arm. "Don't be ridiculous, Molly. You're not riding on any posse."

Molly was feeling no charity toward the Dickerson family tonight after what Max had had to say. Jeremy was the only man who had ever shown the remotest interest in her, and even though she had told herself that his interest was largely due to the ranch, some vestiges of vanity had made her hope that he had wanted her for herself, as well. He'd certainly said so often enough. So it had hurt tonight when Max had said he and his father were disparaging her abilities to operate her ranch. It had hurt more than she wanted to think about. She pulled away from him. "Let go of me, Jeremy. This is the second time this week you've tried to tell me what I can and cannot do, and I suggest that you don't try a third time."

Hiram Dickerson interjected in a conciliatory tone, "Now, Molly, you and Susannah shouldn't even be out here on the street. We have a murderer still at large. Why don't you have Smokey and your new man there escort you back to your ranch before anything happens?"

Smokey stepped forward. "He's right, Molly lass. Let's get on home."

Molly shook her head. "If there's a town posse riding out, the owner of the Lucky Stars is going to be riding with it."

Smokey gave a sigh of resignation and called over the crowd, "Can you reason with her, Max?"

The bathhouse owner had stayed in the background, but when Smokey called to her she moved through the people and put an arm around Molly's shoulders. "You don't have to do this, Molly."

"Maybe not. But I'm going to."

Molly looked dwarfed in the big woman's embrace. Parker felt a quick catch in his chest as he watched her trying once again to take on all comers, her shoulders drawn up as high as she could get them, yet still looking slender in her big coat. So far, Parker had stayed out of the argument. Molly had plenty of advisers at the moment. But he hoped that for once she would give an inch on that stubbornness of hers and listen to them. After watching her the past two days with the cattle, he had no doubt that she could ride as hard and as fast as any of the men who were at this moment mounting up to start their hunt. But he hated to think of what she might have to face when they reached their quarry. He'd seen vigilante justice in the Black Hills, and sometimes it wasn't a pretty sight.

Molly pulled away from Max. "You're all just wasting time railing at me when we should be out hunting a murderer," she said. She pushed through the crowd to where her horse was tied to the hotel hitching post and began to untie him. "I'll need the rifle, Smokey," she said over her shoulder.

Smokey shrugged and laid a comforting hand on Max's back. "Thanks for trying," he said, then followed his mistress over to the railing. "No, you won't. If someone needs to go from the Lucky Stars, I guess it's going to be me."

"No, I'll go," Parker said quickly.

Molly whirled around, reins in her hand. "Neither of you will go. You'll take Susannah back to the ranch immediately. Mary Beth's all by herself. You think I'd leave my sisters unprotected when there's a killer around somewhere?"

Smokey and Parker looked at each other, hesitating, but Molly didn't wait for a decision. She reached over to Smokey's horse, pulled the rifle out of its stock and transferred it to her own saddle. Then she mounted her horse and started to turn it toward the center of the street, causing both men to jump aside in order not to be trampled.

Smokey shook his head. "I guess she's going," he said, his mouth twisting up his beard in annoyance.

Parker watched for a minute as Molly rode across the street to the group of men gathering in front of the sheriff's office. Then he walked around Smokey to swiftly untie Susannah's horse and his own. "Come on," he said tersely. "Let's get out to the ranch and be sure Mary Beth's all right."

Parker's partner, Gabe Hatch, had tried to teach him the rudiments of tracking back in the Black Hills, but without much luck. It had frustrated Parker nearly as much as the cattle herding these past two days. He was used to excelling at most things, whether they took brain or brawn. Within weeks of arriving out West he'd learned to operate a mine, to shoot a squirrel through the head from fifty paces, to drink half the men at Big Jim's place under the table. But he seemed to lack some kind of inner sense when it came to directions and pathfinding. Gabe had bought him a compass finally, and had half-seriously told him to leave a trail of pebbles behind him when he was going to venture farther from his cabin than the creek.

But tonight Parker dared to hope that, for once, he was on the right track. The posse had headed out on the road south, figuring that Ole was probably too drunk to take to the hills. If they stayed on the broad, well-traveled highway, a blind man should be able to find them, Parker told himself.

He and Smokey had ridden hard back to the ranch with Susannah. He'd stopped long enough to be sure that Mary Beth was safely asleep in her bed and to change horses, then he'd headed out to catch up with the posse. He'd left Smokey keeping watch in the big ranch kitchen, two rifles and a six-gun laid out on the table in easy reach. If Ole Pedersson was the killer, the precautions were probably unnecessary. Smokey had insisted once again that there was no way Ole could have killed anyone. But the Dickerson cowhand lay dead, and there was a murderer out there somewhere.

Parker pulled a wool scarf up around his tender ears as he rode along. It was past midnight, and the air had turned sharply icy. He wasn't quite sure what had driven him to follow her. Molly's orders had been plain enough—he was to stay on the ranch with her sisters. Perhaps it had been something about the way Jeremy Dickerson had taken her arm so roughly, and with such an air of ownership. At any rate, he was sure she wouldn't thank him for coming.

The flat prairie landscape turned hilly about five miles south of Canyon City. The road was still broad, but now it weaved a little with the natural curves of the land. Parker's cheeks felt numb with the cold and he was beginning to have doubts about his impulse to ride out. All he needed was another bout with frostbite after disobeying Molly's express orders to go home. She'd have his hide this time, he thought with a grin, ears and all.

He'd almost become convinced that the posse had left the road after all and that he must have ridden past them when he heard the sound of horses and male voices just ahead around a sudden outcropping of limestone that had sprung up from nowhere. The moonlight reflected eerily off the light-colored rock, making it look not quite real.

He spurred his horse ahead. On the other side of the promontory he found them. They had stopped and were gathered around a place where the rocks folded to form a natural shelter. Many of the men were dismounted. They must have found Ole, Parker surmised. He squinted his eyes in the darkness, looking for Molly.

But it wasn't Molly he saw. A sick feeling swirled at the pit of his stomach. He rode forward, his eyes on a scraggly tree that jutted out straight from the rocks about eight feet from the ground. A long dark form twisted slowly back and forth just under its thickest branch. The form was a human being, and it hung suspended from a length of hemp that had been looped around his neck.

As he drew closer, he could make out the man's features—his eyes open and bulging, his tongue lolling unnaturally to one side of thinned, purplish lips.

Parker had never met Ole Pedersson in life, but he hoped the face he was looking at bore little resemblance. He searched in the darkness for Molly, and found her finally, over near the side of the rock face. Jeremy Dickerson was standing behind her, holding both her arms. She didn't seem to be putting up any resistance, and for a moment Parker couldn't tell if he was restraining her or comforting her. But then she spoke.

Her voice was furious. "This isn't over, Jeremy. I intend to report—"

"Report to whom?" Dickerson said calmly. "I told you that you shouldn't have come with us, Molly. This is a matter for men to deal with."

"This is a matter for courts to deal with," she said fiercely.

Parker dismounted and pushed his way toward her through the group of men. "Are you all right, Molly?" he asked in a loud voice.

For a moment he thought she looked pleased to see him, but then her face twisted into a scowl and she said, "You're supposed to be with my sisters."

"Your sisters are fine. Smokey's waiting up with a whole arsenal ready to defend them if necessary. What went on here?"

Belatedly, Molly realized that Jeremy was still holding her against him. The past half hour had been such a shock that she still felt as if her head was not quite attached to the rest of her body. She twisted out of his grasp. She hated to admit it, but Parker's face was like a little piece of sanity in the nightmarish scene.

"Are you all right, Molly?" he asked again in a softer tone as he reached her side.

She took a step away from Dickerson, keeping her head averted from the figure that still swayed grotesquely a few feet away. "No, I'm not. I'm horrified and disgusted, as every one of the rest of you should be," she finished, glaring at the half-dozen men who were nearest to her. "You all may have just lynched an innocent man."

Harv Overstreet, who held the ranch on the other side of the Lazy D, said, "I guess we all knew Ole would come to no good one of these days. If he didn't do it, why did he run away?"

"Of course he did it," Hiram Dickerson added. "Not much point in wasting time on a trial for the town drunk."

Molly looked at both men, her face as hard as the limestone wall behind her. "If my father were still here, this would never have happened."

"Where's the sheriff?" Parker asked.

Molly gave a harsh laugh. "In his bed, I suppose. He left so that the men could act as a vigilante committee, acting on their own in the absence of any available legal means."

"Did he know they were planning to do this?" His eyes darted involuntarily to the hanged man.

"What business is it of yours, Prescott?" Jeremy asked. He had moved away from the cliff and was standing with his hands hanging loosely at his sides. A revolver was strapped to his right hip.

Some primitive side of Parker wished that he, too, had been wearing a gun belt. Dickerson had made it pretty plain that there would never be an understanding between the two of them, and if he'd wanted to settle it then and there, that would have been all right with Parker. He had little doubt who would end up standing after such a contest. He'd seen plenty of gunmen come and go in Deadwood, and there wasn't a one faster than Gabe Hatch. Gabe had been Parker's teacher, and, before the lessons were over, Parker could outdraw him nine times out of ten.

But he'd followed the posse to find Molly, not to fight with her neighbor. Under her angry expression, her normally tan face was pale. "Let's get out of here," he said to her.

She nodded and swung up onto her horse, her fists clenched tightly in its mane. Parker led the way through the posse members. Molly looked back once as they started around the rocks to head north. Harv Overstreet and two other men were cutting the limp body of Ole Pedersson down from the tree.

They rode in silence for several minutes as she tried to swallow down the bile that had gorged her throat. "We can cut across this way," she said finally, pointing to a trail that led up a little hill. "There's no need to go through town."

Parker shifted his horse to one side and let her take the lead. "As long as you know your way. Without the road I'm lost around here, I'm afraid."

At a slightly slower pace they went single file along a path cut through long prairie grasses. Molly tried to concentrate on the movement of her horse, on the whistle of the wind, on the bite of the November cold...on anything other than the memory of Ole Pedersson's gurgling screams as the life had been slowly choked from his body. It was no use.

"I...I'm sorry. I have to stop for a minute," she called to Parker. Miserable and embarrassed, she jumped from her horse, fell to her knees in the grass and spewed up the remains of the Grand Hotel's finest beefsteak.

Parker was at her side instantly. "Damn! I asked if you were all right." He pulled her against him, his voice becoming gentle. "Poor baby." He took a kerchief from his pocket and offered it to her.

Her insides felt better, but she was utterly mortified. A ranch boss didn't throw up and have to be comforted as a "poor baby" by a hired hand. She snatched the cloth from his hand and wiped it across her mouth. Pulling away from his comforting arm, she struggled to her feet. "I'm fine. Let's get going."

Parker stood more slowly. He didn't touch her again, but he bent his head to look into her face. "Not so fast. We're not in any hurry."

"Susannah and Mary Beth—" she began, but he interrupted her.

"I told you, your sisters are fine. Mary Beth was sound asleep when I left, and I'm sure Susannah is, too, by now. You're just feeling a natural anxiety because of what you've been through tonight. Because of what you had to see. I wish I'd been able to keep you from going."

"Because ladies don't know how to deal with those things?" she asked bitterly, mimicking Jeremy. "I guess he was right after all." She nodded toward the grass where she had been sick.

"There's nothing noble about being able to kill a man without conscience," Parker told her. "And there's nothing shameful about having the sensitivity to be revolted by a scene like the one we just left."

"My father used to ride out with the posse. I never saw him coming home to puke his guts out afterward."

"Has the posse ever lynched anyone before?"

She shook her head. "Mostly they'd go after rustlers. One time I remember three young kids came in and tried to rob the general store. Mr. Simon whacked one of them with a broom and they ran away before they could get any money. The posse rounded them up and shipped them over to stand trial in Laramie. Canyon City's just never been what you'd call a lawless town."

"But tonight there was a murder."

"There were two murders," Molly said grimly.

Parker didn't argue. "Are you doing better?" he asked.

The solicitude in his voice unnerved her. Her lip trembled. "I think so. I'm more embarrassed than anything at the moment. And tired."

"Aw, don't be embarrassed, boss lady. I won't tell anyone." He pulled his handkerchief out of her numbed fingers and gave another dab at her mouth. "I'm sorry I don't have anything for you to drink to wash away the bad taste."

Molly gave a wan smile. "I could use my snake-bite medicine."

"Snake-bite medicine?"

"It's whiskey, really. My father always made us carry a little flask when we were out on the range. He believed it had some kind of power to keep people from getting blood poisoning from a wound."

"Well, where is it?"

"What?"

"The snake-bite medicine. Get it out. I don't know about blood poisoning, but it sure as hell is exactly what we need to warm us up enough to make it home without freezing to death."

"I've never actually drunk any of it."

"So tonight will be the first time."

She turned and dug in her saddlebags, pulled out a small tin bottle and handed it to Parker. "You go ahead. I don't think I want any."

Parker untwisted the cap then put the bottle up to her lips. "Just a swallow to wash your mouth out and settle your stomach."

After a moment's hesitation she put her mouth against the bottle and allowed Parker to tip it back. The liquid seared her throat all the way down, then settled into her middle like a toasty little fire. She took another swallow.

Parker nodded. "Now one more to warm you up for the rest of the ride."

"Aren't you having any?"

"You first."

She took the flask from him this time and tipped it herself, downing one hefty gulp, then starting another.

Parker reached out quickly and pulled the bottle away. "That's...ah...probably enough," he said. "That's hitting an empty stomach, you know."

"It feels kind of good, actually," Molly said. And it did. The wind was suddenly nowhere near as biting. And her arms and legs were starting to feel pleasantly a-tingle. "Is this what it means to get drunk?"

The directness and the innocence of her question reminded Parker of Amelia. His sister had always been curious about new experiences, even if they were not ones that would be socially approved back in their upper class New York circle. He had always thought that he'd never meet another girl who could face life as forthrightly as Amelia.

"One more swallow and you'd be just about there, boss lady," he answered with a grin.

"Well, this doesn't feel so bad. I rather like it. Aren't you going to have some?" she asked again.

Parker twisted the cap onto the flask. "I don't think so. And you might have a different opinion when you wake up tomorrow morning."

"I haven't had enough for that, surely?"

He eyed her slight form. "I don't know. You've never drunk the stuff before, and it doesn't seem that it would take much to intoxicate a wisp of a thing like you."

She gave a half laugh and flapped the arms of her big coat. "That's the first time anyone's called me a wisp of a thing."

She looked, in fact, like a child dressing up in adult clothes. Her nose was red from the cold. Her face was still white and strained, making her blue eyes look enormous. "Sorry, boss lady, but I've already figured out that you're not anywhere near as tough as you talk."

She tipped her head to glare at him. "Oh, you have?"

He reached up and tucked a stray lock of hair back up under her hat. "Yes." For just a minute as his hand brushed her cheek he felt a familiar softening in his gut. Before he knew what he was doing, he leaned over and kissed her on the mouth. He pulled away immediately, appalled. What in heaven's name was he thinking?

Molly lifted a hand to her lips, startled. The liquor had set up a hum that resonated through her, moving suddenly now in a great crescendo toward her mouth and at the pit of her stomach. She clutched at Parker's arm to keep from falling off balance.

"I'm sorry," he said quickly. "I . . . I'm sorry," he repeated, as if for lack of any possible explanation to his impulsive action.

Molly straightened and blinked her eyes, trying to get her head clear and her body under control. When she'd been young and still foolish enough to imagine that she would be kissed some day by a lover, she'd pictured it as a grand, formal occasion, the climax to a wonderful courtship of flowers and poetry. She'd never imagined that her first kiss would be from a cowhand who had eyes only for her sister. Never imagined it would be in the middle of the night as she rode home from a hanging, the sour taste of revulsion still lingering at the back of her throat.

"Let's just forget it," she said finally, but her voice sounded shaky.

Parker hesitated a moment, looking as if he wanted to say something more, but finally he nodded and turned away from her to put the flask of whiskey back into her saddlebag. "Are you feeling all right to ride again?" he asked.

She took the reins from him and mounted up, ignoring the hand he offered to help. "I'm fine. I just want to get home." And suddenly her voice was as frigid as the cold November night.

If anyone noticed a strain between Molly and Parker the next day, no one commented on it. There was a good deal of talk about the murder and the subsequent lynching. Mary Beth had cried when she had been told the news. Ole Pedersson had once smiled at her and called her a pretty little thing, which was enough to make her mourn his passing, especially in such a horrible manner.

Molly had had dark circles under her eyes and had winced when Smokey tried to heap some sausages on her breakfast plate. But she had divided up the day's chores with her usual efficiency and had gone off herself to slop the pigs as soon as the meal was finished.

Parker finished up the baling by himself while Smokey rode out with Susannah to check on the cattle they had boxed in. After riding half the night he was just as glad not to have to get up in his saddle, and the baling was just the kind of work he needed at the moment—hard, steady, requiring little thought.

His mind was occupied in other areas today. He didn't know if it was due to the lack of sleep or the inexplicable moment on the road with Molly, but today his head was full of thoughts of Claire. Up to this point, all his flirting with Susannah, his admiring study of all three sisters, had not seemed to have much to do with that part of him where Claire still ruled in his heart. But there had been something different last night. Something about Molly. The way she'd stood up to those men like a staunch little general, then collapsed to her knees in the road, pale and shaking. She had moved him. She'd come close to reaching a place inside him that he didn't want touched. It was Claire's place, locked and barred, and it would hurt too much to open it up again.

When she came by at midmorning to check on his progress, his voice was as detached as hers—polite, respectful, indifferent. Worker to employer. Hired hand to boss lady. He'd do his best to keep things that way.

Chapter Nine

"I just don't see how we can have a traditional Christmas with Papa gone," Mary Beth said sadly, tucking a pine bough around the end of the mantel.

Smokey was filling out the greenery on the other end. "Your father would be the first one to insist on it, child. When your mother passed, he said that the best way to honor the dead was to live well."

Mary Beth gave her gentle smile. "I can picture him saying that. But he didn't completely follow his own advice. He never married again."

"No, he devoted himself to you girls and the ranch, and that was plenty to keep him happy. But I tell you, there was never a Christmas on the Lucky Stars without gifts under the tree and a plum pudding on the table. And this year won't be the first."

"Smokey's right," Molly agreed, entering the big living room with her arms full of garlands. "It's what Papa would have wanted. I'm bringing all the decorations down from the attic, some that we haven't used for years. It will do us good to see them again."

Susannah came in behind her with another armload of boxes and the three sisters sat together on the floor pulling out treasured pieces of the past.

"Remember the time we tried to stay up all night, Mary Beth?" Susannah asked, holding up a candle in a tin star. "We got scared after Papa had put out all the lights so we decided to light the candles on the tree."

"And almost burned the house down," Molly added, laughing.

Mary Beth was cradling an angel in her lap. "I remember the year I said the only thing I wanted for Christmas was a mother." A single tear rolled from the corner of her eye. "Papa said I had the most special mother of all, because my mother was an angel who would be watching over me no matter where I went or what I did."

"And he gave you a Christmas angel that he said looked just like her," Molly added, leaning over to squeeze her sister's hand.

"When Mrs. Barter tried to put it away after Christmas, you bit her," Susannah added.

"I did not!"

"Yes, you did," Susannah and Molly said at once. And then both older sisters put their arms around the youngest. They hugged and giggled as they had so many Christmases past, their wet eyes the only sign of the ache they were all feeling.

Smokey had started the preparations for a Christmas Eve feast that would occupy him much of the day. Mary Beth had volunteered to help. Molly had declared that no work other than the essential chores would be done for the next two days. They would act as if their father was still here, spending this special day decorating the house and smelling the tantalizing odor of apple pie and roast goose coming from the kitchen. Secretly, each person would sneak away to prepare the little gifts of the season that had always been a family tradition.

After breakfast Parker had watched the bustle for a few minutes, looking a little lost and out of place. Then he had said that if there was no work to be done, he'd head out to the bunkhouse.

"We ought to invite Parker in to help with the tree," Susannah said as she stood and began to untangle a garland of stamped tin stars.

"He's probably missing his family on a day like this," Mary Beth added.

Molly jumped to her feet. "He heard what we were planning at breakfast. I suspect if he'd been interested, he'd have stayed."

"He might not have felt welcome," Mary Beth said softly, exchanging a glance with Susannah. Since the night of the lynching of Ole Pedersson, Molly had been unusually curt with their new hand. Susannah and Mary Beth had discussed whether they should talk to their sister about it, but had decided to wait and see if things got better once Molly got over the horror of that night.

"He knows he's welcome," Molly snapped. "He eats here three times a day, doesn't he?"

They went back to work in silence. "I think I'll ask him, just the same," Susannah said after several minutes.

"I think we should," Mary Beth agreed.

Molly didn't say a word. She brushed some clinging angel hair from her buckskin trousers, then turned to head up to the attic for another box.

There would be no snow for Christmas. The remains of the storm that had blanketed the prairie when

Parker had first arrived had long since melted, leaving a shriveled brown landscape that was as desolate as Parker's spirits.

He and Claire had never even had a Christmas together. Not a single one. She'd come into his life with the heady blooming of a new spring... and had left it just as fall was beginning once again to teach its age-old lesson on the inevitability of death. Parker leaned against the door frame of the bunkhouse, looking across the Lucky Stars corral toward the foothills in the west. Is that where he would find peace at last? Past those hills and beyond, to California? Or should he seek it back home? Should he give up this fruitless search for a new life and return to the family he loved—to New York Christmases full of sleigh rides and hot chestnuts on the streets, Yule logs and caroling and mulled cider?

He scanned the horizon and sighed. Amelia and Gabe were having their first Christmas together. The older Prescotts, as usual, would spend part of the day helping out at the soup kitchens, but then the family would gather for a grand dinner. Gabe's nine-year-old son would be there, the son he hadn't known he had until just a few months ago. And the way his sister and Gabe had been after each other, Parker supposed that before long there'd be a new brother or sister for the boy—Gabe and Amelia's this time. Parker would be an uncle. He gave a bleak smile.

It was cold, but he didn't feel like shutting himself up by the stove inside the empty bunkhouse. He blew on his hands and stomped his feet just as the door to the ranch house opened and Susannah came out. She wore no coat, but was wrapped up in a yellow shawl, a bright spot of color against the brown countryside.

"Parker," she called to him, skipping lightly toward him across the yard.

He tried to put some enthusiasm into his smile. "How's the decorating coming?"

She drew nearer. "We've just put up the tree, but we're going to wait to trim it until after lunch. Molly and Mary Beth are helping Smokey." She shivered and pulled the shawl around her. "Aren't you cold standing out here?"

He hesitated a moment, then stepped to one side to allow her access to the bunkhouse. "Come in, if you like. The stove's still going from last night."

Susannah peered in the door as if she expected to see a naked man hiding underneath one of the empty beds. "We were never allowed in here when Papa..." Her voice trailed off as she stepped over the threshold.

"Forbidden territory, eh?" Parker asked with a grin.

She smiled back at him. "There was a lot of forbidden territory when Papa was around," she said, her expression turning mischievous.

"I'm sure he was just trying to protect you all."

He followed her into the room, leaving the door open. She stepped around him and firmly closed it, looking at him with a glint of daring in her eyes. "You'll let out all the heat."

Parker moved a little uneasily into the center of the room. "Maybe your sister wouldn't like you being out here with me."

"I thought we'd settled that the other day. I'm too old for her rules anymore." She looked around, then chose a bunk and sat on it, smoothing her skirts around her. With a nod toward the other end of the bed, she added, "Come on and sit down with me."

Parker looked amused. Susannah was not practiced at the art of flirting, but it didn't make the least bit of difference. She just naturally had that indefinable quality that made a man want to take her in his arms almost the minute he saw her. It was more than beauty and an attractive figure. It was a kind of openness—no guards, no barriers to cross. Totally unlike her older sister, who seemed to live inside a walled fortress.

"I don't think I should sit there beside you, Susannah," he said lightly.

"Why not?" Her perfect little nose wrinkled.

"Well, for one thing, if your sister came in and saw us on a bed together, she'd probably carve me up and serve me for your Christmas dinner tonight." He sat on a bunk directly across from her.

Susannah gave a little puff of annoyance. "Now, see. Why does that have to be?"

Her lip trembled a little, and Parker suddenly realized that, impossible as it seemed, Susannah might truly not know the answer to that question. His voice softened. "Maybe it's because she knows that there's not a man in the territory who could sit close beside you without wanting to kiss that lovely mouth of yours...and more."

"Including you?"

Parker gave a little laugh. "Including me."

"And what if I said...that I didn't think that would be so terrible?"

"I might be inclined to advise you to listen to your sister."

"I'm nearly twenty-one years old, Parker, and I've never even been kissed." Her eyes were serious, expectant, and where she had let the shawl slip down around her, her high breasts rose and fell with rapid, shallow breaths.

Parker rubbed a hand across his mouth. It would be one hell of a way to celebrate Christmas, that was for sure. Forget scruples, forget memories, forget the dreary, winter-dead prairie outside and lose himself in the arms of a beautiful woman who was overripe for learning about lovemaking. His body was telling him that it would be happy to cooperate.

"Susannah," he said slowly. "There's nothing I'd rather do than walk over there and kiss you, but I can't do it. I made a promise to your sister when I signed on here, and while I'm still taking wages from her, I intend to honor it."

Even as he said the words, he knew that it was not the whole reason for his reticence. He couldn't entirely explain it even to himself. It was tied up with the protective way Molly had made him feel the other night when she'd been sick along the side of the road.

"Well, then, I guess I've thrown myself at you enough for one day." Susannah's sweet voice had turned brittle. "I'd best get back up to the house. You're to come up to eat in a half hour or so, and you're welcome to stay afterward to help with the tree."

She stood, bright eyes shuttered. "It's not you, Susannah..." he began, but she put up a hand as if to ward off further explanation.

"I'll see you at lunch," she said, and quickly made her way out the door.

*　*　*

Parker had lain back on his bunk, not eager to arrive for lunch early. The other night he'd managed to anger the oldest Hanks sister. Now he'd upset Susannah. If it weren't the dead of winter he'd be tempted to get up on his horse and ride out of here, away from both of them.

He lay with his arm shading his eyes from the light of the oil lamp. It was time to bank the stove and head over to the big house, but his body didn't seem to want to move.

The knock was so faint that he almost thought he'd imagined it. He sat up as the door creaked open and Mary Beth's tiny face appeared in the crack.

"Hello," he greeted her uncertainly. Was he supposed to have a fight with the third sister, too?

She opened the door another inch or two. "Hello."

"Come on in," he said, swinging his feet to the floor.

"Were you sleeping?"

"No." He combed his fingers back through his mussed hair. "No, of course not. I was just enjoying the day off. Come in," he repeated. She swung the door halfway open and looked cautiously inside. "I know," Parker said with a little smile. "When your father was alive, you weren't supposed to come in here."

Mary Beth nodded and smiled gently in return. "It was a dangerous place, full of potentially wicked cowboys."

"Well, there's only me now. I don't know about the wicked, but I sure as heck don't feel much like a cowboy yet."

She pushed the door wide and stepped in. "You're learning, Parker. You're doing very well."

"Your sister doesn't seem too impressed with my work the past few days."

"That's just Molly. She gets her moods, but you shouldn't take it to heart."

"Would you like to sit down?" He swatted the dust from the end of an unused bunk.

"No. I just came to tell you that you are welcome to trim the tree with us this afternoon."

"Thank you. Susannah already invited me, as a matter of fact."

Mary Beth turned her head around as if looking for her. "Oh, good. She's shut up in her bedroom and I didn't think she'd been out here."

"Shut up in her bedroom?"

Mary Beth's eyes twinkled. "Well, you know. It's Christmas. People have little secrets on a day like today."

Parker was not at all sure that Susannah had shut herself up to wrap Christmas presents, but he said, "I guess so."

Mary Beth's smile died at the uncertainty in his voice. "I'm sorry, Parker. I know you must be missing your family today. Did you have wonderful Christmas celebrations back in New York?"

Mary Beth was such an intuitive, sensitive little creature. Parker tried to make his smile reassuring. "We had wonderful Christmases, and you're right— I'm feeling a bit homesick."

"Oh, but you mustn't. You must let all of us be your family for today."

A little of his melancholy lifted. Her tenderhearted sympathy was exactly the remedy he needed to lighten his mood. Unlike Susannah's offering of a kiss, he could accept Mary Beth's suggestion without misgivings. "I'd be honored," he said with a little bow.

She took his arm in both her hands and started pulling him toward the door. "Come on over to the house right now. Just for today, we'll pretend that you're our brother. I think that everyone should be with people they love at Christmastime."

There was a bit of an odd note when Mary Beth said the word *love,* but Parker was too startled at being categorized as a brother to take much note of it.

"So, you're one of the family, all right?" Mary Beth repeated with gentle insistence.

He looked down at Mary Beth's tiny hand on his arm and felt a surge of affection. Of the three sisters, it would be easiest to develop brotherly feelings for her. Susannah was just too damn beautiful and Molly was... He didn't know how the hell he should feel about Molly. All he knew was that when he had kissed her the other night, he hadn't felt the least bit brotherly.

After his gloomy mood that morning, Parker had a surprisingly delightful afternoon with Smokey and the girls. The tree-trimming had turned into a regular competition with spirited arguments over whose string of cranberries and popcorn was the most perfect. Then Smokey had chided Parker for eating up too many of the decorations and had finally slapped his hand away from the popcorn bowl with a dish towel. The bowl had overturned in the process, and a popcorn-flicking fight had ensued between the two men, who taunted each other like rival schoolboys and looked thoroughly silly.

Susannah had been quiet when she had arrived at the lunch table a little late, but her humor was restored as the afternoon wore on, though she avoided Parker's eyes. Even Molly seemed to be having a good time, for once letting herself laugh along with her sisters and forget that she was the one in control.

Smokey had been in and out of the parlor all afternoon as he tended his meal. He'd had the ingredients for his famous plum pudding "plumping" for days and had gotten up before dawn to begin working on the other savory dishes he had planned.

When the eight-foot tree was filled to the top with adornments and all the other preparations were finished, Parker headed back out to the bunkhouse, whistling and realizing that he was looking forward to Christmas Eve after all.

He dressed up for the occasion in the rough silk shirt he'd brought from New York. It was the first time he'd worn it since he'd come West. It was wrinkled from being packed with his things, but he figured it would smooth out respectably enough against the heat of his skin.

Susannah and Mary Beth had also taken out their best finery. Susannah's gown was a delicate pink, with a smocked bodice that emphasized her shapely figure. Mary Beth was dressed in a bright green shirtwaist that made her eyes take on a turquoise cast. Even Smokey had cleaned up. His denims had been replaced by a pair of slick serge trousers that squeezed him a bit at the middle. His normally scraggly beard was trimmed and neatly curled out to each side with some kind of pomade.

"Whooee, old timer," Parker exclaimed as Smokey joined them in the parlor. "You smell downright pretty. Another minute and I'm going to be asking you to dance with me.''

"You do and you'll find your head spun round the wrong direction on your shoulders, you young pup.''

Mary Beth and Susannah laughed. "You look very nice, Smokey,'' Mary Beth added in soothing tones. "We all do, I think.''

"Well, the supper's ready. Where's Molly?'' Smokey said.

"Still up in her room, I guess,'' Susannah answered, getting to her feet. "She took the washtub up there for a bath.''

Just as Smokey and Mary Beth were digesting this unusual piece of information, Molly shouted from the top of the stairs, "I'll be right there.''

All heads turned toward the big staircase as the missing sister appeared around the curve. Smokey's jaw dropped halfway to his knees and Mary Beth breathed, "Oh, Molly. You look so beautiful.''

Parker felt as if he'd been hit in the stomach. It was Molly, all right, but not the dirty, tough, scrappy female who'd threatened to blow his tongue off with her buffalo rifle. Not the skillful horsewoman who'd bullied and nagged him as he tried to learn how to move cattle. Not even the tearful, stubborn vigilante he'd held after she'd gotten sick by the side of the road. This Molly was a stunning woman—no, a *lady*—with her hair swept up into a graceful twist that set off her slender neck, her figure poured into a crystal-colored dress that shimmered as she carefully descended the stairs. Parker could swear that she was even wearing a corset under the shiny taffeta. The sleeves were puffy and short, revealing long, white arms, which Parker found oddly sensual. Molly always wore long-sleeved clothes. Even on the few warm days they'd had, when Susannah and Mary Beth had dressed in lightweight summer wear, Molly had never bared her arms, nor any other part of her. Now, in the scooping neckline, she was bare all the way to... quite bare. Parker swallowed, his mouth suddenly dry.

It was almost a relief when she reached the bottom step and burst out laughing, bringing back at least the sound of the old Molly. "You lost your bet, Susannah," she said gaily. "I did wear it. So there. But there's no way I'm going to be able to fit any of Smokey's goose inside this thing with me. So I think I'll just run back on upstairs and change into—"

Susannah ran over to her and grabbed her arm. "Oh, no, you don't. You look stunning, sis, and you're going to stay that way. And besides, you don't win the bet until you wear it to the Overstreets' party tomorrow."

"Oh, do keep it on, Molly," Mary Beth urged. "You look like a princess."

"A star," Smokey agreed. "Your father always said you three were his lucky stars. And I have a feeling he's up there watching us tonight."

Molly's eyes misted at the old cook's words. "I think so, too," she said softly. She looked up at the ceiling, held her arms out to the side and twirled. "Can you see me, Papa? Do I look like one of your stars?"

Mary Beth and Susannah each seized one of her hands. "Here we are, Papa," Susannah said loudly. "Your three stars, all dressed up for Christmas and for you."

"Your papa would be so proud of you girls," Smokey murmured. "You're like a trio of angels."

"Amen to that." Parker found his voice for the first time. Now that she was laughing with her sisters, Molly was looking a little bit more like herself. Her soft brown hair had come out of its knot in places and made wispy tendrils against her neck. She'd kicked off the slippers that had added to her stature as she'd descended the stairs, saying, "Well, I'm sure as shooting not wearing these torturous things all night." But nevertheless, the transformation was amazing. He'd suspected that her figure would rival her sisters', but he hadn't known it would be such perfection. He found his eyes darting constantly to the smooth white expanse of her bare neck and chest.

"Do you like it, Parker?" Molly asked, a little catch in her voice that made her sound more like Mary Beth than herself.

"Yes, ma'am." Parker tried to keep his voice light. "That getup's a sight prettier than two-year-old buckskins, if you ask me."

She stuck her tongue out at him while Mary Beth chided, "You're supposed to say something gallant, Parker."

He gave a grin he was not entirely feeling. "I agree with Smokey—you're the prettiest trio west of the Mississippi."

"But not as pretty as the girls in New York?" Susannah asked a little caustically.

He shifted his gaze slowly, studying each of the three of them in turn. "Ladies, I'd wager you'd turn heads in any city of the world, including New York."

They looked satisfied with his answer and turned happily, arm in arm, toward the dining room. Smokey lumbered after them, leaving Parker standing in the middle of the parlor, wondering why he felt as if his world had just gotten much more complex than it had been only a few hours ago.

After gorging themselves on Smokey's supper, they heaped praises on his culinary abilities until he was pink with pleasure.

"I've never had a finer meal at Delmonico's in the heart of New York," Parker had declared, which had led to another round of questions from Susannah and Mary Beth about life back in the glamorous big city.

Finally they retired to the parlor to open the gifts that had been snuck under the tree during the course of the day by members of the household. Parker had purchased fine leather riding gloves for each of the sisters and a meerschaum pipe for Smokey, to replace the battered old one the cook pulled out each evening after finishing up the dishes. The gifts were much finer than would be expected from a typical cowhand, but not, Molly supposed, out of the ordinary for the son of a New York banker.

Susannah exclaimed with delight when she opened her pair, which had been dyed blue, and crossed the room to bend and give Parker a quick kiss of thanks on the cheek, looking defiantly at her sister as she straightened.

Molly let the gesture pass without comment. She would probably let a band of armed Indians pass without comment this evening. She was having trouble enough keeping her head sitting straight on her shoulders. When Susannah had taunted her about buying a real dress for once, she hadn't admitted to herself that Parker was a large part of the reason she had accepted the dare. But tonight, as she'd seen his eyes on her again and again with that admiring, almost predatory glint in them, she realized that she'd wanted to impress him. Of course, he'd looked at Susannah that way, too, and Molly certainly couldn't compete with her sister in attracting male attention. The fact that tonight Parker's gaze was more often on her than on either of her curvier, blond sisters was simply because of the novelty of it all. But nevertheless, she'd felt a strange fluttering inside her every time she saw that particular look.

The dress seemed to make her more aware of herself and everything else around her—the gentle sway of it alongside her hips as she moved, the cool air on her bare arms, the heat of the fire against her chest. And under it all, that not unpleasant flutter. Was this why women went through what they did to dress in such impractical garb?

"Here's another one for you, Molly." Mary Beth was kneeling next to the tree, digging out the last of the packages.

Molly went to claim her gift and bent to pick up another cloth-wrapped bundle at its side. "This one's for you, Parker," she said self-consciously. Now that it had come time to give it to him, she'd begun to feel a little embarrassed about the gift she'd chosen for him.

He stood to take it from her, a warm smile on his face. He was wearing a loose shirt of some kind of fine, white material that contrasted sharply with his tanned face and dark brown hair. She'd never seen such a shirt before on a man, Molly realized. It gave him a dashing air that added to his stark good looks. She handed him the package, her heart speeding up a little as his fingers brushed over hers. Hell's bells, she was mooning more than Susannah. Just because they had a handsome man working for them didn't mean that she had to turn into a ninny. She backed away from him. Perhaps, after all, she'd best march on upstairs and get back into her trousers.

"Thank you," Parker was saying. "You folks didn't need to do this." His flowy shirt moved right along with his muscles as he sat back down and began to untie his gift. It was a leather-bound book entitled *Roughing It.*

Molly watched his reaction anxiously, her words tumbling out. "It's about a man's adventures coming out West. Mr. Simon over at the general store told me about it. I thought you might...since you've come out here yourself...and you like book learning and all..." She stopped and bit her lip. Why couldn't she have just bought him the tin of tobacco her father always had given the hands?

"Mark Twain, of course."

"You've read it?" she asked, dismayed.

"No. I've read *Innocents Abroad,* about his travels in Europe. He's brilliant—very funny. It's a perfect gift, Molly, thank you. Thank all of you," he said, including the rest of them in his smile.

"Susannah and I have our own presents for you," Mary Beth said, jumping to her feet and crossing over to him with two more packages.

Everyone watched him open them. Mary Beth had knit him a gray wool scarf. In the other package was a kerchief on which Susannah had chain stitched PP in each corner. As he finished, Smokey threw a pair of unwrapped wool socks into his lap. "To keep you warm out there in the bunkhouse," the cook said gruffly.

Parker sat back in his chair and surveyed the group. "I'm overwhelmed. I don't know what to say."

"Just say it's a very merry Christmas," Mary Beth suggested with a smile.

He rubbed his fingers along the tooled edge of the book Molly had given him. "That it is, Mary Beth. It's a very merry Christmas indeed."

Smokey had insisted that no one would be cleaning up the kitchen in their Christmas finery. It would wait until tomorrow, he assured them. So they sat around the big parlor fireplace, drinking Smokey's spicy hot Christmas punch and singing Christmas carols, stopping every now and then for a bittersweet remembrance of Christmases past.

"What was your favorite gift when you were little, Parker?" Mary Beth asked.

Parker stared into the flames, remembering. "When I was eight and my sister was seven, we each got a pony. Mine was a dapple gray named Cloudy. I suppose out here on the ranch that wouldn't be so remarkable, but to a little boy in New York City, I thought I'd never seen anything so pretty in all my life. I rode her every day."

"And now all these years later you've come out West to learn how to ride a real horse," Molly said dryly.

Her elegant dress had not completely softened her tongue, Parker noted ruefully. He answered her with a smile, refusing to be baited. "I've been riding real horses for some time now, Molly. But I am learning a lot out here—thanks to all of you."

"Hell, he rides better than half the rummies we've had come through this place," Smokey said.

"When I can ride and rope better than this place's mistresses—that's when I'll be satisfied," Parker replied.

"You've set your sights high there, my boy," Smokey said.

Molly gave a disparaging huff and added, "That'll be the day, tenderfoot."

Parker grinned. "Sounds like a challenge to me."

"Don't worry about it, Parker," Mary Beth said in her conciliatory tone. "You already ride and rope better than I can."

Smokey stood and stretched his back. "The day you can rope better'n Molly and ride better'n Susannah is the day I shave this beard off my face."

"You'll look good clean shaven, old man," Parker taunted.

"I don't intend to live that long. And I won't, either, if I don't get some sleep. I'm getting too old to get up before dawn to start all the fixings for a fancy supper."

His comment brought another round of compliments from all on the excellent feast he'd prepared. Then Susannah and Mary Beth both got to their feet.

"We all need to get to bed. We'll be dancing until dawn tomorrow night."

Molly gave a little shudder. "I don't know if I even want to go. The last time I saw most of those men was when they were murdering Ole Pedersson."

"It wasn't murder, Molly," Susannah objected. "Ole had killed a man."

"He was *suspected* of killing a man."

"Well, there haven't been any other problems since he was hanged. And no clues to any other killer. He must have done it."

Smokey shook his head sadly. "I still don't see Ole as a killer, but the drink'll take a man sometimes. Puts a demon in them."

"Even if he was the killer, he should have had a trial." They'd been through this countless times. When she'd first come back from that night, Molly had been almost obsessed by it. She'd ridden into town the next day to protest to the sheriff, without getting any satisfaction. Then she'd sent a letter to the territorial marshal over in Laramie. But as time had passed, the horror of the night had faded a little. Everyone said that Ole was the killer. And, while it was illegal, vigilante justice was often the accepted practice in smaller towns when the circuit judge came around only twice a year. Molly regretted having brought up the subject, spoiling the happy Christmas mood.

As if reading her thoughts, Parker changed the subject. "So this Christmas party tomorrow... are cowpokes invited?"

"Of course you're coming with us," Susannah said quickly. "Who do you think we're counting on for all our dances?"

Parker looked at Smokey. "It's two of us and three of them, old timer. Do you think we can handle it?"

"When I was your age, I could handle 'em six at a time. Of course, I wasn't a fancy Eastern pup like you."

Parker grinned. "I'll just have to do my best."

Smokey gave a little wave and headed toward the kitchen. Susannah and Mary Beth turned toward the stairs. "I'll be right up after I check the barn," Molly said.

"Let me do it," Parker urged. "You're too dressed up to go out there tonight."

"No, thank you," she said stiffly, hitching up her silvery skirts and walking toward the door. For as long as she could remember her father had checked the barn every night before he went to bed. It had given him a sense of peace to know that the animals were quiet, the latches closed, all in order. The first day he'd been too sick to make his nightly rounds, she'd gone for him. She'd gone every night since and, fancy dress or no, she wasn't about to hand the job over to a tenderfoot in a silk shirt.

Chapter Ten

Parker followed her out the door. "I want to thank you again, Molly," he said to her back. "It really was a wonderful Christmas Eve. I'd never expected to be so content tonight."

Something in his voice made her turn around to look at him. "Because you missed your family back in New York?"

"That and...other things. Christmas could have been tough for me this year. Instead, I felt...welcome. As if I was among good friends."

His usual glib confidence was gone. A sudden glint of pain in his dark eyes made Molly answer softly, "I think we are your friends, Parker. I hope so, anyway."

A little timidly, she put a hand on his forearm. Under the thin material of his shirt, it felt rock hard. She started to move away, but his hand came up to capture hers, keeping it there, pressed against him. As the night wind raised chill bumps on her bare chest, her heart started to pound.

"I think so, too," he said. "We're certainly good enough friends for me to claim your first waltz tomorrow."

She could feel the pounding all the way to her ears. She swallowed and said quickly, "Oh, no. I don't dance. Unless it's a reel."

"Nonsense. How could you not dance?"

She pulled more forcefully and her hand slipped out from under his. "I just don't, is all."

Parker took a step back and put his hands on his hips. "You mean to tell me the men in this territory would let a pretty girl like you get away with sitting in the corner like the little old ladies?"

He looked so dumbfounded that Molly couldn't help believing that he meant what he said. He considered it amazing that men wouldn't want to dance with her. And he considered her pretty. She felt a quick flush of heat on her cheeks. "I get asked sometimes, but mostly I imagine it looks too ridiculous to see two sets of trousers out there dancing with each other."

"You've always worn trousers to the dances?"

She nodded.

He was quiet a long minute. "Now, why exactly is that, boss lady?"

His tone was kind, gentle. Molly couldn't detect any pity, but that didn't mean it wasn't there. She stiffened. "It's what I wear. And why I wear it is none of your business."

He nodded. "You're right. To tell you the truth, I think you look darn cute in those pants. But you're not going to wear trousers tomorrow, right?"

"Well, I have to win my bet with Susannah."

"Right. So tomorrow you'll dance more than the reels."

The cold had finally reached inside her and she began to shiver. She turned away toward the barn. "I don't know how," she said dismissively over her shoulder.

In one long stride he caught up to her and stopped her with a hand on her shoulder. "If I can learn to rope cattle, I guess you can learn how to dance."

She glared at him. "Will you stop yammering at me, Parker, and let me get my work done? I'm freezing to death out here."

He ran his hands briskly up and down her bare arms. "You're like to catch your death. Why don't you go back on inside and let me finish up?"

His hands were rough and his touch businesslike, but Molly felt the pounding again. It was like having a bad fever that ebbed and peaked, leaving you out of your head and weakened. "If you'd just let me alone, I could finish up and go on in where it's warm."

He took a step back from her and held up both hands as if in surrender. "Fine. Go."

She hurried away from him toward the sanctuary of the barn. Out of the corner of her eye she saw him walking to the bunkhouse. They reached their destinations at the same time. "Good night, Parker," she called. "Merry Christmas."

He waved at her and yelled back, "The first waltz, Molly...it's mine." Then he disappeared into the dark bunkhouse.

The Christmas night dance had been a tradition for the past several years. Back in the sixties it had often been held at the Lucky Stars, until Charlie Hanks had started to get too nervous about all the handsome bucks buzzing around his little daughters. Recently it had been at neighboring ranches, and the Hanks family had said their goodbyes promptly at midnight, before any of the young men had gotten too rowdy on spiked cider.

Harvey Overstreet was a widower, but he was a sociable fellow, and his two married daughters came up from Cheyenne to act as hostesses when he wanted to have a gathering. They were there tonight with their husbands and a total of nine children between them. Traditionally the children were given their own room at the party, and each brought a favorite Christmas toy to keep them occupied.

Except for the logistical difficulty of keeping at least one eye on each of three daughters, Charlie Hanks had always enjoyed Christmas night. As one of the oldest settlers in the region, he had been looked up to by the ranchers, and they had listened to his stories with flattering respect. The ladies had liked him, too. He'd had a gallant tongue and an appreciative eye, though everyone knew his attentions would never go beyond the bounds of propriety. Charlie Hanks had been that rare kind of man—totally satisfied with his lot in life and not interested in trying to change it.

It felt strange to be arriving at the party without him, Molly decided as they got out of the old carriage that Smokey had insisted on dragging out of the back of the barn for the occasion. Almost as strange as arriving in her new silver dress. She shivered underneath her warm coat. Then she shivered again as Parker took her arm in one hand and Susannah's in the other. Neither girl needed help walking the short distance from the carriage to the Overstreets' front porch, but Parker said in his most courtly Eastern way, "Please allow me to escort you inside, ladies," and Molly didn't dare protest.

Smokey followed Parker's lead, and laughingly offered his arm to Mary Beth. "Might as well do this proper," he said.

Once inside, it was plenty warm and Molly let Parker slip her coat off. Her shivers had subsided. She took a deep breath and squared her shoulders. She wasn't at all sure what the reaction of her neighbors would be to her outfit. It wouldn't be the first time she had shocked them. But it would be the first time she had shocked them by doing the normal thing.

"You look stunning. They'll all be astounded," Parker whispered from behind her, as if reading her thoughts.

"I'd give anything for my buckskins right now," she confessed.

He walked around to stand in front of her, his eyes skimming down the length of her figure. "Just wait. I predict it will take you about two minutes out there to feel comfortable. Then you're going to start having the time of your life."

"I'm always a little nervous at these things. I'm better with cattle than with people. I never know what to say."

Parker put his arm at her waist and swept her out into the Overstreets' big living room, which had been mostly cleared of furniture for the dance. "You won't have to say anything, Molly, believe me."

And he was right. Suddenly the neighborhood men with whom she'd never done more than discuss cattle prices and feed mixtures and drought remedies were swarming around her like bees at a hive. The older ladies who had turned up their noses when she'd attended the barn dances or the husking bees in her men's attire were suddenly smiling at her and calling her "dear Molly."

After several minutes it all became too much. She felt the room closing in around her as if she was about to faint for the first time in her life. Her skin was flushed and hot. She was looking around the room for the easiest path to the door when suddenly Parker was at her side, a strong hand on her arm, leading her through the crowd.

They reached the little entry hall, and she took a deep breath. "Whew. I've felt more comfortable in the middle of a cattle stampede," she said shakily.

"I told you that you'd cause a ruckus," Parker said, his eyes alight as they rested on her.

She fanned a hand at her face. "It's not fair, you know. Clothes shouldn't make that much difference. I'm exactly the same person I was when I was wearing my buckskins."

"Maybe you're not."

"What's that supposed to mean?"

He leaned into the coat room and pulled out her coat, then put it around her shoulders and led her out the door. There was a cane swing at the end of the wide front porch. "Shall we sit out here while you catch your breath?" he asked.

She let him lead her to the seat, but repeated her question. "What do you mean, I may not be the same person?"

"It's only that…" He struggled for the words. "Of course you're the same person you are in buckskins, but sometimes what we wear reflects what we're feeling about ourselves. The fact that you've decided to go to the trouble of dressing yourself up may say something about what's going on inside you."

Molly looked sideways at Parker, astonished. She had expected him to agree with her that all the fuss over her new "look" was silly. But instead he had put the matter in a whole new perspective. She didn't know if his comment had just been a lucky guess or if he was simply extremely wise in the ways of human nature. She only knew that he was dead right. She hadn't worn the dress to win a bet with Susannah. She was feeling different about life, about herself, about a lot of things these days. And a large part of the reason was the man sitting next to her on the swing. It made her nervous as a field mouse to think about it.

"Hell's bells!" she exclaimed. "Can't a girl put on a dress now and then without everyone thinking she's gone soft?"

Parker chuckled. "Now, you see. You're using bad language to try to show me that you haven't changed any—that you're as tough as ever. It's part of what we do—dress differently, talk differently, depending on how we want to present ourselves to the world. For a long time you've felt the need to present yourself as the hard-as-nails, no-nonsense owner of the Lucky Stars."

"Which is exactly who I am."

"But you're also a twenty-one-year-old girl with—"

"Twenty-two."

"A twenty-two-year-old girl with a whole life ahead and a natural desire to get on with living it."

His thigh rested against hers on the tiny swing. She shifted uneasily. "You talk like you know all about it, Parker. You're not more than twenty-two yourself."

"Twenty-three." He grinned at her.

She leaned against the back of the swing with a big sigh, setting it in motion. "I *did* want to look pretty— just for once," she admitted.

"And what's wrong with that? No one's going to think you're less of a rancher because you've come to a dance in a dress."

She pushed with her foot to keep the swing rocking. "No one thinks I'm much of a rancher, anyway."

"Then they're fools, and you shouldn't care what they think."

The vehemence of his defense surprised and pleased her, but his arguments had only added to the evening's confusion. "You see, that's why I can't dress up like my sisters. Once they think I'm just like them, they'll never take me seriously."

Parker planted his foot down to stop the swaying. Then he reached for her hand. "Molly, you are one of the strongest women I've met in my life—and one of the smartest. You decided to wear men's clothing because you weren't about to let anyone dictate your attire. Now you should feel free to wear a dress if you want to for the same reason."

When he put it that way, it suddenly made very good sense. Parker was right. She'd always sworn to wear what she darned well pleased. Right now it pleased her to wear a silvery dress and sit in the moonlight with a handsome man. Or better yet...

"How about that waltz you threatened me with, tenderfoot?"

Parker was on his feet in an instant, pulling her after him. "I thought you'd never ask," he said with a wink.

* * *

The music for the dancing was supplied by Harv Overstreet's brother, Norbert, and Mr. Simon, the owner of the general store. Their fiddles sang out in peaceful harmony most of the time, though on a couple of the reels Norbert insisted on going at a tempo that was a little faster than Mr. Simon's skill could manage, leaving him to trail a couple of measures behind like an out-of-tune echo.

The crowd minded not at all. By midnight the older folk had mostly retired to the row of chairs along the wall or had joined the group in the Overstreets' book-lined library. The dance floor was left to the younger set, who seemed to get more energy as the night wore on.

Parker watched with some amusement as Molly and her partner glided by in a perfect waltz. For a girl who had never danced before, she'd certainly gotten the hang of it quickly enough. But then, he had yet to discover anything that Molly couldn't do well when she had the mind to.

She'd been claimed by a score of partners, outshining even Susannah. Parker himself had managed only two dances. He'd danced three times each with Susannah and Mary Beth and, dutifully, one time each with several of the matronly ranch wives. He'd avoided the other single women. For a man who'd sworn off romance, he already had enough trouble living with three women.

The Dickersons had arrived at the party late. Parker had watched as Molly had waited for Jeremy's reaction to her new appearance, and he'd noted the quickly hidden disappointment in her expression when her neighbor had greeted her with only a cool "You look lovely tonight, Molly. It's nice to see you in a dress for a change.''

She deserved much more in a man than Jeremy Dickerson, that was for sure. She deserved ... *Passion* was the word that leapt to his mind, though Parker found the image made him somewhat uncomfortable.

The waltz ended and almost immediately the fiddlers started in on another. Molly was pulling away from her partner with a laughing shake of her head, her hand against her slender throat. Parker darted around a twirling couple to reach her side. ''I believe this was the dance you promised me,'' he said, whisking her into his arms with a nod of apology to her partner.

He matched his steps with hers, but she protested, ''I'm winded. I don't think I can dance another step.''

''I could see that,'' he said, and whirled her into the dining room to a precision stop right next to the punch bowl. ''You need a drink.''

He served her a cup and watched as she gulped it down in big, thirsty swallows. ''So that was a rescue?'' she asked.

''Yes, ma'am.''

''You're a useful person to have around, Parker Prescott.''

''I try to be.'' He smiled at her and plucked the punch cup from her fingers. ''Do you want more?''

She shook her head. The dining room was empty. Only a few morsels of food remained scattered around the trays on the big plank table. ''It looks like we're out of luck if you're hungry,'' he said.

''I'm not.''

At the far end of the dining room an archway led into a small music room with a spinet. Parker nodded in that direction. "Do you want to sit down for a minute?"

"Anywhere but the dance floor."

He took her elbow and led her around the messy table. "So, you've enjoyed your evening after all?" he asked.

She nodded. "Yes. And I may have you to thank for it. Once I stopped worrying about what other people thought of my dress, I was able to relax."

"And waltz."

She smiled. "It wasn't so hard after all."

His arm moved from her elbow to her waist. "I was hoping to get another dance with you myself."

She gave a happy laugh. "It's not my fault if you can't speak up fast enough, Mr. Prescott. All you had to do was ask."

He pulled her to a stop, then pointed above her head. "I'm asking," he said, his voice suddenly thick.

She looked up to catch a brief glimpse of a hanging ball of mistletoe, just before his lips came down on hers.

Parker had meant the gesture to be friendly, light-hearted. But even before he had reached her mouth he knew that it was going to be more than that. The last thing he saw before closing his eyes was the quick rise and fall of her half-bare breasts above the clinging silver of her gown. His body swelled instantly. The arm around her waist involuntarily tightened, drawing her closer. He kissed her once, dry and hot, and then, when she breathed out a half-startled moan, he moistened his own lips and hers with his tongue and kissed her again. In earnest. Deep and satisfying, with the entire length of her body drawn up against his as waves of sensation swept downward and settled around his groin with spectacular urgency.

He released her almost at once, stepping back as if he'd been burned, expecting a slap or, at the very least, the harsh lash of her tongue.

She stood watching him for a long moment, her breathing altered. Then, to his astonishment, she said softly, "Thank you." Her eyes skittered down to the floor.

Parker took a long, calming breath. "Thank you?" he asked, unsure as to whether the sudden surge of lust had affected his hearing.

She raised her gaze, looking more herself again—in control, but a little defensive. "It completes my fantasy, you see. I wanted to feel beautiful and desirable for at least one night. Maybe I even wanted to be kissed."

Parker ran his hand back through his hair and gave an off-balance laugh. "Well, jumpin' Jehoshaphat, Molly. All you had to do was ask."

"Asking would have spoiled it." She sounded wistful, as if the moment was already a memory to tuck away.

He put his arm back around her waist. "I... ah... could try it again, just for the sake of the fantasy."

She stepped backward and shook her head. "No. Then I'd have to fire you."

"Tarnation, boss lady. Make up your mind."

She smiled apologetically. "You know as well as I do that we shouldn't have done it. But I guess I was in the mood to break the rules tonight. And besides, it was... nice."

"It was *damn* nice."

"But not anything we can let happen again. Ever again," she added sternly.

Parker gave a shrug that was much more indifferent than he was feeling. Was the woman made of ice after all? Hadn't she felt what had just happened between them? Maybe she didn't have enough experience with kissing to realize that not every kiss turns into that kind of explosion. Or perhaps the explosion had been one-sided. It was hard to believe, but as she stood there lecturing him, cool as a schoolmarm, he wondered.

"So if I kiss you again, I lose my job?"

"You'd better believe it, cowboy."

"Hmm." The decision took him about three seconds. He snatched her against him again. Using more finesse this time, he skillfully mated their lips and tongues until he was *darn* sure he hadn't left her indifferent. Just before he felt his control about to snap once again, he released her, stepped back and held up his hands, waiting for her reaction.

Her eyes were closed, her lips blurry, and he thought he could detect the slightest bit of a quiver.

"There you are, Molly. It's time for the midnight toast and we couldn't find you." Susannah's voice hit both of them like a splash of water.

Molly turned guiltily toward the door at the far end of the room where her sister's graceful form was silhouetted in the dim light. "We were . . . having a glass of punch."

Her voice was shaky, but Parker recovered more quickly. "They've worn your sister out tonight, Susannah," he said smoothly. "She's the belle of the ball in her new finery. Of course, I haven't noticed you lacking for partners." With a hand that barely touched her lower back, Parker guided Molly smoothly across the dining room. "I'd hate to have to judge a competition between you two."

Susannah did not seem suspicious of her sister's unsettled appearance. "I told you it would be fun, Molly. Admit it, now. You've had a good time."

Molly shot a sideways glance at Parker. It wasn't friendly, but it didn't look as if she was about to dig out her buffalo gun, either. "Yes, sis. I did have a good time. But I'm more tuckered than if I'd spent the day hog-tying cattle."

Susannah laughed and reached for her sister's hand, pulling her through the door and onto the dance floor. "Well, you don't look like you've spent the day hog-tying cattle. Come on, let's go break a few more hearts before we find Mary Beth and head home."

Parker stood in the recesses of the dining-room door for several more minutes watching the sisters move across the room, gathering men about them like a tumbleweed adding on dried twigs. It had been quite a night for Miss Molly. So much had happened, it was possible that the kisses under the mistletoe might not have been as staggering to her as they had been to him. But he had the feeling that things had changed between him and his boss lady. Whether or not either one of them was ready for it to happen.

Everyone always slept late the day after Christmas at the Lucky Stars. But no one had bothered to tell Parker. The kitchen was cold and dark when he came up for breakfast. He lit an oil lamp and started a fire in the stove. The short night's sleep had left him a little less confident than he had been last night about

Molly's reaction to his behavior. Everything looked different by the dawning light of the new day. But it was too late to do anything about it now. If she had regrets, so be it. There was one thing he knew for certain—he hadn't been the sole participant in those kisses.

The tin pot was nearly full of yesterday's coffee, and he put it on to heat up. He wasn't especially hungry. A cold biscuit would do for now, then he'd go on out to see to the animals, who hadn't danced into the wee morning hours and were undoubtedly expecting breakfast as usual.

He didn't admit that he would just as soon get out of the kitchen before Molly came down. He'd have to face her, of course, but he'd rather it would be when the entire family was around. He laughed out loud at his own cowardice. *Buck up, Prescott. Since when have you been one to let a slip of a woman scare you? Even one with a buffalo rifle twice her size?* He wouldn't even wait for the coffee, he decided, clapping on his hat and turning toward the door.

"What's so funny?" Molly appeared at the foot of the kitchen stairs. Her transformation back to boss lady was complete. She had on her buckskins and her hair was pulled back into severe braids.

Parker took off the hat and threw it on the table with a sigh of resignation. "Nothing," he said bluntly. "I was just about to go out and get to work. Assuming I still have a job."

"Aren't you going to have breakfast?"

"Do I?" he insisted.

"Have a job?"

He nodded, waiting.

"I s'pose."

"Now, there's a ringing endorsement."

He was wrong. She wasn't completely trans-formed. There was a little quiver around her mouth, a hint of vulnerability in her blue eyes. "What do you expect me to say, Parker? We can't deny what happened last night, but I'd appreciate it if you would help me forget about it."

He grabbed the coffeepot with his shirttail, poured a cup and took a step toward her, offering it. "So you're sure you want to forget about it."

She looked at his hand holding the cup as if it were a rattlesnake. "Of course I do. I acted . . . like a fool."

"There's nothing foolish about kissing. People do it all the time."

"Like a hoyden, then. I . . . I kissed you back."

"Yes, ma'am, you did." Parker restrained a grin.

"Well, it won't happen again."

"If that's the way you want it."

"It is."

Parker took a step closer, reached for her hand and put the coffee cup in it, bending her fingers around the handle. His face was inches from hers. "But I still have a job," he confirmed softly.

"Yes." Her voice changed pitch halfway through the word.

"Good."

He turned on his heel, snatched up his hat once again and walked out of the room.

Chapter Eleven

It seemed as if winter had just been waiting for the Christmas festivities to end before arriving in full force. The day after Christmas was cold and blustery, and by midafternoon it had started to snow—not the big wet flakes of the earlier snowstorm that had frozen Parker's ears, but tiny ice pellets of fierce, driving snow. Before the storm started, Parker and Smokey had ridden out to check on the cattle in the boxed canyon. The snow caught them as they neared Cougar Creek, which was now frozen except for a few places where water bubbled up from underneath the built-up ice.

"We should head back," Smokey yelled. "This looks like it could be a nasty one."

"We might as well just take a look now that we're this far. It'll relieve Molly's mind to hear that her babies are still behaving."

Smokey laughed. "Shake a leg, then, son. Let's take a quick peek and skedaddle on out of here."

Parker turned his horse away from the rough creek bank and headed toward the canyon, scanning the horizon for signs of the cattle, his expression becoming tighter. It seemed to him that he should be able to see the herd from this point. The snow cut down on their visibility, but before long they were close enough to see that the carefully rounded up herd had once again scattered. "They're gone!" he said unnecessarily.

Smokey sat up in his stirrups, looking all around. "Dogies do like to roam."

"You think they went off by themselves?"

"What else? Unless a cougar or something came by and spooked them."

"Or something," Parker said in a low voice.

"Well, there's not much we can do about it today with this storm coming on. Bejeezus, Molly will be spitting nails."

Parker slapped a gloved hand against his thigh. Molly had as much as admitted that things needed to go smoothly if she was to be able to keep this place going. She needed every one of her cattle, and she needed them near enough to bring in next spring with a minimum of men.

They'd turned back toward the house when Parker's attention was caught by three animals grouped together a little upstream. Shouting over the wind, he pointed them out to Smokey.

"They're calves," the cook called back. "But I don't see any sign of the mamas."

"What shall we do?"

Smokey reined in his horse and lifted his face to the snow. "Bring 'em in, I guess. They're like to die out here without any of the bigger animals for shelter."

Working as quickly as they could, they cornered the three strays and zigzagged with them back to the corrals. "I'll put them in the barn with Moonlight," Parker hollered. "You go on inside."

The three calves appeared more than willing to be led out of the howling wind. With no more than a slap on the rump, each went easily into the big stall, where Moonlight gave a halfhearted bleat of welcome. It was a small victory, but Parker felt pleased. This cattle business wasn't so bad after all. Especially when the cattle were no bigger than he was. He grinned and saw that they had plenty of water and hay. Then he said, "Sleep tight, little dogies," and started up to the house to see if Smokey had broken the bad news to Molly.

The storm outside made supper seem cozier than usual, or perhaps it was a lingering Christmas spirit that hovered over the table. After Molly's initial explosion at word of the missing cattle, she calmed down and let the good humor of the others take her mind off the subject. They ate the last of the Christmas goose and went over last night's party in exaggerated detail.

"Did you see how the Widow Fosseen wouldn't let Harv Overstreet out of her sight all night long?" Susannah asked with a little giggle.

"Well, good for her. Harv hasn't had enough to keep him busy since Roberta passed away," Molly said. Then she grinned. "And I noticed Max McClanahan seemed to make herself conspicuous whenever Smokey got anywhere near."

"Was Max there?" Mary Beth asked. "I didn't even see her."

"You never were around," Susannah observed. "Where were you off to most of the evening?"

Molly gave her youngest sister a sharp look, but Mary Beth answered calmly. "Just because I don't have to dance twice with every man at the party under the age of ninety doesn't mean I wasn't enjoying myself. I had a nice long talk with Frannie Copplemeyer, for one.''

''How's her hip?'' Susannah asked.

But Molly interrupted her question. ''It's hard to imagine anyone not knowing when Max is in the room, but she did leave early to go on over to nurse Cynthia Baxter's mother-in-law. She's got the croup, and at her age...''

Parker listened to the accounts in silence. He didn't know most of these people, but he was struck by the sense of community among them all. Back home, his mother spent hours each week working in the poorhouses and the homes for fallen girls, but then she would come home to her upper-class mansion and join her proper social stratum for the main part of her life. It had been one of the reasons Parker had left—the layering, the impersonality of it all.

''And did you have a good time at your first ranch party, Parker?'' Susannah was asking him.

He looked quickly over at Molly, but she was studying the crystal pattern in the top of the butter dish. Turning back to Susannah, he said blandly, ''I had a wonderful time. Your neighbors appear to be very nice people. I especially liked the fact that everyone was invited. It doesn't seem to matter here if you're a cowhand or a...banker.''

''It matters to the mamas,'' Smokey contradicted. ''They stand around the edge of the room like chicken hawks, and when one of their sweet young things dances one too many dances with a no-account wrangler, they swoop down and carry them off to safety, or to the nearest suitable prospect.''

''So cowboys aren't considered suitable prospects?''

"It depends on the cowboy," Susannah said with a bat of her long lashes.

Molly stood. "We all should get to bed. If the storm stops, I want to ride out tomorrow and see where those critters have taken themselves off to."

Parker glanced over at the window where the storm was rattling away in fury. He got to his feet slowly. "I'll say good night, then."

Molly followed the direction of his gaze. "I guess you'd better stay in here tonight, Parker." When everyone looked at her in surprise, she added tartly, "I'm not an ogre, you know. It would be stupid for him to stay out there in this storm."

"I appreciate it," Parker said simply. "If you'd get me a couple of blankets I can just roll up over by the fireplace...."

"You can stay in Papa's room. As long as we have a free bed, you might as well use it." She looked around the room as if daring anyone to question her decision. No one said a word. "Well, let's get going, then. I told you there'd be work to do tomorrow."

The next day the snow had been replaced by bitter cold. The inside of the big window in the master bedroom was covered with a thick layer of frost. Parker huddled under the covers. For a moment he wished that he was a boy again back in New York City with the maid coming to bring him a cup of hot chocolate and light the fire before he had to get up into the cold room.

There were no uniformed servants at the Lucky Stars, and the only way he was likely to get warm was to remember for the hundredth time those kisses he had shared the other night with Molly. Which was not, he had already discovered, the most sensible way to get a productive start to the morning.

He jumped out of bed, grimacing as the frigid air hit him. He'd slept in his long underwear, and he didn't intend to remove it for a morning wash. His standards of cleanliness had diminished somewhat since coming West. And, hell, it was too cold to smell bad, anyway.

He had pulled on his pants and was buttoning his flannel shirt when there was a knock on the door. He opened it to find Molly on the other side, her expression thunderous.

"Smokey said you bedded down those calves last night."

"I did." He'd checked the stall latches twice, and had even tied a length of twine around one that looked loose.

"What did you feed them?"

Parker looked puzzled. "Feed them? I just gave them hay."

"Well, they're down."

"Down?"

"Bloated. Something has sickened them."

He could see that she was extremely upset, fighting for control. "Maybe something they ate out on the range before we rounded them up."

"It's all four of them—Moonlight, too."

"What can we do for them?"

She closed her eyes for a minute. "I don't know." Her voice grew softer. "I'm sorry, Parker. It probably wasn't anything you did. I only thought that maybe you'd given them something...."

"I wouldn't do that. I don't know much about ranching, but I know enough not to go making up the rules on my own."

She nodded, fighting tears. "It's just that... I need these animals, Parker. I need every single one."

He quickly tucked his shirttails into his pants and stepped out the door, taking her arm. "Well, then, boss lady, let's get busy and save them."

They'd stayed in the freezing barn all day, going into the house only when their hands became so numb they could no longer move them to work. One of the calves had died almost immediately, justifying the worst of Molly's fears. The other three lay on their sides, kicking their legs every now and then and bleating in agony.

Smokey had said that the only thing to do with a bloated calf was to feed it oil. They tried to funnel some down their throats, but without much success. By midafternoon the distension of the animals' left sides was painfully obvious.

Moonlight's writhing had become increasingly frantic. Her eyes had turned dull, and her tongue lolled out of her mouth.

"We're going to lose them," Molly said grimly.

But Parker was not ready to give up. During his summers upstate he'd sometimes worked with the veterinarians who came to treat the horses. Once in a case of severe colic they'd considered puncturing a hole into the animal's intestine. "The way you do with bloated cattle," the doctor had said.

"How about if we just make a hole and let the gas come out?" he suggested.

Smokey looked as if Parker had taken leave of his senses, but Molly's eyes brightened. "Yes. I've heard of that."

All three eyed the fallen calves. The skin over their swollen middles was stretched so tautly it almost looked as if they might explode on their own.

"You mean just poke 'em—like a pig's bladder?" Smokey asked warily.

Parker had already walked over to the shelf to search for the awl they used to repair leather. "They're going to die if we don't do something."

Molly knelt next to Moonlight, rubbing her soft ears. "It doesn't look like we have a choice."

Parker entered the stall beside her and held out the instrument. "Do you want to do it?"

She gave a little shudder. "Would you?" ·

He took a deep breath. "I never did anything like this back in the bank," he mumbled as he knelt beside her. "Where do you suppose I should stick her?"

Molly ran her hand over the bulge in the animal's side. "I guess here where it's sticking out the most."

Parker puffed out his cheeks. "All right. Here goes." With a swift downward stab, he pierced the animal's skin. Immediately a foul-smelling liquid shot straight up in the air, splattering them both.

"Whew!" Smokey said with a grin. "It looks like that just might work, but you two are going to be smellier than a skunk in a briar patch."

Parker and Molly looked at each other and laughed, their noses twitching. Almost immediately Moonlight stopped writhing. In a few minutes she was standing. Molly and Smokey tied a strip of cloth around her middle to cover up the tiny wound while Parker proceeded to carry out the treatment with the other two calves.

By late afternoon all three animals were on their feet. Their distended stomachs had shrunk and the complaining moos had stopped.

"We did it," Molly said wearily.

In spite of the odor that still clung to them both, Parker gave her a quick hug of victory. "We sure did, boss lady. For these three, anyway. Too bad we couldn't have saved their buddy, too."

"You're the one who saved them, Parker. You just might turn out to be something of a cattleman after all."

Parker smiled. "I'll remind you of that when we start rounding them up again."

She straightened and looked at him. "Seriously, thank you. I would have given up when the oil didn't work. We would have lost all four without you."

Smokey and the girls had gone inside to start supper. Parker put a comforting hand on Molly's shoulder. Now that the crisis was past, the battle lines were gone from her face, replaced by a soft fatigue. It was odd, these feelings she engendered, unlike anything he'd ever quite experienced. He'd felt protective with Claire, too, but then it had been understandable. Claire had been a fragile wisp of a beauty who had ultimately proven too delicate for this world. There was nothing fragile about Molly. But at the moment he wished he could pull her head to his shoulder and make all her problems go away. That is, he thought with a grin, he *would* wish that if they both didn't smell so terrible.

"I reckon they won't let us in up at the house in these clothes."

Molly looked down at herself and wrinkled her nose. "I should have told Smokey to bring something out here for me to put on."

"Come on over to the bunkhouse. You can put on something of mine."

"Then we'll smell up your place."

"I don't care. It's better than stinking up the house where people are going to be eating in a few minutes."

After a moment's thought, she agreed and they walked across the yard to the bunkhouse. Once inside, Parker shut the door behind them. Molly gave him a wary look. "I'm not going to ravish you, boss lady. Frankly, you don't smell too appealing at the moment."

She laughed. "You'd rival a bed of skunk cabbage yourself, tenderfoot."

He stripped off his jacket and shirt and dumped them in a pile by the door. "I'll scrub all these clothes after dinner. Does Smokey have some lye?"

Smelly or not, Molly had to swallow hard at the sudden sight of Parker's well-muscled chest. It tapered to a narrow waist where at the moment his hands were beginning to unfasten the buttons of his trousers. "Ah . . . lye?" she asked stupidly.

Parker grinned at her obvious reaction to him. He stopped unfastening his trousers and said, "I'll change first and then wait outside while you wash up. You can turn around if it makes you uncomfortable."

She did so, a little reluctantly. And she kept her back turned as she heard the sounds of him sloshing water from the pail that served as his nightstand. "There," he said finally. "That'll do for the time being. I'm decent now, boss lady. You can turn around."

He was now wearing the silky shirt he had worn on Christmas. It was tucked into snug Levi's. He gave an apologetic shrug. "I'm out of clean shirts, other than this one," he said, holding out a plaid flannel to her.

"You...ah...look fine," she said.

"There's the rest of your ensemble, my lady." He pointed to a pair of his trousers that he'd laid out across his bunk. "I'll wait right outside, and I promise not to peek," he added with a wink.

Molly quickly took off her smelly clothes, gave herself a perfunctory wash in the bucket and dried her wet body with the flannel shirt. Then she donned it and the pants and went over to open the door.

Parker was waiting on the stoop. "That's what I like," he teased. "A lady who can dress for dinner in five minutes."

He stepped back inside and used his foot to kick the pile of dirty clothes out the door. "Those can just stay outside until I'm ready to wash them up."

Molly shook her head. "Are you sure you were a banker in New York, Parker?"

"Born and bred," he answered. "If my father had had his way, I'd be there still. Pushing papers. Counting other people's money."

"Well, you've saved *me* a pile of money today. I'll let you help me count it when we sell those heifers."

They shared a smile. "I think it was a mutual effort, boss lady, but if I helped, I'm glad."

"You did. Thank you again."

"I hope you'll continue to let me help you. You don't have to do everything alone, you know."

The smile died and her eyes became wary. "Now you're starting to sound like Jeremy. 'A woman can't expect to run a ranch alone,'" she mimicked in a low voice.

Parker sighed. "Just because someone offers to help out doesn't mean that you aren't good enough, Molly. Everyone needs help—men and women. It's not a weakness."

"So you think I should let the Dickersons sashay on over here and start to give orders?"

It seemed as if she had shed the vulnerability and the weariness of the past couple of hours along with her smelly clothes. Parker sighed again. "Of course not. I didn't say you needed their kind of help, but, gol-dang it, Molly, sometimes it seems that you're not willing to accept support from anyone—even your own sisters."

"I've accepted it from you," she said defensively. She hugged her arms around her middle and looked up at him with something like anger in her eyes. "I've accepted more than that from you, Parker."

A few minutes ago he'd wanted to put his arms around her and protect her. Now suddenly she was glaring at him like a prizefighter in the opposite cor-ner. Keeping a rein on his patience, he said, "Well, you've accepted a couple of kisses. You're right about that."

She mumbled something about tradition and mis-tletoe, but he interrupted her, still speaking calmly. "I've kissed under the mistletoe before, Molly. That's not what we were doing the other night."

"What were we doing, then?"

Her face was stony, and Parker fought off the urge to put his hands on her and watch it soften. "We were kissing each other, Molly, rather thoroughly. And I'm standing here thinking very seriously about doing it again."

She blinked hard, then looked down at his flannel shirt, which hung all the way to her knees. With a half-sad smile she said, "I'm hardly dressed in satin today...."

His restraint snapped. He gripped her arms and moved closer. "Blast it, Molly. It's not a pretty dress or scents or a Christmas social that makes the connection between two people. It's what's inside you—what you feel. It's how your stomach takes that little jump when you hear the other person's voice. It's how you can't wait to tell them when something good happens to you. It's how you feel that you just might die if you have to wait one more minute to put your lips together."

Molly didn't want to hear the words as they bombarded her, as stinging and as unwelcome as the tiny ice pellets of yesterday's storm. She didn't want to have them batter against the defenses she'd so carefully built up for herself over the years. She'd sworn when she was still a child to be as good as a man, to run her father's ranch the way a son would. She'd sworn never to turn into one of those simpering, love-sick females who hadn't a thought in their heads except for their beaux. Only the weak needed to be in love. And the fact that Parker's hands around her arms were making her feel like jelly inside was perfect proof of just how debilitating it could be.

He was watching her intently, waiting, as her doubts flickered across her eyes. She took a deep breath. "I liked kissing you, Parker. It was a new experience. It was...educational. But it's not anything I'm interested in pursuing. I'll have to ask you not to bring up the subject again."

Parker's jaw dropped. *Educational?* He stared at her impassive features. Maybe Molly Hanks was exactly as tough as she said. Maybe behind the facade of this woman there was a core of ice that wouldn't be melted with any amount of passion. For a moment she almost had him convinced. But then he noticed the telltale flush creeping up her neck. He saw that the tips of her fingers, just barely showing out the sleeves of his shirt, were shaking.

She wasn't tough—she was scared. Well, that made two of them, Parker thought grimly. Because the last thing he'd expected to find in the barren stretches of Wyoming prairie was a feisty young woman who would open wounds that had barely stopped bleeding.

Educational? To hell with that. He reached behind him and slammed the door shut, then picked her up by both arms and brought his mouth against hers—two stiff, cold pairs of lips melding, sucking and drawing heat from within to create a tiny, focused, wet inferno of sensation in the frigid bunkhouse. He leaned backward against the door and let her body ride his. His hands moved, slipping underneath the flannel shirt to find her firm, slim rib cage. His strong fingers held her there against him, then moved to seek the softness farther up her body—the same tantalizing swells of breasts he had watched rise in passion when he had kissed her on Christmas night. He wanted to feel them bare and rising into his palms. He wanted to kiss her there and hear her moan as he suckled her. She moaned now, but there was distress in the sound, and immediately his hands stopped their search.

He pulled away from her mouth, the moisture on his lips turning immediately cold. He put his hands on her waist and let her slide down him until her boots touched the floor again. She straightened without looking at him and stepped from between his legs. The flush now reached all the way to her hairline.

He waited for her to speak, to look at him, to get angry...to do something. When she just stood there, he gave a little sigh and pushed himself away from the door. "All right," he said. "If that's the way you want it, boss lady, I'll try not to bring the subject up again."

Then he pulled open the door and gestured for her to leave.

They spent the next two days riding in the snow, gathering cattle from the far reaches of the ranch. Molly was angry with herself. She should have branded last summer, even if she'd had to do every blasted calf herself. At least Moonlight and the two surviving strays that Parker and Smokey had brought back would not be lost. She'd decided to keep all three wintered in the barn. It was still a mystery as to why they had separated from their mothers. But then, why had the herd scattered in the first place? If there was a mountain lion on the loose, she wished they'd find it.

She pushed herself hard, trying to keep her mind on the cattle and off Parker Prescott. But she couldn't help spending a little time watching him, silently admiring how quickly he'd learned to handle his horse and move the animals like a seasoned cowhand. He'd kept his promise and not mentioned anything about what had happened between them. In fact, he'd barely spoken to her. But then, there'd been little time for conversation. They were working too hard.

The dry prairie was covered with neck-deep drifts in some areas and, unlike the earlier storm, this snow wouldn't melt off till spring. They couldn't possibly expect to find all the cattle. She could only hope that they hadn't wandered out of Lucky Stars territory, at least the unmarked ones.

As they rode back to the ranch she leaned forward and rubbed Midnight's neck. "We've done our best, girl," she told the animal. "We'll just hope the winter's mild and that next spring they'll all be loping in, fat and happy." The mare gave a toss of her head as if in agreement. Molly smiled. The two days of riding had worked most of the irritability out of her system. At the moment she felt as if she could handle the ranch—and Parker Prescott, as well. She looked up at the overcast winter sky. "Don't worry about us, Papa. I'm taking care of it. Everything's going to be just fine."

Parker watched Molly stroking the neck of her horse. Midnight was not the showiest animal. At the Westhills Riding Club back home, she probably wouldn't have even been allowed a stable. But she was the most surefooted gol-danged critter Parker had ever seen. And she never flagged, never seemed to get tired. Sort of like her mistress, he thought ruefully. Molly's energy out on the range was boundless. When everyone else had headed back to the barn, Molly kept working, well after dark. And Parker had stayed working with her, unwilling to leave her out on the range by herself. But whereas he'd come in each day with his thighs aching and a ladder of twinges running up his back, she'd seemed as steady and brisk as when they'd set out in the morning.

He'd tried to keep his mind off her, but he couldn't keep his eyes from drifting her way, watching her skillfully cut and turn with Midnight as if the two were one creature. Her determined face was set in lines of total concentration, eyes lively, cheeks rosy with cold. It was hard to imagine that he had once thought her sister more attractive. Susannah was a beauty, and rode with speed and grace, but Molly had an inner fire that no male clothes could disguise.

She turned now and waved at him to follow her home. He trotted a distance behind, making no move to catch up to her. The snow had made his decision to stay at the Lucky Stars irrevocable. There was no way he'd be able to head across the mountains until spring. And he just wasn't quite sure what he was going to do about the way his gut had begun to twist every time he looked at her. It wasn't something he was ready for, and he had no intention of acting on his feelings. But he'd wager his entire winter's pay that before the snow disappeared he and his boss lady would have to get back to talking about more than cattle.

He followed her back to the barn at a distance, not eager for conversation in his current state of mind. She'd already tended to her horse and gone into the house by the time he came in, but Smokey was standing in the middle of the barn, idly examining a row of cinches that were draped across one of the stalls.

"Haven't you frozen your behind enough for one day, you old biscuit shooter?" Parker called to him, jumping from his horse. "What are you doing out here?"

Smokey did not smile at his taunt. "I was waiting for you, I reckon."

Parker led his horse toward its stall and began to remove the bridle. "What's the matter?"

"I wanted to show you something. See what you make of it."

Parker left his horse saddled and walked over to the cook. "Is there something wrong with the cinches?"

"No. But something else is wrong. The roof was dripping out back—melted away a patch of snow. And underneath it I found this." He reached behind the stall wall and pulled out a dirty cloth bag.

Parker took it from him and examined it. "What is it?"

"Looks to me like a fifty-pound sack of sugar."

Smokey's voice was grave, but Parker had no idea why. "Did someone steal it from your kitchen, or something?"

"I've never seen it before. But all I know is that it's empty and I found it in back of our barn—the same barn where them heifers took sick."

Realization slowly dawned. "You mean *sugar* could have made them bloat up like that? I thought it was bad alfalfa that did it."

"Those calves didn't have any alfalfa. There wasn't anything out here that could have made them sick like that." He reached out and took the bag back from Parker. "Unless they had help doing it."

Parker felt a little sick himself. "Why in hell would anyone do something like that? Do you think it was some of the cowboys in town who've been kicking up trouble about a woman trying to run a ranch?"

Smokey shrugged. "I don't know. It'd take someone belly high to a snake for something that mean."

"Have you told Molly?"

"Nope. She got so darned upset when she thought she was going to lose these animals, I just don't have the heart to make it worse for her."

"But she's got to know."

Smokey put a hand on Parker's shoulder. "Molly's got the responsibility for every darned thing that goes on around this place. Maybe this is one little item you and I should keep to ourselves."

"But we should be notifying the sheriff, looking for the culprits."

Smokey gave a snort of disgust. "Sheriff Benton's about as good as a street lamp when it comes to solving problems. And how would we go about tracking down the varmints who did this? We don't have any more clues than one empty bag of sugar—the kind any sidewinder with cash can buy any day of the week over at Simon's store."

Parker looked from the empty sack over to the three surviving heifers, chewing contentedly in their stall. "It seems to me that Molly should know."

"Then you tell her. I'm not giving her one more damned thing to worry about."

Parker took in a deep breath. "If we don't say anything, it'll be up to you and me to keep watch around here. We can hope this was a one-time trick by some mean-spirited cowboy with a grudge against women. But if anything else happens . . ."

Smokey nodded. "We'll keep our eyes open. If that varmint shows his face again around here, we'll be ready for him."

In a rare girlish gesture Molly had decided to play Cupid and had invited Max McClanahan to dine with them on New Year's Eve. She'd known it would be a difficult occasion, ushering in the first New Year they would spend without their father. Last year at this time he had just developed the hacking cough that would finally ravage him and take his life.

Jeremy Dickerson had ridden over earlier with an invitation for them all to dine at the Lazy D, but, to Parker's relief, Molly had greeted him coolly and had sent regrets to his father.

Max arrived well before supper, riding out from town in her own little two-wheeled buggy. Molly, after a few moments of indecision, had once again donned the silver dress.

"Land sakes, girl," Max boomed. "You look like the fairy queen in that thing. Who'd have thought it? I always knew you'd decide to come out of your cocoon one of these days, and that when you did, you'd be the prettiest butterfly of all."

They were up in Molly's bedroom, waiting for the supper hour. "It's just the dress," Molly said, pleased.

"Hogwash. It's the girl in the dress, just the way I've always told you. You're a rare one, Molly, and it was about time you came into your own and started to realize it." She cocked her head at the blushing girl. "It appears to me that handsome pilgrim you hired on knows it well enough."

Molly turned away to look in the mirror as she combed her hair. She'd decided to leave it down tonight. "What a thing to say, Max," she said, keeping her voice casual.

"You sayin' he's not interested?"

"Of course not. He did look hard a time or two at Susannah when he first came, but we straightened that out. Now he just works for us. He's a decent man."

Max barked a laugh. "No man's *that* decent. If he doesn't look at Susannah anymore it's 'cause he's spending all his time mooning over you."

Molly pulled hard at the tangles. "That's ridiculous. He . . . he calls me boss lady."

"And I call him pilgrim—doesn't mean I want to pray with him." She gave a comical waggle of her eyebrows.

Molly laughed. "He is attractive, isn't he?"

"Criminy, child, he's downright bonny. Smart, too. And if you want my advice, you'll go after him."

"I've always valued your advice, Max, but this is one time where you're dead wrong. Imagine what a coil it would be to get mixed up with one of my drovers. I'd never get the men in the territory to take me seriously."

"They don't take you seriously now, so what's the difference? And what do you care, anyway? Where's the twelve-year-old girl who decided she'd dress and act and live exactly the way she pleased?"

Molly put the brush down with a grimace into the mirror. She should have put her wispy, flyaway hair up after all, but it was too late now. Turning around to Max she said wistfully, "I think she still feels like she's twelve sometimes."

Max stood up from the bed, put her plump arm around Molly's shoulders and gave her a hug. "So do we all, child," she said. "So do we all."

Max's words wouldn't leave her head all through supper. Smokey had outdone himself again with pork roast and apple sage dressing, but she scarcely tasted the food. Parker had on his silk shirt tonight with a black jacket that Molly couldn't remember having seen before. He looked every bit the gallant, but, for the life of her, she could detect no difference in his treatment toward the women at the table. He complimented Mary Beth on her hair and teased Susannah about her dimples. He pulled out Molly's chair at the beginning of the meal and said that he'd never begun a New Year with such a collection of feminine beauty. He even had Max blushing with his blatant flattery, leaving poor Smokey shifting in his chair and searching for something to say that would compete.

Molly had meant what she'd said to Max. It would be ridiculous to think about any kind of relationship with Parker. But the very fact that she was analyzing the possibility, she had to admit, showed how much the idea had been on her mind. The year was about to turn. Perhaps it was time for her to turn over a new page, too. Thanks to her father, she had no experience with men, at least not in these areas. Romance had always been something for simpering females— for dime novels and opry houses. Molly had had a ranch to run.

The paperback novels that Mary Beth read always had the hero saving the heroine from a dire fate and finally, on the last page, kissing her. The end. Parker had already kissed her. But somehow Molly had the feeling that that wasn't the end of it, not by a long shot.

"I'm too damn old to stay up till all hours just to hear a clock chime," Smokey complained as they finished cleaning up the supper dishes.

Max took his arm and said, "I'll sing to you, you old coot, and keep you awake."

"You've got to stay up, Smokey," Mary Beth had agreed.

The others had added their urging, so they had all gathered in the parlor and built up the fire for the evening. And for a pleasant while Max did sing to them—barroom ballads that she had learned during her days in the Colorado silver mining towns. Some were a touch scandalous, but she sang those verses quickly, and with such an impish look on her face, that no one thought to be offended.

When she declared that her golden throat would not warble a single note more, Molly suggested popcorn, in spite of the big supper they'd had. If nothing else, it would give them something to do as they all battled yawns, waiting for the hall clock to chime twelve times.

"I'll heat up some cider to go with it," Smokey said, but Parker stood and motioned him to stay in his chair.

"You've done your share today. Let me fix it. What do I put in it?"

"Just a little cinnamon and cloves—not too much."

"I think I can handle that," he said with a grin and started toward the kitchen.

Susannah jumped up to follow him. "I'll help," she said, and the two disappeared behind the kitchen door.

Molly watched them go, hoping that the sudden twist she'd had inside hadn't been jealousy. After all, Max had said that it was Molly whom Parker appeared to be interested in. And *she* was the one he'd kissed. He was always nice to Susannah, even flirtatious at times, but since that first day when they had ridden out together, Molly had seen to it that they had never been alone. There was no way Parker could have kissed her sister the way he had kissed her on three separate occasions.

"Do you want to do the corn?" Mary Beth asked her, taking the long-handled popper down from its hook next to the fire.

"No, you do it," Molly answered absently.

Smokey boosted himself from his armchair. "Popping corn takes an expert hand, ladies. If you'll permit me…" He reached for the popper and Mary Beth surrendered it to him with a giggle.

"I always suspected you'd be an expert hand, Smokey," Max said coyly. Smokey turned around and winked at her.

"I'll just see if they need help with the cider," Molly said suddenly. She jumped up and marched toward the kitchen. She didn't know why she'd suddenly felt so uneasy. But she discovered the reason as she pushed open the kitchen door.

A jug of cider sat on the kitchen table next to an empty pan and a bottle of cinnamon. Behind it, Susannah stood with her back pressed against the stove. Her arms were around Parker's neck, and he was kissing her.

Chapter Twelve

Molly felt as if her throat was closing, choking off her air. At the creak of the door, Parker and Susannah broke apart. Both their heads snapped toward her. "Molly!" Susannah exclaimed. Then she took a step backward.

Parker frowned, his eyes troubled. "It's not her fault," he said. "I . . . ah . . . we were just wishing each other happy New Year."

Molly tried to swallow, but the saliva had pooled in the back of her throat. Susannah came toward her. "Molly, you look as if you'd been shot. It was just a silly kiss." She came up to her sister and embraced her lightly. "It's like I told you, I'm a big girl now. You don't have to be watching out for me all the time."

Molly let herself be hugged. Susannah's lavender fragrance seemed overpowering, and for a moment she thought she might be sick.

"It wasn't what you're thinking, Molly," Parker said again.

Molly put her hands back against the doorjamb for support and spoke as steadily as she could. "This is my fault. I've made a mistake letting you get so close to all of us, Parker. It's not the way a ranch should be run."

He narrowed his eyes and watched her for a long moment. Then he said lightly, "Don't fraternize with the help. That's the rule, right?"

"No." Her voice was hard. "The rule is, don't let the help lay hands on my sister. I want you to move back into the bunkhouse—tonight. And in the future you'll come into this house only for meals."

"Molly, I was the one—" Susannah began in distress, but Parker interrupted her.

"That's all right, Susannah. Your sister's the boss around here, remember? She's the one who pays me, which means she gives the orders." His jaw was set, his eyes dark.

"That's right, I do," Molly said, unrelenting.

He studied her for another minute, then strode across the kitchen and pushed his way past her out the door. Neither Susannah nor Molly moved until they heard the big front door close with a convincing slam.

Parker had not asked permission to ride into town. He'd be darned if he'd spend another Sunday all by himself out in the bunkhouse freezing his hindquarters. It had been three weeks since the New Year's Eve debacle and, though the January weather had been mild, the atmosphere around the Lucky Stars had been colder than a Canadian norther.

On three occasions Parker had cornered Molly alone to try to discuss the matter, but she'd waved away his explanations. It didn't help that he felt one hundred percent in the wrong, even though Susannah had been the instigator of the kiss.

There had always been a flirtatious side to Susannah, but lately she seemed to be developing it with more confidence and determination. It was as if her declaration of independence to Molly when Parker had first arrived had boosted her one step up into womanhood, and she was reveling in the newfound power. At the Christmas night party she'd seemed utterly in control as the young swains of the territory practically worshiped at her feet. It had made it easier for Parker not to feel bad about his increasing preference for Molly. He'd been sure that, though Susannah found him attractive, she'd not be unduly upset over his lack of attention. But New Year's Eve he'd been the only man around, except for Smokey, and it appeared that Susannah was disposed to reach out and take what was available.

"I've never kissed a boy on New Year's, Parker," she'd said, smiling and throwing her arms around him.

Nevertheless, he'd been at fault for not pushing her away immediately. Though he'd never been shy with the ladies and had been told a time or two that he was a more than adequate lover, he'd never been one to take lovemaking lightly. When he'd kissed Molly, it had been because she was the one who had captured his attention. He never had any intention of letting his earlier flirtation with her sister develop one bit further. He was horrified to think that in the same week he'd kissed two sisters. Molly had a right to be angry. But he also had a right to be heard with his side of the story, and she hadn't given him that chance. He'd tried three times, and that was enough. From now on he'd forget about both sisters. He'd work another couple of months, stay out in the bunkhouse where he belonged and then be on his way.

But today he'd enjoy himself, try to find some people who would talk to him without turning their noses up as if he smelled bad. Max, for example. The big woman's hearty humor was exactly what he needed at the moment, he decided, turning his horse toward the bathhouse.

Music was floating out from inside the Grizzly Bear, and there was a crowd inside from the looks of it through the frosted glass door. No Sunday liquor ordinances in Canyon City, apparently. Perhaps the Grizzly would be his next stop. He'd learned back in Deadwood that whiskey didn't help much when it came to drowning out grief and loneliness, but at least there'd be noise there, and friendly people.

Max was sitting in her front waiting area in a rocker, knitting.

"You look like my saintly old grandma," Parker teased as he walked in. The room was steamy compared to the cold outside air. Sunday must be bath day for a lot of folks.

"Saintly, my arse," she boomed, throwing the knitting to one side of her chair. "Come in, pilgrim, and let me look at you."

Parker closed the door behind him and walked over to take a seat on a little stool near her chair. "Don't you want to wait until I'm in the tub?" he teased.

"I'll look then, too. But first I want to talk to you and ask you what in tarnation happened out at your place on New Year's. Molly was madder than a dog with his first porcupine, and she wouldn't tell anyone what was going on."

Parker stretched his feet out from the low stool with a big sigh. "Remember how I went to fix the cider?"

At her nod, he continued, "Well, Susannah followed me. When Molly came to find us, we were kissing."

Max looked troubled. "I never took you for one of them dirty, four-flusher types, pilgrim. Wasn't one sister enough for you?"

"It wasn't like that. Susannah all of a sudden said she wanted a New Year's kiss and threw her arms around me."

"And, of course, she's so big and strong and you're so puny that you couldn't fight her off."

He shrugged. "It all happened so fast. I've apologized and I've tried to explain to Molly, but she'll hardly even talk to me. More than once I've thought of packing up my gear and riding on out of there."

"So why haven't you?"

This wasn't the kind of distraction he'd been looking for today. He'd wanted some music and laughter and a good hot bath where he wouldn't have to go over and over his own thoughts the way he had been for the past three weeks. He was tired of thinking about it.

"Hell, Max. I don't know. I guess because I promised Molly I'd stick it out through the spring. No one else seems willing to hire on out there, and she's worked so hard to keep the place going." He reached to rub the back of his neck. Max sat back in her chair, a slow smile creeping across her face as he continued, "And she's sitting there at the mercy of that mangy cur, Dickerson—"

"So it *is* Molly you're sweet on, after all," she interrupted. "I knew it."

Parker straightened. "I'm not sweet on anyone..." he began, then stopped and said slowly, "I admire Molly. I've never met anyone quite like her.

But if there ever was a chance for anything between us, it's gone now."

"Because you kissed her sister."

"Darn right! Imagine how that must make her feel."

Max nodded her head. She was still smiling. "How?"

"How? Well...terrible. I don't know."

"Jealous?" Max suggested.

Parker thought for a minute. "Jealous," he confirmed with a nod.

"Well, there you have it. Molly Hanks is not a girl to develop a feeling lightly. If she's still mad at you, pilgrim, I'd say it's because she was already in up to her stirrups over you before this ever happened. So now she feels betrayed. What it all boils down to is that the lass is more than halfway in love with you."

Parker stood and walked over to the door to the bath room. "Is this empty?"

Max pushed herself up out of her chair. "Did you hear what I said? The girl's in love with you."

Parker closed his eyes. "I don't think so, Max. And even if that is true, I'm not sure I'm ready to have anyone in love with me. Maybe riding out of here would be the biggest favor I could do her."

Max's bosom gave a great heave. "Men! The biggest favor you could do her would be to ride on out to the Lucky Stars and make her understand that you aren't waltzing around with her sister behind her back and haven't the least intention of doing so."

"I told you, she won't talk about it."

"Then you do the talking, pilgrim. I've never known words to stick in your mouth."

Parker was silent for a long moment. He didn't want to admit how good Max's words were making him feel after three weeks of misery. He reached for the doorknob. "Can I take a bath first?"

Max grinned at him. "On the house," she said, then added with a wink, "You go on ahead and I'll bring you a towel in a few minutes."

Parker hadn't stopped at the Grizzly Bear after all. The bathwater at Max's had been scalding hot, but he hadn't stayed to enjoy a slow cool down. Instead he had dressed quickly and bidden goodbye to Max with a smacking kiss on her plump cheek.

All the way back to the ranch he thought about the conversation they'd had. After three weeks of thinking, how had he missed the fact that Molly's anger had been out of proportion to the offense unless it had sprung from jealousy?

He knew firsthand what the green-eyed monster could do to a person's temperament. When he'd first fallen in love with Claire, Parker couldn't always scrape up the money to buy her time for the evening at Mattie Smith's brothel, so she'd had to entertain other customers. Mattie had eventually taken pity on the young couple and had allowed them to be together without any money exchanging hands. But up to that point, Parker had spent evenings pacing and cursing and emptying more than his share of bottles of Big Jim Driscoll's rotgut whiskey.

Of course, he couldn't imagine that he and Molly would ever have what he had experienced with Claire. And he hadn't noticed her pacing or cursing or staggering tipsily around the barn when she came for her nightly check. But now that Max had opened his eyes, he could see the signs. Molly, who had for years denied that she could ever be a match for her sisters in attracting a man, had evidently convinced herself that Susannah had won him away from her. Or perhaps she thought that he'd been playing to both sisters at the same time. Whatever the misconception was, he intended to clear it up, if he had to hog-tie her to do it, which might, he reflected with a rueful grin, be a very real possibility.

He'd have to see her alone, which wouldn't be easy if the past three weeks were any indication. He'd have to create the opportunity, and by the time he'd arrived back at the dark bunkhouse he knew exactly how he was going to do it.

Molly sat as patiently as possible holding up the skein of yarn that Mary Beth was rolling into a ball. It was the third one they'd done and Molly's arms were beginning to ache, but she didn't complain. She considered it a kind of penance for how out of sorts she'd been with everyone all day. Parker hadn't come to Sunday dinner or supper. Smokey had gone out to the bunkhouse to fetch him and had come back to report that he was gone, along with his horse. Molly had had a sudden stab of fear that he had decided to leave without telling them—to head on out to California, in spite of the snow. But Smokey had said that his things were still there and that he was probably just letting off some steam in town like any normal cowpoke on a day off. He didn't say what they all were thinking—that Parker was hardly any normal cowpoke. And he didn't speculate on why Parker might have to let off steam after three weeks of frigid treatment from the lady of the house. But Molly had felt her sisters' reproachful eyes on her. And she had resolved that, while she would never again let the man inside her guard, she would do her best to be civil to him when they all started work again tomorrow.

"That should be enough to make scarves for the entire Seventh Cavalry, Beth," she told her sister finally, standing and shaking out her skirts.

"It's enough for tonight," her sister agreed. "But I'm making a sweater and it takes a lot of yarn."

"A sweater for who?"

Mary Beth's hands shook a little as she packed yarn and needles away in her tapestry sewing bag. "I...I haven't decided yet. I've just had a hankering to make a sweater."

Molly looked sharply at her sister. Was it for Parker? she wondered immediately. Hell's bells. Were *both* her sisters besotted with the man? "Fine," she said wearily. "We'll wind some more tomorrow night if you need it. But now it's time to sleep." She turned toward Smokey, who sat in his usual chair by the fireplace. "Off to bed, Smokey. You've been nodding into your beard this past hour or more."

The old cook stood and yawned. "I've been listening to every word."

"We haven't been saying anything," Molly observed.

"Let's go, Susannah," Mary Beth said. "Are you coming up, Molly?"

"As soon as I check out in the barn."

It was a beautiful night. The wintry air seemed to make the starlight sharper and more brilliant. Molly pulled a shawl around her and walked slowly across the yard. Her thoughts were still on Parker's day-long disappearance. The bunkhouse looked dark and there was no smoke coming up from the little stovepipe chimney. She would be nicer to him tomorrow, she resolved again. It had been wrong for him to kiss her sister, but she had known from the beginning that he was an Eastern charmer, undoubtedly used to regular female conquests. It wasn't his fault that she'd allowed his kisses to awaken something inside her that she had no business letting into her life.

She pulled open the barn door and went in, taking a deep breath of cold, hay-smelling air. There was something very satisfying about her nightly visits to the barn—the animals tossing their heads in indifferent greeting, the lantern bobbing at her side as she walked, tossing its light around the stalls and wooden beams of the tall ceiling. It was a ritual that made her feel at peace with her world.

"You're later than usual."

The voice came from the shadows behind the last stall. Molly jumped, bumping the lantern with her knee and sending it clattering to the ground.

In an instant Parker was by her side, retrieving it. "You'll set the place on fire," he chided.

"You scared me out of a year's growth."

Parker sent a quick glance along the length of her lean body. "I don't reckon you'll miss it any." She reached her hand for the lantern, but he shook his head and said, "I'll hold it."

"What are you doing here?"

"I was waiting for you." His voice was low with an extra vibration to it that set up one of those flutterings in her middle.

She blinked. In spite of her resolution to be nicer to him, the sudden start to her nerves made her voice caustic. "Why?"

"Because I wanted to talk to you."

The flutters accelerated. "It's late, Parker. It can wait until morning."

"No," he said, taking her elbow. "It can't."

He pulled her gently along the row of stalls to the end where the clean hay was piled. He *had* been waiting for her, she realized at once. His quilts from the bunkhouse were spread out neatly over a patch of hay. She looked at him questioningly.

"Have a seat," he said with a flourish of the lantern. "It's a little cold out here, but at least we won't be interrupted. I would have invited you to the bunkhouse where there's a stove, but I figured you might refuse to come into the wolf's own lair. Was I right?"

His eyes on her were intense in the lantern light. His hair curled over the collar of his wool coat. Every inch of her felt the touch of his hand on her arm, but she answered as calmly as possible, "I see no need to talk with you in the bunkhouse or anywhere else—especially not at this time of night. So if you'll excuse me..."

As she started to pull away, he set the lantern on the ground and said, "That's what I was afraid of."

Before she knew what was happening he had lifted her up and laid her down on the blankets. Then he swung himself over her, planting a knee on either side of her, just at her waist. He sat back, his knees keeping most of his weight off her thighs. Their bodies warmed where the shared heat began to build.

"Get off me!" she sputtered, struggling to sit up.

He reached out to her chest with one long arm and held her easily against the ground. "Sorry, boss lady. I can't do that. Because if I get up, you'll leave. And you can't leave until you hear what I have to tell you."

His voice was as calm as if he had been discussing the weather. His hand felt like a branding iron in the middle of her chest.

She gave a huff of surrender. "Talk, then. And make it good, Prescott. Because, I swear, tomorrow I'm turning you off this place. I don't care if we're in the middle of the worst blizzard of the decade."

Parker gave her an infuriating grin. "Well, then, that means we only have tonight to get this settled."

She glared at him but she stopped squirming, which was a good thing, Parker thought ruefully. He'd never sat on a woman in quite this way. He hadn't realized it would be so... provocative. They were both fully clothed, but their private parts were nearly touching, as if they were about to make love. The entire lower portion of his anatomy had begun to throb. "Hell," he said under his breath. He'd come out here to make her listen to his apology, not to seduce her.

"What's the matter now?" she asked grumpily.

He wondered for an instant if their proximity was doing similar things inside her own body. His experience last summer with Claire had given him a lifetime of knowledge about women. She'd been a prostitute, and she'd taught him a lot about sex and pleasure. But more important, she'd opened herself up to him, shared her feelings and emotions, in a way that he'd never believed possible. Sweet, ethereal Claire. Though they were as different as two humans could be, he had the odd feeling that Claire would have approved of Molly Hanks. She would have applauded her courage. She would have admired her willingness to make her way in a man's world. In a way, Claire had been forced to do the same thing, and she'd done it with dignity and on her own terms.

He tore his thoughts away from the past. "Nothing's the matter," he said. "It's just a little too cold out here for comfort, so we need to get on with our talk."

"So, talk."

"About New Year's Eve when you thought I was kissing your sister—"

"When you *were* kissing my sister," she interrupted. Her small jaw was set and the misery in her eyes resembled Parker's own those early days with Claire. Max had been right—it was jealousy, and there was nothing that was better at gnawing on your gut from the inside out.

"When I *was* kissing your sister," he agreed quietly. "It didn't mean anything."

"I'm sure Susannah would be flattered to hear you say that."

He shifted slightly on her legs. "I imagine Susannah would agree with me."

Now there was a flare of anger in her blue eyes. "Listen, Parker Prescott, just because we're three single women living by ourselves doesn't mean that we're willing to kiss any man that comes along, like a houseful of joy ladies. If Susannah let you kiss her, it was because she..." She stopped for a minute to swallow. "It was because she's falling in love with you."

Parker felt a wave of tenderness. She'd been so tough and so cold for three weeks—why hadn't he seen that she'd been utterly miserable? Why hadn't he forced her to speak with him about it the very next day? It would have saved them both a lot of grief. "Susannah's not falling in love with me," he said gently. "Susannah's falling in love with the idea of love. Now that your father's gone, she's finally getting a taste of something that is normal and natural for girls your age. Something that most girls discover much younger."

Molly stopped squirming for a minute as she appeared to give his words some thought. Finally she said with a reluctant touch of humor, "Now you're calling us old maids."

"Hardly. But it appears that your father might have been just as happy if you had ended up that way." He held up a hand as she tried to interrupt. "I'm sure he was a wonderful man, Molly. He certainly raised three great daughters. It's just hard sometimes for fathers to realize that it's time for their girls to grow up."

Hard for brothers, too, he thought, remembering how he had wanted to kill Gabe Hatch when he'd found out he'd slept with Amelia.

Molly's forehead was knit in thought. "How do you know this about Susannah?"

"By watching her . . . by hearing her talk, seeing the way she moves. By seeing how she's blossomed into such an attractive and, yes, flirtatious woman. She's reaching out for what life has to offer her—especially love."

"Maybe she's reaching out for you."

She seemed to hold a breath as she waited for his answer. He shook his head slowly. "I don't think so. I hope not. Because it's hard for me to even listen to Susannah anymore. I'm too busy trying to keep from mooning after her sister."

"I haven't noticed you mooning." Her smile was faint but unmistakable.

"You haven't been watching me, then."

She bit her lip, then said very deliberately, "Yes, tenderfoot, I most assuredly *have* been watching you."

She looked up at him as if she had just bet her entire pile of chips on a pair of jacks. Her eyes dared him to believe that her words were some kind of declaration. He reached to touch her hair where it lay spread out in tangled waves. "That makes two of us, boss lady." His voice had grown husky. "And I don't know exactly what we're going to do about it. But maybe the first thing is to kiss and make up."

He leaned over her, his hands on either side of her head, and brought his mouth slowly down on hers. He'd meant to be careful, but the instant their lips touched, the chaste caress wasn't enough. He slid his legs back along hers and gathered her in his arms so that they were lying together, his body pressing her into the soft wool blanket. The ache at his groin made him moan a little as it suddenly seemed that they couldn't hold each other tightly enough.

He moved his hands to hold her head as his mouth mated with hers, deep and hot, until they were both breathing hard and wanting more. It wasn't the apology he had intended, he thought between the surges of desire, but he suspected that it would serve the purpose.

She made a sound in the back of her throat and he pulled away, shifting to the side a little to relieve her of his weight. "Are we made up yet?" he asked, nudging the soft skin of her neck with his nose.

She gave a short, throaty laugh. "You're a hard man to stay angry with, tenderfoot."

He was hard, period, he thought to himself, moving uncomfortably, but he had no intention of doing anything about it. He hadn't come out here for a quick tumble in the hay with no thought to the consequences. Molly deserved much more than that, and, however much he wanted her, he wasn't convinced that he was the man to give her what she needed.

He kissed her lightly. "That's all I wanted to hear. So we're made up? You won't be turning me off the place tomorrow with that .50 caliber Sharps of yours?"

Her cheeks turned pink in the lantern light and she shook her head. "I reckon I never had any intention of doing that. I need you here, Parker."

The statement was made with her typical directness, but Parker was quite sure that it was not a sentiment she had expressed often in her life. He kissed her forehead, then the bridge of her nose. "Well, you've got me," he told her tenderly. Then he let his head fall back on the blanket and settled her more firmly in his arms. Even under her bulky clothing, he could feel her slender shape mold to his as she nestled contentedly.

They lay peacefully without talking for several minutes. Then Parker felt Molly's slender hand on his cheek, turning his head toward her. He smiled at her, but didn't move.

"Parker?" she said, her voice uncharacteristically shy.

"What is it?"

She leaned near him and spoke so low he could hardly hear. "Let's make up some more."

It took him just a minute to assimilate the words, then he rolled toward her and sought her mouth. "My pleasure, boss lady," he whispered back.

Chapter Thirteen

The traditional February thaw came early and lasted through the month. It was as if the weather had decided to emulate the benevolent mood that reigned at the Lucky Stars these days. Molly felt it all around her. Smokey whistled more often as he cooked supper each evening, and he'd taken to riding into town twice a week to spend the evening with Max. Mary Beth was her usual quiet self, but there was often a smile on her lips, and she whizzed through her chores without a word of complaint. Molly herself had moments of feeling as giddy as a schoolgirl. Since her meeting in the barn with Parker, he'd started to act like an honest-to-goodness suitor, opening up doors for her and complimenting her one day on her hair and the next on the tidy way she'd whiplashed a broken hayrack. Twice he'd gone to town and come back with a paper of candy—just for her.

She'd made some purchases in town herself—a calico dress and a green linen skirt with a white dimity blouse. Though Parker treated her with the same attention and courtesy no matter what she was wearing, she'd begun to enjoy putting aside her buckskins in the evening. Now and then she would feel Parker's eyes on her in the more shapely clothing and get pleasantly tingly. And occasionally, it would be more than a tingle. There would be a kind of heavy ache in the pit of her stomach, a mixture of longing and curiosity that was slowly driving her crazy.

Because the only thing Parker hadn't done was kiss her again. They'd been alone together several times. In fact, she'd brazenly seen to it that they would be. But he'd kept his distance, smiling and warm and courteous. She'd seen the same flare of desire in his eyes that she'd noticed when he'd kissed her. But it had been carefully banked, like an all-night fire.

Still, just being around him was making her happy. When she'd sworn never to be dependent on a man, she'd had no idea how satisfying it could be to *share* with a man—share problems, decisions, ideas. Parker, in spite of his inexperience, was a quick learner and, as he had with the sick heifers, brought a wealth of academic knowledge that complemented Molly's broader practical education. It made her happy to sit with him at the end of the day discussing her plans for the future. And when he declared that when spring came he and Smokey would scour the town for some hands who would help get her unmarked cattle branded, she agreed without a twinge to let them do it.

It took Jeremy Dickerson to deflate her good humor. They hadn't seen much of the Dickersons all winter, and Molly was beginning to think Jeremy had given up his plans to win both her and the ranch.

With all the good weather, the winter repairs and other chores had all been done, leaving the Lucky Stars group with a lot of idle time. The day the Dickersons rode up, Susannah and Parker had arranged an impromptu riding competition.

"I want to make it just like the fancy rich people back East," Susannah had exclaimed. "A real steeplechase."

"It's awfully muddy for a steeplechase," Parker had said. "And the saddles are different, you know."

She would not be dissuaded. "It will be a *Western* steeplechase."

So they had set out a course with buckets for turn markers and hay bales for jumps. Molly, Mary Beth and Smokey had declared the corral fence would be their grandstand and promised to serve as cheering onlookers.

Diamond pranced around a little nervously, waiting for Parker to give her direction. It was as if she knew that her master was about to pull something entirely new on her.

But before the race could begin, the Dickerson brothers were spotted coming across the western field. Molly recognized them at once and jumped down from the fence to greet them.

"Good afternoon, Jeremy, Ned. What brings you over this way?"

Jeremy surveyed the makeshift racecourse with a look of disdain. His glance flickered over Parker without acknowledgment, then returned to Molly with a smile. "It's been too long, Molly, dear, since we've been to visit. I've neglected my duty."

"Are you saying that visiting us is a duty, Jeremy?" Molly asked. She looked over to include Ned in the question, but his eyes were on Mary Beth and Smokey, still sitting on the fence rail.

"Of course not," Jeremy said smoothly, dismounting. He walked toward her and gave a little bow.

"Forgive my phrasing. Nothing so pleasant could ever be considered a duty."

Molly smiled. She was in too good a mood to let Jeremy's imperious ways bother her. "Well, in that case, you're welcome. You've arrived just in time to witness our great Western steeplechase."

Jeremy gave Parker another dismissive glance. "I do hope you'll try to find yourself some *real* cowhands before spring, Molly."

His words were deliberately loud enough for Parker to hear them. Molly could almost see the hair bristle on the back of his neck. But he stayed calmly where he was, his face impassive.

Her smile dimmed. "I'd put Parker up against any two cowhands you'd like to name, Jeremy," she said.

Jeremy looked surprised at her quick defense. He eyed Parker, his expression calculating. "Indeed?" he said.

Ned had dismounted and come to stand next to his brother. "We came over to tell you about your mule, Molly."

"My mule?"

Jeremy took over the tale. "We found that old mule of your father's—under a melting snowdrift."

"Not Beatrice?" Mary Beth cried.

"I'm afraid so," Ned confirmed. He sent her a look of sympathy.

"Poor Beatrice," Molly said. "We kept hoping all winter that she'd come wandering back one day, but she probably never made it through that first storm."

"Well . . ." Ned gave Mary Beth a troubled glance. "She'd been shot."

"Shot!" all three sisters exclaimed at once.

"Shot through the head," Jeremy added.

"Who would shoot Beatrice?" Mary Beth asked.

"Maybe she'd broken a leg or something and some passerby put her out of her misery," Molly suggested.

Jeremy nodded. "It's possible. But the cadaver has stayed in pretty good shape under the snow, and there's no sign of any other injury."

"How very odd." Molly's distress was obvious in the tone of her voice. Parker got off his horse and walked across the corral toward her.

"Where did you find the mule, Dickerson?" he asked.

At first it appeared that Jeremy would ignore Parker's question, but finally he said curtly, "On our property—over by Levitt's Hill."

"Poor Beatrice," Molly said again with a sigh. "What in the world was she doing way over there?"

"Something must have spooked her over there," Smokey chimed in for the first time. "Maybe the same thing that spooked the calf over to your place."

"Are you still thinking that there might be a cougar around?" Ned asked.

Smokey exchanged a glance with Parker, who gave an imperceptible shake of his head. "A cougar or somethin'," he said with a shrug.

"Well, anyway, we thought you'd want to know about it," Jeremy said briskly, "seeing as how your pa was fond of the critter. I've had my men see to the carcass."

"Thank you," Molly said. The good spirit of the play horse race had disappeared. For a minute no one spoke. "Would you like to come in for some coffee?" she asked finally.

Secretly she hoped that for once the Dickersons would refuse her hospitality. But the brothers accepted with nodded thanks.

"Perhaps we could do the race later?" she asked, sending Parker a pleading look.

"Sure," he said, taking a step back from his position at her side.

Jeremy took his horse's reins and handed them to Parker. "You'll see to our horses, won't you?" he asked.

Parker took the reins of both horses. "At your service, gentlemen," he said with a little tip of his hat. Molly watched with a frown as he turned his back and led the horses toward the barn.

The Dickersons had stayed through supper, and Parker had not joined them. Molly wasn't surprised that he stayed away, but it made her feel odd after the closeness they'd developed in the past few days. When Ned and Jeremy left, she fixed a plate with a couple of pieces of cold chicken and some leftover biscuits.

"Is that for Parker?" Susannah asked.

"Yes."

"I'll take it out to him," Susannah suggested with a coy smile.

Molly smiled back. The green worm of jealousy still squirmed inside her sometimes when she saw Parker looking at Susannah. It was still hard for her to believe that he could possibly prefer her over Susannah's willowy beauty. But each time she pushed the feeling away. By now even Susannah could tell that it was Molly who held Parker's interest. She'd good-naturedly declared her sister the victor in this particular competition and had begun to treat Parker like the brother she suspected he was likely to become.

"I think I can handle it," Molly said, picking up the plate. "I'll just drop it off with him before I check on the animals. I should be back in a minute."

"If I were you and I had a man like that panting after me, I wouldn't be back in any minute," her sister declared firmly.

"Susannah!"

"Well, he is. You should see how he looks at you when you're not looking."

Molly hesitated. "How?" she asked softly.

Susannah gave an airy wave. "Never mind. I wouldn't want to offend you."

"You won't."

Susannah ducked her head to whisper as if in a conspiracy. "Like a bull moose in mating season."

"Susannah!" she exclaimed again.

Susannah shrugged. "I warned you. The trouble with you, Molly, is you think you're so darned independent and free, but you're just as tied up inside as the old biddies in the church quilting circle. You should try relaxing those stern standards one of these days—you might find it's a lot of fun."

Molly pondered her sister's words as she walked out to the bunkhouse. She'd told herself that she was going out there because her hired hand had missed supper. She had a duty to be sure that he was well fed. And she wanted to be sure that Jeremy's remarks had not upset him, though she couldn't really imagine that Parker would care one way or another what Jeremy Dickerson had to say about him.

But as she neared the low wooden building she felt her heart begin a now familiar pounding. The palms of her hands began to sweat, in spite of the cold. She wasn't heading to the bunkhouse to offer Parker some supper, she realized with sudden clarity. She was going out there to offer him herself.

Parker had braided and unbraided his strips of whit leather until the rawhide was crinkled. A dozen times he'd gotten up from his bunk, grabbed his hat and started toward the door to head over to the house. Then he'd stop, picture Jeremy Dickerson's supercilious face sitting across the table from Molly as if he were already master of the house, and he'd change his mind, throwing his hat off in disgust.

He hoped they were having a miserable time. Molly had never given any indication that she was receptive to Dickerson's suit, but he remembered that when he had arrived at the Lucky Stars, Susannah had informed him that Jeremy and her sister were as good as engaged.

Molly herself had admitted that the union of the two ranches had been her father's wish, and Parker knew that Charlie Hanks's wishes were still a powerful force acting in Molly's life. And, hell. Who was to say that it wasn't a good idea after all? Joining the Lucky Stars and the Lazy D would create a cattle empire that would dominate this section of Wyoming. And Molly had always made it clear that the ranch came first, above all other interests.

It was almost as if his thoughts had conjured her. The bunkhouse door opened without warning and she stood there silhouetted against the black night. "Molly!" he said, scrambling to his feet.

Now that she was here, Molly could hardly keep her hands from shaking as she gripped the tin plate. "Ah . . . hello, Parker."

He stood and began to button his flannel shirt, which hung open to the waist. Red long underwear sculpted the muscles of his chest. "I didn't expect any visitors."

"No, don't . . . worry," she said nervously, motioning toward his shirt. All at once she realized that there was no way she could express the vague notions and longings that had been in her head. She had envisioned this scene a hundred times in her dreams, but the reality was totally different. She'd imagined something like the night in the barn, when the dim light and eerie vastness of the building had lent a dreamlike quality to their lovemaking. Here the big lantern on the center table cast a brilliant light around the small room. The heat radiating off the stove smelled like steamy wool clothes. And Parker, instead of looking at her with the hooded desire she had seen before in his eyes, was staring, puzzled, looking perhaps as if she had just awakened him.

"I brought you some supper," she said, a little too loudly. She set the plate quickly on the table, then clasped her hands behind her back to stop the trembling.

Parker gave her one of the smiles that crinkled the corners of his eyes. "Thank you, ma'am."

She smiled back, relaxing a little. "I'm sorry you didn't come in to eat with us."

"I preferred the company of the spiders out here."

Molly laughed. "I'm sorry if Jeremy upset you."

"There's no reason for you to apologize for him. He has nothing to do with you." He watched her as he finished buttoning his shirt and tucked it into his pants. "Or does he?"

"No."

He came around the table toward her and asked directly, "So you have no plans to marry him and join your ranches the way your father had hoped?"

He looked big and rumpled. His broad chest was just inches from hers. Her pulse had begun to race, and all at once it was hard for her to breathe. It had been a mistake to come out here, she realized in a panic. What had he asked her about Jeremy? "No...I don't know."

Now he stood over her, near enough for her to see the heavy stubble of his whiskers. "Well, which is it?" he demanded. "'No' or 'I don't know'?"

"No." Her answer came out as a whisper.

Parker took hold of her arms. "Good," he whispered back. Then he pulled her against him and kissed her thoroughly. By now their mouths had begun to learn each other. He could tell exactly when she wanted the kiss to deepen, could sense when to withdraw, to soften, to let the tension build. Neither one of them moved any part of their bodies other than their lips and tongues, but Parker could feel the invisible tugs of desire streaking throughout, racing to set up demands that were even more strident than when he had lain on top of her that night in the barn.

He dropped his hands from her arms and stepped back, his breathing hard. "You'd better head on out of here, boss lady."

He sounded almost angry with her, giving Molly pause for a minute. She'd been thoroughly enjoying his kisses. The pleasant tingling had come once again, then had dissolved into stronger waves of sensation that left her wanting something more.

"I don't want to leave," she said, her direct eyes meeting his.

He looked startled and, for once, appeared to be at a loss for words. "You don't know what you're saying," he concluded finally.

"Yes, I do. Susannah says you look at me like a...a bull moose in season, but you've kissed me now... several times...and each time you end up chasing me away."

Parker gave a reluctant grin. "A bull moose?"

She nodded, her face defiant, daring him to mock her.

The ache of his desire had subsided a little, replaced by something resembling fear. Parker blew out his cheeks and let out a puff of air. "You are the most damned direct woman I've ever known, Molly Hanks."

She didn't feel direct. Her insides were feeling as shaky as her hands had been a few minutes ago. But she'd rather play out the scene than run away once more to her cold bedroom to spend the night in restless, indefinable dreams. "So...what are you going to do about it, tenderfoot?" she asked softly.

They stood inches apart, not touching but each feeling the pull of attraction between them as real as a caress. "I once had a boss who told me I'd end up as buzzard meat if I didn't keep my hands off the Hanks sisters." Parker tried once more to keep his voice light.

"You don't strike me as the type that always follows orders."

Her lips were pressed tightly together, but instead of making her look stern, it simply made her look vulnerable, made him want to kiss them open again to find the warmth within. Her shawl had fallen unheeded to the floor when they'd kissed. She was wearing the calico dress that stretched tightly across her trim breasts. So tightly that he could see her state of arousal by the hardened peaks. But Molly was a virgin. And he didn't feel he had the right to change that unless he was also willing to commit to her with his whole heart—the heart that had been broken and buried with Claire back in Deadwood. He held his hands up in the air as if renouncing any claim to her. "You're wrong. I do follow orders, boss lady."

Molly gave a snort of impatience. "Then consider the orders rescinded," she said, and flung her arms around his neck.

For several seconds he didn't respond. But this time she kissed *him,* and it set Molly's blood racing even faster than their previous kisses had. She felt the sensitive tips of her breasts against his hard chest, the warm hollow of her abdomen against the hard ridge of his manhood. She'd been raised on a ranch—she knew how procreation occurred, but she'd never imagined the reality of it all. She'd never expected the urgency, the pounding, the ache.

Parker made a sound at the back of his throat, surrendering to the inevitable. With one hand he reached to douse the wick of the lantern. Then he lifted her in his arms and made his way unerringly in the dark to his bunk. "Well, you're the boss," he whispered, setting her down on the hard mattress.

He leaned down and pulled off his boots, then settled back against the wall and pulled her once again into his arms. If it was going to happen, it wouldn't be in a rush. He couldn't remember ever being quite so desperate for a woman before, but he was determined to make himself go slowly enough to make it good for her. The one positive thing about Claire's unfortunate profession had been that she'd been able to introduce Parker to a whole new world of sensuality. She'd taught him that a woman's desire could be as strong as his own and that frank and open sharing between a man and a woman could lead to heightened pleasure for them both.

He nestled Molly in his arms and began with short, tender kisses that covered her face. When she sought his mouth, he pulled away. "This is the last time I'm going to give you the chance to get up and walk out of this room," he said huskily.

"I don't think I could if I wanted to," she whispered back. "My legs feel like jelly."

He'd seen her strong limbs in trousers, hugging the sides of her horse. He'd seen them outlined by the shimmery satin of her silver dress. He'd seen them in his dreams, entwined with his own. He ran a hand along the length of first one, then the other. "No, they don't," he murmured. "They feel firm and long—just like the rest of your beautiful body."

His hands moved to her waist, then upward to the swell of her breasts. "Firm and beautiful," he said again, touching their fullness for the first time. "I want to feel them bare in my hands, Molly. May I?"

Without waiting for permission, he moved her a distance away and started to remove her clothing. Molly had ceased thinking the minute his hands had begun their exploration. She had almost ceased breathing, until a sudden tightness in her chest made her take a deep gulp of air. She was grateful for the darkness as she felt the unfamiliar sensation of a man's hands tending to her like a chamber maid. He seemed more than familiar with women's clothing, but she pushed the implications of that thought out of her mind. Tonight she didn't care. She wanted Parker and she wanted to learn what it was to make love. Tomorrow, if necessary, she'd deal with any aftereffects, ramifications, guilt.

He'd shed his own clothing, too, and now laid her back against the blankets and began to explore with gentle strokes. "You've a body meant for love, Molly," he said in her ear. "You quiver like a drawn bow when I touch you."

"I can feel your fingertips all the way inside me," she said with wonder. Then she gave a little gasp as the tips reached her nipples and began a rhythmic massage.

"You'll feel this, too." He bent to replace his fingers with his lips and gently sucked. She lay passively beneath him. "You feel it all the way to here, don't you, sweetheart?" He laid his hand carefully over her private woman's place. And it was true. The tugging at her breast seemed to radiate downward until she felt swollen there, though he had yet to touch her. "Do you feel it?" he asked again, placing one finger barely inside her.

She moaned then, and there was no more time for talking as he released her breast and once again took possession of her mouth. With increasing desperation he stoked the fire that had flared inside them both, waiting to make himself one with her until she was open and seeking, holding back at the last minute for fear he would hurt her.

But here her well-honed horsewoman's body worked to his advantage. She welcomed him into her without a murmur and joined the frenzied thrust and pull of their bodies with a passion to rival his own. In fact, she was the first to clutch at him as the quick, white-hot climax overtook them both.

They lay very still afterward, stone heavy. Parker's head was on her chest. After a moment he chuckled, which was the last reaction Molly had been expecting. "What's funny?" she asked warily.

He rolled to one side and leaned his head on his arm. Their eyes had grown accustomed to the dark, and the starlight through the bunkhouse's solitary window was enough to allow him to see the white curves of her body. He traced a finger limply along from her neck to her navel and tried to answer her question. "You...me. I don't know. I was going to try to be so careful and controlled because it was your first time, and instead..." He leaned down to kiss her mouth. "I was about as controlled as a prize stallion."

"Isn't it always like that?"

He chuckled again at the sweet naiveté in her voice. "Hardly."

"Well, that's too bad, because I think I rather liked it that way."

He dropped his head heavily to her chest once again. "I can almost assure you that you'll have the chance to do it that way again," he said dryly.

"Although slow might be nice, too, now that I think about it. Is slow nice, too?"

Parker groaned. "Yes, slow's nice, too. But you might want to take things a little easy, sweetheart. This is your first time."

Molly appeared to consider for a minute. "I'm not at all tired," she said matter-of-factly. "I don't see any reason to stop yet."

Parker smiled in the darkness as he felt the familiar surges. His body evidently shared Molly's opinion. He lifted his head. "Well, we'll take it slow, then, this time, shall we, sweetheart?"

"Yes, please," she whispered.

Chapter Fourteen

Molly briefly considered staying with Parker until morning. She had found their lovemaking so wonderful that she felt she didn't care if the entire world knew about it. But then she thought about how scandalized her sisters and Smokey would be, and she decided that she had better, for perhaps the first time, keep a momentous event in her life to herself.

Parker walked with her back to the house before dawn and kissed her at the doorway before he let her go.

"You could invite me to move back into your father's bedroom," he teased gently. "Then you'd just have to sneak down a little bitty hall to my bed."

"Do you think I'm a coward for keeping it secret?"

He planted a kiss on her nose. "Of course not. What we had last night was a private thing—it's no one else's business but ours. I just don't know how long we're going to be able to keep it secret when every time you look at me like...like you're looking at me now, I'm going to want to snatch you up in my arms and carry you off to the nearest pile of soft hay."

Molly laughed and bent the top of her head into his chest. "But you will restrain the impulse, right?"

He ruffled his hands through her thoroughly mussed hair. "As long as I know I can have you in my bed after everyone else is asleep."

She turned up her face for a kiss. "I'm already wishing it was night again."

Parker looked off to the east. "We might have another half hour or so before it gets light...."

She pushed on his chest and he stumbled backward on the porch. "I thought you said we should be taking it easy, since it was...you know...my first time."

"I did, but that was before I realized that I'd tangled myself up with some kind of Amazon woman."

Molly wrinkled up her nose. "Amazon?"

"From mythology. They were supposedly a race of women who were tremendously strong. They kept men around solely to serve their needs."

"Smart ladies."

"Yeah, well, I don't know how some Amazons got transported all the way out to Wyoming, but I'm starting to feel like that's where I've ended up."

"Hmm. You sound as if you're not too happy about it. Perhaps you're the one who needs the rest, tenderfoot. Should I not bother to come out to you tonight?"

He grabbed her against him and kissed her thoroughly until she went pliant in his arms. "Only if you want me coming in to get you. I'm fine either way."

"But then you might have to tangle with my Am...Amazon sisters."

He leaned close and bit her earlobe, then whispered, "I'd fight a whole army of Amazons to get to you, boss lady."

She laughed happily, kissing him yet again, then finally, reluctantly, opened the front door and slipped inside.

It was a good thing she hadn't decided to declare her new relationship and stay with Parker, she realized as she went down to breakfast to find an early visitor sitting at the table with Smokey. It was a man she'd never seen before, but he had a marshal's gold badge pinned on his leather vest. Both men stood as she entered the room.

"Good morning, Molly," Smokey said. "This is Marshal Tichenor over from Laramie. He's come about your letter."

It took a couple of minutes for Molly to realize what letter Smokey was talking about, then she was embarrassed at how something so important could have slid into the background. She'd always heard that falling in love made people crazier than a coyote on locoweed, and now she knew what they'd been talking about.

"My letter about the lynching, of course. I'm glad you've come, Marshal. It's been hard for me to believe that no one has done anything about such a travesty of justice."

She motioned to the marshal to resume his seat, and he did so with a little nod. He was a tall, good-looking man, surprisingly young for such an important position. "I've talked to Sheriff Benton, Miss Hanks," he said. "He claims that the men that night were duly deputized and that a trial was held."

She took her seat across from him. "There was no trial, Marshal. Not even a semblance of one."

"And you'd swear in court to that fact?"

He had a no-nonsense demeanor that Molly liked instantly, quite a change from Sam Benton, whose weak-kneed groveling to the richest ranchers in the territory was well-known. Every rancher's son sowing his oats knew that Canyon City was safe haven. Any trouble with the law and Sheriff Benton would be more than happy to overlook it after the right threats or bribes.

"I'd swear to it, Marshal."

"If you don't mind my putting this plain, Miss Hanks, are you sure you've thought this through? You're not likely to make any friends with your neighbors if you have me pursue this matter."

"Pursue what matter?" Parker appeared in the dining-room doorway.

Molly turned to him and tried to keep the quick flush of pleasure from showing on her face. In a clean white shirt and tight jeans, he looked more handsome than ever. And his smile for her was so personal, it almost felt as if he had touched her.

"Parker, this is Marshal Tichenor. He's here to investigate the lynching of Ole Pedersson. He's warning me that people won't like it if I testify about what really happened. But that seems a little irrelevant at the moment. After all, a man's dead."

Parker paused a moment. Could the mysterious accidents around the Lucky Stars have something to do with the vigilantes? he wondered. The cattle had been scattered before the night of the lynching, but perhaps that had been just a cougar after all. He walked across the room and reached to shake hands with the marshal, introducing himself with a smile and a firm nod. "Parker Prescott, Marshal." Then he turned to Molly and said, "He might have a point. You'll make a lot of enemies if you try to tell about that night. I, however, can tell the story just as well, and I'm not worried about reprisals."

"I'd want a deposition from both of you," the marshal told them. "Whether it would ever come to testifying in court, I have my doubts. The territory has been terribly lax with vigilantism up to now. It's something I'd like to see changed."

Molly had been absently toying with the biscuit on her plate. She hadn't eaten a bite. Though she was still feeling a glow from Parker's presence, the horrors of that night had begun to come back to her. "We'll do whatever's necessary, Marshal."

Tichenor gave a nod of approval. "You're a brave lady. I'd like to start out with a list of the men who were on the posse. Do you think you can remember?"

Molly's eyes met those of Parker, who smiled his encouragement. "I can remember," she said grimly.

"What's the matter with you, Molly?" Susannah asked sharply. "That's the third time you've jabbed me with those things."

Molly had promised to cut her sister's hair that evening, but her mind was already out in the darkened bunkhouse where Parker was waiting for her. There had been three more long nights since they first made love, each more wondrous than the last. And she found that the experience seemed to have possessed every moment of her day—waking and sleeping. She had no desire to eat. She lost track of conversations in midsentence. She had absolutely no concentration. Susannah was right to complain—she could cut her sister's throat without even realizing it.

"I'm sorry. My hands just don't seem to want to do what I tell them today." She held out the scissors. "Why don't you have Mary Beth cut it?"

"Mary Beth's gone to sleep. I declare, she takes to her bed earlier and earlier these days. I don't understand it."

"These last days of winter are tedious. But spring's not far away. Then she'll feel better."

"I don't notice you in any doldrums," Susannah observed. "In fact, if I didn't know that the idea was ridiculous, I'd say my big sister has fallen in love."

"Why do you think it's ridiculous?" She took the scissors back and snipped absently at Susannah's golden curls.

"Why, because my big sister always told me that love was for...'simpering ninnies' I believe was the term."

Molly smiled ruefully. "Was I that insufferable?"

"More. But I forgive you. So...*are* you?"

"Falling in love?"

"No...planning the spring roundup. *Yes,* falling in love."

Molly didn't know how to answer her sister. Was the exhilaration of these past four nights love? Was it the way Parker's smile and his voice and his walk and everything about him sang in her heart all day long—was that love? "I guess I am," she said slowly.

Susannah gave a whoop of triumph. "Who'd have ever thought that you'd be the first of us? Of course, it's supposed to be the oldest first, but I'd always considered that you'd *die* before you'd let a man turn your head."

"People change, I guess."

"I *guess*. Well, now you'll have to help me find someone. Have you told Jeremy yet?" She whooped again. "He'll have a fit."

"There's...I haven't told Jeremy anything. There's nothing to tell."

"He'd undoubtedly disagree with you there. He thinks he's staked a claim on you, sis."

"Well, he can think again. No man has a claim on me—not Jeremy, not Parker." She threw the scissors down in exasperation. "That'll do for now. It looks fine."

Susannah looked into the hand mirror with a dubious expression. "I'll get Mary Beth to work with it in the morning," she said with a sigh. "Are you going out to the *barn* now?"

"I always go out to the barn at this time of night."

"But it didn't used to take you half the night to check on a few stall latches." Molly blushed and started toward the door. "Ah, young love," Susannah continued breezily. When the door had closed behind her sister, Susannah smiled and said to herself softly, "You may not realize it yet, Molly, but sometimes claims are staked and filed when we're not even looking."

Molly hesitated before opening the door to the bunkhouse. The conversation with Susannah had disturbed her a little. She had been so caught up in the excitement of her union with Parker, she hadn't given thought to what it all meant—to her, to her sisters, to the ranch. She didn't want to think about Jeremy Dickerson's reaction to her liaison with the hired hand. She didn't want to know if Parker considered he had staked a claim on her. They'd never discussed it. Indeed, they'd been too busy exploring one another to discuss much of anything. But she was sure of one thing—he'd never used the word *love*. Not once.

The door opened and Parker stood there, bootless, his shirt hanging open. "I thought I heard your step. Why didn't you come in?"

His voice alone was enough to send a wave of feeling plummeting through her middle. "Maybe I was wondering if you really wanted me here. I've come every night. Perhaps you're tired."

Parker looked at her as if she'd lost her mind. Then his dark eyes narrowed and he asked, "What's wrong?"

She took a deep breath. "Nothing. I just... Susannah knows about us."

The concern in his eyes was replaced by a look of relief. "Oh, is *that* all? Well, I told you we wouldn't be able to keep it a secret."

"She thinks I'm falling in love with you." Molly drew in a breath and held it.

Parker frowned. He bent his head and tried to read her expression. Something was wrong—more than just Susannah finding out about their trysts. He took her hand and led her toward the bunk. "It's a natural assumption, sweetheart. It normally goes along with—" he gestured toward the bed "—with what we've been doing."

It wasn't quite the declaration Molly had been hoping for. It just skirted the edge of things—talking around it without any real commitment. "Do *you* think I'm falling in love with you?" she asked.

He seated her on the bed and sat beside her, leaving a little distance between them. "I don't know, Amazon," he said lightly. "You haven't left me much time or strength to discuss the matter."

"So it's just been . . . physical."

Parker rolled his eyes. He supposed the uncomplicated bliss of the past few nights could not be expected to last, but blast it if females didn't have a way of making simple things hard. "Of course it hasn't been just *physical,* Molly. Two people can't experience together what we have if it's just physical."

"Truly?"

"Truly," he said firmly, reaching for her with a vain hope that the discussion was over.

She pushed him back, her natural curiosity momentarily superseding the other issues. "Then how do you explain that men—you know—*pay* for women to do what we've been doing?"

Parker was taken aback once again by her bluntness. "Jesus, Molly. It's not the same thing at all. You're trying to compare a strictly physical sensation with a—" he groped for the words "—a very special communion between two people who care about each other . . . who . . ."

"Who love each other?" she asked softly.

Parker was silent for a long time. Too long.

She looked down at her hands. "It's that girl, isn't it? The one you called for when you were sick."

Parker leaned over and tried to weave his fingers into her clasped hands. She moved them away. "Is she waiting for you out in California?" she asked.

Parker slid backward on the bunk to lean against the wall. Months had passed, he thought angrily. It shouldn't be this hard. In Deadwood he hadn't been able to talk about Claire's death with anyone—not even his sister. But he'd headed west to make a new beginning. And part of that process should include freeing himself from the past, or at least turning the memories into friends instead of enemies who were set to shoot down every chance he had at happiness. "She's dead," he said tersely, and the words were even harder than he had feared.

Molly waited for him to continue, but when he remained silent, she said, "I'm sorry." Her throat was full and her eyes misted. And she *was* sorry. For Parker, for his poor lost love whose life had been cut short, and for herself—who had at long last torn down the wall she had built up around herself over the years, only to find a thicker, much more painful wall on the other side.

Perhaps with time, perhaps if he would talk with her... "What was her name?" she asked gently.

Parker's expression had tightened. "Claire. Claire Devereaux."

He said the name as if it were poetry, and used an odd, French inflection. "Was she French?" Molly asked.

He stared into space, a bittersweet smile on his lips. "She was an orphan, born in France but raised in this country. She always wanted... we were going to go to Paris together. I was teaching her the language," he added wistfully, now thoroughly lost in the memories.

Molly could understand grief—she'd been through it recently enough with her father. But she felt her heart sinking as she listened to him talk about his beautiful French love. Someday Parker would love again, she felt certain. He had too much life in him to spend it longing for the past. But when he chose someone, it would hardly be a "boss lady" like Molly.

His Claire had obviously been refined and delicate. An ethereal beauty, he described it. Which was just about as far from Molly Hanks of Wyoming as that fancy Delmonico's was from the Grizzly Bear Saloon. She'd been a fool to think a cultivated Easterner like Parker would ever fall for her.

"And you're still in love with her," she said with a brittle smile.

Parker winced. "It wouldn't make sense to be in love with a ghost, now would it?"

"Well, let me put it this way. You're not yet ready to fall in love with anyone else."

His silence was achingly eloquent.

She shivered. It felt as if a casing of ice was forming around her heart. This was what came of letting down the guard she'd carefully built up since she was twelve. She'd let herself be swept away by Parker's charm and good looks, by the way his eyes smoldered when they looked at her, by the way his hands could make her body sing. Going against all the principles she'd established for herself, she'd been on the verge of trusting her happiness to a man.

"I reckon what all this means, Parker," she said stiffly, "is that I won't be coming out to visit you nights anymore."

Parker's dark eyes were unreadable. "If that's the way you want it."

Tears sprang to her eyes and she blinked them back furiously. "That's not the way I want it, as I think you well know."

He hung his head. "I'm sorry I can't offer you everything you need, Molly."

"I'm sorry, too."

"Do you want me to leave?"

She shook her head. "If you're willing to stay on, I still need the help, especially now that spring's coming."

"I'm willing," he said in a low voice. "I'll stay as long as you need me."

No, you won't, Parker, she thought, pushing back a sob that wanted to fight its way out of her throat. *Because that would mean you'd stay forever.* There, she'd admitted it. She wasn't just falling in love with him—she was already there, totally and irrevocably. But she would now take that love and tuck it away, as she had her crinolines and ribbons when she was twelve years old. She stood. "I appreciate that," she said briskly. "I'll try not to...confuse matters again."

Parker shook his head. "Molly, it doesn't have to be like that...." He reached for her hand, but she'd already turned toward the door.

She paused for a minute before leaving and, without looking back at him, said sadly, "I'm afraid it does, Parker. I'm afraid it has to be like that."

"Jeremy's spitting mad about your sister," Ned told Mary Beth after he had kissed her and tied up her horse outside the little abandoned cabin where they had met throughout the winter.

She returned his embrace and stayed in the circle of his arm as they went inside. "What's he angry about? He hasn't even been around our place since the day you brought word about the mule."

"He's been unhappy ever since the Christmas dance when he got the idea in his head that Molly was getting interested in that hired man of yours."

Mary Beth thought for a moment. "You know, I thought the same thing myself for a while. In fact, I was almost sure of it, but lately things have been different. I even asked Molly if they'd had a fight, but she told me to mind my own business."

Ned chuckled and pressed Mary Beth to his side. "She does tend to speak plain, doesn't she?"

Mary Beth smiled. "It's just Molly's way. We're used to it. So it's Parker that's making your brother upset?"

The cabin had no furniture, but they'd brought a collection of old quilts and blankets and made a little nest for themselves in front of the big stone fireplace, which Ned had supplied with plenty of wood. He gestured for her to sit down while he began to build up a fire. "No, it's not just the cowhand. He's riled because evidently Molly talked to the territorial marshal about the night Ole Pedersson was hanged."

"Oh! She was dreadfully disturbed by all that."

"Well, I wasn't there that night, as you well know, Bethy." He leaned down and gave her a kiss on the mouth. "But Pa says that he and Jeremy told Molly that a posse was no place for a lady, and she just wouldn't listen."

Mary Beth hugged her knees tightly as she defended her sister. "Don't you think that's a little beside the point, Ned? Males or females—the posse had no right to hang a man without a fair trial."

Ned dropped a match on his carefully stacked fire, then eased down beside her with a sigh. "Don't you turn all preachy now like your sister. She'll have you sounding like one of those—what do you call them—female suffragers."

"Suffragists," she corrected. "And there's certainly nothing wrong with that. It's only logical to think that women should be able to have a voice in the way they're governed."

Ned groaned. "I suppose next you and your sisters will decide to ride on into town and chop up the Grizzly Bear with a hatchet."

"Why, Ned Dickerson, you're being mean. Just because we believe women should be treated fairly. We aren't even teetotalers."

He tumbled her backward on the blanket. "Are we having our first fight, my love? Because I've heard that making up can be an awful lot of fun."

"I declare, Ned. Sometimes it seems that's the only thing you think about." Her smile softened the words.

His voice lowered as he began to kiss her. "It's hard to think about anything else when I'm with you, Bethy. I can't seem to get enough of you."

"I know. I'll be glad when my birthday comes and we can be together openly—all the time."

"All the time," he agreed, nuzzling her neck.

"And your family won't object? It won't matter that Jeremy's angry with my sister?"

"It sure as hell won't matter to me," he said fervently. "Jeremy and Molly will just have to work things out for themselves. He still plans to marry her, you know. I've heard him say so."

Mary Beth widened her eyes in surprise. "Well, he's got a funny way of showing it—getting angry and ignoring her for weeks on end."

"Jeremy's not the courtin' type. And I don't mean to hurt your feelings, Bethy, but Molly's not exactly the type of woman who inspires that kind of thing."

Mary Beth set her mouth in a firm line. "Inspired or not—if your brother wants to marry Molly, he'd better start taking a few pains to show her so."

Ned stopped kissing her as he thought for a moment about her remark. "You may be right, Bethy. I'll pass along your advice."

"To what do we owe the pleasure, Jeremy? Have more of my animals managed to find their way over to your place?"

Molly's tone was more caustic than usual. She hadn't slept well for the past week since her break with Parker. And, in general, life just didn't seem very joyous to her at the moment. She was faced with mounting debts and dwindling money. She'd have to try to sell off a good portion of her herd this summer. But first she had to find the men who would help her round them up and brand all the ones they'd missed last year. The household wasn't being of much help. Mary Beth still had that odd, dreamy look about her. Susannah had begun taking off regularly on excursions with some of the other young folks in the neighborhood. One night last week Fred Baumgarten had brought her home close to midnight and Molly had smelled sherry on her breath! Smokey was continuing to see Max on a regular basis. And Parker had taken to riding in with him. Molly had no idea what he'd found in town to occupy himself—one of the dance girls at the Grizzly, probably. Anyway, as he had told her when she'd inquired, what he did once his chores were completed wasn't her concern.

"I just came to see you, Molly," Jeremy said almost sweetly. "I've brought you a cattle magazine I thought you'd find interesting."

Molly reached out for the publication. It was not as romantic a gift as Parker's candies, but it was much more practical. Sort of like the difference between

Parker and Jeremy themselves. And it felt good to have someone paying attention to her. She smiled. "Thank you, Jeremy. That was very thoughtful."

"You may not believe that I think about you, Molly, but I do. If I haven't been around much this winter, it was only because it seemed that you weren't that interested in having me here."

"I'm always happy to have you here, Jeremy, except when you start barking and telling me what to do."

He laughed. "Fair enough. I'll try to be less authoritative if you'll try to be a little more willing to listen to my *suggestions*. I only have your welfare at heart, you know."

Molly nodded. The welfare of her ranch was what he meant. But he'd come with a peace offering and she was in the mood to accept it. She held out her hand. "It's a deal."

She ushered him into the small formal sitting room on the other side of the hall from the family parlor. It made her feel a little uncomfortable, because they never used this room. The last time had been when the minister had come to talk with them about her father's funeral.

"Shall I tell Smokey that you're staying to supper?" she asked him.

"I was hoping to convince you to ride back with me to the Lazy D. I'd like to have you spend more time there, Molly."

From virtually ignoring her for most of the winter he was suddenly sounding once again like a suitor. It was almost as if he had known about her temporary detour to Parker and knew that after her hired hand's rejection, she was more vulnerable than ever before.

"I've always enjoyed visiting the Lazy D," she said carefully. "But I've work yet to do today. Perhaps I could ride over with my sisters some day later this week."

They were sitting on either end of the straight-backed sofa. He leaned toward her and said, "Your sisters are welcome, of course, but I was hoping that I'd be able to have you to myself for once. I think we need time alone together."

Molly felt a great lump at the base of her throat. This wasn't the way it was supposed to feel. Obviously, Jeremy was trying to court her. It had, after all, been talked about between their fathers since Molly and Jeremy had been children. But instead of making her feel excited at the prospect of finding someone to share her life with, it was making her want to weep. She'd found only one person with whom she wanted to share, and he wasn't interested. But she'd be darned if she'd cry in front of Jeremy. Or anyone else, for that matter.

"I'd be happy to come by myself, Jeremy. Would Thursday be convenient?"

He stood and bent over her hand. "I'll be looking forward to it."

"So will I," she lied.

Chapter Fifteen

Parker had started to like Harry Tichenor. It had taken some time to warm up to the taciturn marshal, but now that they had ridden out together several times and ended more than one evening sharing a bottle at the Grizzly, he'd begun to appreciate the man's honesty and simple value system. To Harry, there was no such thing as bending the law. In a wild territory like Wyoming most marshals wouldn't have spent a day investigating the lynching of a town drunk. Nor, Parker imagined, would most marshals have taken the time to listen to Parker's suspicions about the problems at the Lucky Stars ranch. Marshal Tichenor did both and promised Parker that he wouldn't be giving up on either matter until some kind of resolution had been reached—even if it took months or years. He was just that kind of man.

The first day Parker had ridden into town to look for the marshal, he'd found him in the restaurant at the Grand Hotel. Tichenor had told him that he had decided against using Sheriff Benton's office as a base for his investigation. For some time he hadn't much approved of Benton's version of justice in Canyon

City, he'd explained to Parker, but he hadn't had any real leads to go after him until now.

Parker was happy to help out. For one thing, he believed in what the marshal was doing, and, for another, it gave him a good excuse to spend a lot of time away from the Lucky Stars. The two men sometimes met at McClanahan's Bath House, since it afforded some privacy and was run by a woman who could be trusted to keep her mouth shut. But today they'd been out to interview one of the men who'd been part of the posse, and when they came back they decided they'd stop at the Grizzly before calling it a night.

"So if we can get Overstreet's testimony along with mine, will that be enough for a hearing?" Parker asked as they walked along the sidewalk toward the saloon. The main street of town was nearly deserted and the early-March wind blew down the center of it like a freight train.

"Along with Miss Hanks's statement."

"I was hoping we could leave her out of this."

Tichenor stopped and turned to his new friend. "You've got it bad for that gal, haven't you?"

Parker rubbed his whiskery chin. He couldn't remember the last time he had shaved, but it had been several days. "No. Molly Hanks is my boss, nothing more."

Tichenor's face remained impassive except for one errant eyebrow that shot way up. "If I were a betting man, that's one bluff I'd call in a heartbeat, Prescott."

Parker gave a reluctant smile. "She's quite a woman, I'll grant you. But I'm not the man for her. She needs someone who can settle down with her and help her save her precious ranch."

"Someone like Jeremy Dickerson?"

Parker shrugged. "I guess he's the most likely candidate."

"He's a sidewinder, far as I can tell."

"I've gotten the same impression, but Susannah tells me that he's starting to act a bit more decent these days. She thinks he may really be in love with Molly." Parker ignored the roiling in his gut that started every time he thought about Molly and Dickerson together. She'd been riding over to the Dickerson ranch regularly the past couple of weeks.

"Now, that Susannah...*she's* special."

Parker looked over at the marshal, amazed at the vehemence of his observation. In his several meetings with Harry, he'd never known him to get that excited about anything. "She's easy on the eyes, that's for sure," Parker agreed.

"Easy! Hell, she's downright blistering on the eyes, if you ask me. I've never seen such a beauty."

Parker chuckled. "Sounds to me like you're smitten, marshal. Is that allowed when you're on duty?"

Harry shook his head and laughed. "No. Why do you think I'm spending my evening with a lousy, no-account cowpoke like you instead of camped out on her doorstep?"

"Hey, there, you'll offend Max if you call me lousy. She makes sure I bathe at least once a month, delousing included."

They both were laughing when they suddenly became aware that two men had come up quietly behind them. "You're just the man we wanted to see, Marshal."

Parker recognized Jeremy Dickerson's arrogant tone. They turned around to face him and his companion, Sheriff Benton. "What can I do for you, gentlemen?" Tichenor asked quietly.

"I understand you've been asking a lot of questions about the night some of us were deputized by the sheriff here to help him with a legal matter."

"If you're referring to the night Ole Pedersson was hanged, I am. It seems a report was never filed on the incident."

"It was a local matter," Benton chimed in. "No need to go to the territory with it."

"All capital offenses go through the territory, Benton. You should know that much, at least."

Dickerson smiled and clapped a hand on Tichenor's shoulder. "Hell, Marshal, Ole's been cold in his grave for months now, and to tell the truth he wasn't any good to anybody when he was still warm. Can't we just let the thing rest? I know my pa'd appreciate it. And it never hurts to have the Lazy D on your side when it comes to those damned territorial politics. Why, I've heard that men get their jobs whisked out from under them faster than you can say Jack Sprat. Good men, sometimes."

The implication was lost on no one, but Tichenor's calm expression didn't waver by so much as a hair. "I'll be sure and let you and your father know the outcome of my investigation, Mr. Dickerson. Now, if you'll excuse us, my friend and I were about to go in for a beer."

Dickerson shot a look at Parker. "One more thing, Marshal. I believe you've interrogated Molly Hanks on this matter."

"I've talked to Miss Hanks."

"From now on, if you need to speak with her, I'd appreciate it if you would do so through me."

Tichenor's eyebrow rose. "And why would I do that, Mr. Dickerson?"

"I consider all the Hanks sisters to be my responsibility now that their father is gone. And Molly and I are practically affianced."

"Practically affianced?" the marshal drawled. "You understand that lingo, Parker?"

Parker, whose stomach had tightened at the first sound of Jeremy's voice, stopped grinding his teeth long enough to answer. "It means he's doing everything he can to get his hooks into Molly's ranch."

"Oh," the marshal said. "I thought it meant something like that."

Jeremy's face took on an almost purple cast in the dimly lit street. His hand flexed and hovered over a revolver that was tucked into the front of his pants. "You won't be talking so pretty when Molly and I announce our engagement, Prescott. Because you'll be packing up your gear that same day."

"If you and Molly announce your engagement, I'll be packed and halfway to Montana that same *hour*. Until that time, I'm staying—for as long as Molly wants me."

Tichenor seemed to sense the escalating tension between the two men. He grasped Parker's arm and pulled him toward the saloon. "Like I said, we'll keep you informed of the investigation, Mr. Dickerson. Good evening, gentlemen."

Benton and Dickerson did not follow them into the Grizzly. For a moment Parker thought he was going to be sick as the bright lights of the bar and the strong odor of cigar smoke overwhelmed him. "Are you all right?" Tichenor asked.

"Yeah. That fellow sticks in my craw."

"Mine, too," the marshal agreed easily. "And I'm not even jealous of the son of a bitch."

Parker gave him a sideways look. "Meaning that I am?"

Tichenor nodded solemnly. "Wretchedly."

Parker didn't argue. "Damn," he said simply.

"There's only one thing to do about jealousy."

"What's that?"

"Stake your claim."

They'd walked up to the bar and the marshal had signaled the bartender to give them two beers. He pushed one toward Parker, who drank half the mug without stopping. "I don't have a claim," he said finally, swiping a hand across his dripping mouth.

"Well, see. That's your problem. You've got to get out there, pound in your stakes and take possession. Then you'll be able to sleep at night."

Parker looked at the marshal with a look of amazement. How did Tichenor know that it had been weeks since he'd had a good night's sleep? "Pound in my stakes, eh?"

Tichenor took a gulp of beer and nodded. "Yup. Stop sittin' here every night making chin music with me and get to it."

Suddenly Harry's words made absolute, brilliant sense. Parker stood up from the stool and clapped on his hat. "You want me to pound in one or two around Susannah while I'm at it?" he asked with a grin.

Tichenor took another swallow of beer. "Nope. I plan on staking out that filly myself one of these days. You can just leave her plumb alone."

Once he'd made up his mind, Parker couldn't get back to the ranch fast enough. He apologized silently to Diamond for pushing so hard after a long day, but he wanted to get back before Molly had turned in for the night. What he had to say wouldn't wait until morning.

As it turned out, his timing was perfect. When he rode into the barn she was there, standing in the stall next to Moonlight the calf and talking to it softly. She was wearing her buckskins. She hadn't put on a dress for supper as often in recent days, though Parker had noted with some irritation that she did seem to don her female attire lately every time she headed over to the Lazy D. Of course, as he had told her, she looked every bit as appealing in the buckskins. In fact, there were times when she moved around and he watched how the soft leather molded itself around her firm little bottom... He felt it now—the familiar tugging through his midsection.

"Hello, Parker." Her greeting was frosty. "I trust you had another *pleasant* evening in town."

He swung down from his horse and began to unsaddle her. "It was pleasant enough, except for a not-so-pleasant run-in with your friend Dickerson."

"Jeremy?"

He lifted the saddle and blanket off Diamond's back and began to rub her down. "Yes. The charming Jeremy."

Molly looked as if she wanted to appear indifferent, but curiosity got the better of her. "What was it about?" Then she added, "And he *can* be charming when he wants to be, you know. He's been very nice to me."

Parker gave Diamond's rump a gentle slap to send her into a stall. "You mean he can be charming when he's angling to get control of a prime piece of property—like the Lucky Stars.''

Almost instantly he regretted his statement. She winced, almost as if he had hit her, and then her eyes took on the same hurt expression that she'd had the night they'd talked about Claire. She looked young and vulnerable, and he realized that, however brave a front Molly might be putting on, she had lost some of the confidence she'd begun to gain when she'd been falling in love with Parker. It was obvious that she, too, believed Dickerson's interest in her was based solely on his desire to control the ranch. Parker sighed. He had some amends to make. Some repair work to do.

He walked toward her slowly. ''I'm not saying that he *only* wants the ranch, Molly.''

Her nose had that defiant tilt he had learned to expect when she'd been hurt. ''Yes, you were. It's what everyone says, and I expect it's true.''

Yesterday as she'd left the Lazy D, Jeremy had kissed her. She'd told herself that it was a good sign, that it meant he cared about her as well as the ranch. So she'd kissed him back, willing herself to feel something. She'd hoped that his kisses would help blot out her memories of those few impassioned nights with Parker. But it hadn't worked. Jeremy's kisses had only filled her with a mild distaste, and she'd cried all the way home.

Parker took her chin in his big hand. ''It's not true. I can't imagine any man getting near enough to look into those blue eyes and still keep his mind on cattle and grazing land.''

She pulled her face away. It felt too good to feel his fingers on her skin. Good and awful at the same time.

She felt a surge of resentment. She'd been rejected once by Parker. He had no right to come in and stir things up again.

"I suppose he thinks about a thing or two besides cattle when he kisses me," she said with deliberate nonchalance. It was a slight exaggeration of the status of her relationship with Jeremy, but she saw that the barb had hooked as Parker's nostrils flared in quick anger.

"When he kisses you," he repeated slowly.

She nodded.

Parker reached toward a nearby stall and wound his fist around a bridle that was hanging over the wall. "Then Susannah was right all along. Jeremy's the one you want."

"Jeremy and I make sense. It would be a good move for both our ranches."

"Ah, yes, the ranches. Let's forget about the kissing and talk about what makes sense for the ranches."

Molly had never heard such tight anger in his voice. The knuckles of the hand holding the bridle were white. She backed away a step. "It's my life, Parker," she said softly. "The ranch is my life."

"Do you love him?"

Molly looked away from the intense scrutiny of his dark eyes. "That's none of your business, Mr. Prescott." She started to turn away toward the door, but he grabbed her arm.

"The hell it's not." She was in his arms then and he didn't make any effort to be gentle. His lips smashed against hers and opened her mouth to the fierce onslaught of his kisses. He held her uncorseted body against his with both hands, her breasts crushed into his chest, her thighs tightly pressed to his. Then he put his hands on her waist and turned her so that her back was against the wooden wall of the stall, and he kissed her some more, filling his hands with her softness and bending his legs to nest his stiff arousal in the hollow below her belly.

The moist heat of her mouth burned him, incinerating a streak down his middle, ending in an explosive fury at the juncture of his legs. He'd never felt anything quite so extraordinary... or so devastating. It was a combination of lust and anger. He wanted to lose himself in her body, to pour inside her all the rage he'd been saving up underneath his carefree manner—rage against Claire for leaving him alone, against Molly for waking up his heart so that he could once again feel the pain of loving someone. And blinding, scalding rage against Dickerson for daring to touch her.

"Did it feel like this when he kissed you, Molly?" he growled against her softened lips.

She pushed against him and bit the side of his lip. But the struggle was halfhearted and the bite inflamed rather than punished. Parker retaliated by biting her back.

"What was I, boss lady?" he asked between deep, rhythmic kisses. "What was the lovemaking we shared? A training run with the hired hand?"

She brought her hand up to slap him, but he caught it and held it inches from her face. "Is that what it was?" he asked again in a low, deadly voice.

She twisted her wrist suddenly to escape his grasp and slid out from beneath him. "You've been drinking, Parker," she said, taking deep breaths.

For just a minute there was a look of something like fear in her eyes, and it stopped Parker cold. He knew

that he hadn't drunk enough at the Grizzly to intoxicate a bumblebee, but, nevertheless, he *had* lost control. He'd ridden out here planning to talk with Molly
about a possible future for the two of them. Instead,
when she'd told him that Dickerson had kissed her,
he'd thrown her up against a wall and come close to
ravishing her.

He squatted on the ground and dropped his head
into his hands. "I'm sorry," he said, taking a deep,
shuddering breath. "I'm not drunk, Molly. I'm
just . . . I don't know what the hell I am."

Molly looked down at him. The truth—the awful
truth that even now had her head ringing—was that
she'd been utterly aroused by Parker's rough kisses.
She'd wanted more. She still did.

"Sure you do, tenderfoot," she said lightly. She
rested a hand on his bent head. Of their own volition
her fingers threaded into the dark waves. "You're a
fast-talking Easterner who came out West expressly to
break the hearts of us simple ranch girls."

Parker looked up at her and spoke softly. "Did I
break your heart, Molly?"

She grimaced. "Bent it a little. I'm too tough to
break."

He tugged on her hand to pull her down beside him
and they both fell backward onto a pile of horse blankets stacked against the stall wall. "Is that why you've
been spending so much time over at Dickerson's
place?"

"The one thing has nothing to do with the other. I
visited the Dickersons regularly before you ever
showed up here, and I will continue to do so after you
leave."

"And continue to let Dickerson kiss you?"

She leaned back against the rough wood slats and held up a hand as if asking for peace. "Don't start in again, Parker. You haven't got a case here. It's none of your business who I let kiss me."

He looked at her soberly for a long minute. "I'm making it my business, Molly."

Molly's breath caught in her throat. "Don't say that, Parker, unless you mean something by it. Please. My heart's starting to look like a parade ground after a hard rain from all the stompin' it's taken."

Parker stood suddenly and, before Molly could say anything, bent over and picked her up. "Have the folks over at the house turned in for the night?"

"Yes," she whispered.

"Good. 'Cause I wouldn't want them waiting up for you."

He started walking with her out of the barn. "Parker, what are you doing? Put me down."

She bounced against him as he made his way toward the bunkhouse. "Parker!" she said again.

He stopped, but didn't loosen his hold on her. "Listen, boss lady. In a couple of minutes I intend to close up that beautiful mouth of yours, but for the time being maybe you could manage to shut it all on your own."

He kissed her hard, quickly, then resumed his walk. Her soft, leather-clad bottom rubbed against his forearm as he walked. "And stop squirming," he added, "or I'm going to have to stop and make love to you right here on the cold ground."

A surge went through his middle at his own words, and evidently they affected Molly as well, since she stopped protesting and instead tucked her head above his shoulder and began soft nips along the line of his jaw.

"You haven't shaved," she whispered.

"I didn't figure to be entertaining a lady tonight."

Suddenly she remembered her suspicions about all his recent trips into town. "What did you figure to be doing?" she asked.

He'd reached the door and kicked it open with his boot. "Now, see? I knew you wouldn't be able to keep that mouth closed all by yourself. I reckon I'm going to have to do it myself."

"But I just wanted to know—"

She couldn't finish her question. He'd taken her mouth again in a head-spinning kiss. "I've never kissed anyone in trousers before," he teased when he'd left her thoroughly dazed.

"Do you mind?" she whispered.

"No, ma'am." He spread his hands over the seat of her pants and pushed her against him. "Does that feel like I mind? And anyway—" his hands moved to the ties of her shirt "—you won't be in 'em for long."

Sunlight was streaming in the bunkhouse window when Molly awoke with a start. Her first impulse was to jump up and get back to the house before her absence was discovered, but after a moment of thought she sank back into the pillows next to Parker. It was time, after all, that the rest of the family knew how things were between them. Though they hadn't exactly talked about marriage during their long, drugging night of lovemaking, Parker had made it plain that he was ready to consider the idea of building their relationship into something more permanent. Molly knew she'd be in for some hearty teasing by her sisters after all the years she'd spent warning them about falling for a man. But they'd been used to sharing everything, and she wasn't going to shut them out now, just because her life had taken such an unexpected turn.

Parker's voice startled her. "I thought the moonlight on your skin last night was the most beautiful sight I'd ever see, but you're even prettier with the sunbeams dancing in those big blue eyes."

His smile reached deep inside her, warming her all the way to her toes. "You're not too bad a sight to wake up to yourself, tenderfoot."

He grinned and pulled her down beside him. "Tenderfoot? I was hoping after last night I'd have worked my way up to wrangler."

She giggled and snuggled more closely against him. "I think I'll move you all the way up to trail boss, Mr. Prescott."

He pulled her underneath him and started nibbling at her lips. "Don't do me any favors now, boss lady. I don't want anything I haven't earned."

She made a sound in the back of her throat as he moved down her body to swirl his tongue around her nipple. His beard prickled against the tender skin of her breasts. They were both morning sensitive and ready. He entered her almost immediately and after only a few slow thrusts she clutched his arms and cried out. He increased the tempo, his eyes open, watching her, and ended with a long sigh of satisfaction.

She smiled shyly. "I think you've earned it, cowboy."

He grinned. "Are you sure? I'd be happy to keep working at it."

She daringly reached down and gave a slap to his bare rear. "How about you save some of your strength for the cattle?"

"I've plenty of strength to go around, sweetheart, but I'm going to get up now anyway and let you get dressed. As much as I hate to have all that covered up—" he boosted himself up on his hands and looked down the length of her limp, sated body "—I don't want Smokey or your sisters showing up looking for us."

They pulled each other out of the bed amidst more laughter and kisses. Molly didn't think she'd ever been so happy in her whole life. Was it only two days ago that she'd ridden home from the Lazy D in tears?

"I'll have to tell my sisters something," Molly observed as they were smoothing out the bedding, one on each end.

"About us?"

"Yes, about us." Men were exasperatingly dim at times. "They'll know I spent the night here."

"Oh. Well, tell them the truth—that you've fallen madly in love with me."

She gave the quilt an extra hard flip, pulling it out of his hands. "Humph. How about if I tell them that you've fallen madly in love with me?"

Parker grinned. "How about if we tell them that the tenderfoot and the boss lady have fallen in love with each other?"

She smiled. "That sounds like a good plan." She held out her hand and he took it as they headed together up to the ranch house.

The teasing at breakfast had not been as bad as Molly had feared. Smokey and Mary Beth had both appeared to be too delighted with the news to taunt. And Susannah had been oddly restrained about the whole thing. Perhaps now that she was spending so much time with the young folks of the neighborhood, she was imagining that she, too, would be in a romantic relationship before long, so it didn't behoove her to make fun of Molly's.

Spring was officially just around the corner, and after the mild winter, Molly had decided that they would start the roundup any day now. The only thing stopping them was the lack of help. As he had promised, Parker agreed to ride into town with Smokey and convince some of the cowboys to sign on at the Lucky Stars.

"Tell them we have a male trail boss, if you think that will help," she told him archly as they saddled up their horses.

He leaned over to kiss her. "I ain't about to show off my trail boss *credentials* to a rowdy bunch like that," he said with a wiggle of his eyebrows and a swift look down at his privates, which seemed to be in a state of half arousal these days whenever Molly was in the same room.

Molly chuckled. "I would hope not."

He seized her waist. "I could show them off to you, though, boss lady. Just one more time before we start to work—over there in that nice soft pile of hay."

"Take your randy hands off me, Parker Prescott. You've got me a crew to find, and I've got my own things to get done."

He leaned over and spoke softly. "You think about what you're missing as you ride along in that hard saddle today."

"Parker!"

"Well, lady. What do you expect me to have on my mind after a night like you just gave me?"

"Work. The ranch."

"Ah, yes. The ranch." He released her and gave a shrug of resignation. "So, what are you going to do today?"

She hesitated for a moment. "I'm riding over to the Lazy D."

His teasing expression dropped in an instant. "The hell you are."

Molly bristled. "I beg your pardon?"

"You expect me to let you ride on over so Dickerson can put his hands on you again?"

Molly let out a slow breath. The fresh spring breeze suddenly seemed colder. "I don't expect you to *let* me do anything, Parker. I'm still the boss around here, remember?"

He'd shaved that morning and now he drew the back of his hand across his smooth cheek as if it had been slapped. "I remember," he said quietly. "But I don't want you going over to the Lazy D. Not unless I'm with you."

Molly looked at him, dumbfounded. "You're not being serious, I hope," she said, though he appeared in deadly earnest.

"Yes, I am."

They stared at each other for a long moment, at an impasse. Molly felt like pinching herself to see if the entire night they had just spent and the past two minutes of conversation were both part of some kind of dream—or nightmare. Before she had met Parker she had sworn she would never fall in love, never give a man control over her life. He had changed that. His easy charm and uninhibited ability to laugh at himself had made her believe that this was a man who would never expect her to subjugate herself in any way to his will. Now they weren't even engaged yet, and he was forbidding her from riding over to visit her neighbors. She could scarcely believe her own ears.

She pulled herself up stiffly. "You have your orders for the day, cowboy. I'll see you at supper." She turned away from him and tugged at her horse's cinch.

"I don't like Jeremy," Parker said, making his tone a little less dictatorial. "And I don't trust him. Yesterday he threatened to make Harry Tichenor lose his job if he didn't drop the investigation of the lynching."

"He's nervous about it. So are a lot of the men who were on the posse that night. But I know most of them, and they're good people at heart."

"Yeah, well, Dickerson's not one of your good people."

"I guess I can be the judge of that."

"Molly, I—"

She shook her head and interrupted him. "I don't want to hear it, Parker. If you aren't going to be able to let me run my life the way I've been doing perfectly well for some ten years now, then what we thought we were beginning last night is going to end right now."

Parker gave a growl of exasperation and kicked at a clump of hay. "You are the most damned stubborn woman I've ever..."

But before he could even finish his sentence she'd swung up on Midnight's back and ridden out of the barn.

Chapter Sixteen

Parker was mad enough to kick a cow chip all the way to the Pacific Ocean, but he retained enough sanity to realize that it wasn't fair to take his temper out on the laconic Harry Tichenor. Harry had put up with his ill mood all morning, and the only comment he'd made on the subject was a brief "You New York gents do get grouchy sometimes, don't ya?"

The remark had been enough to make Parker pause for a moment. For the truth was, he'd *never* been the grouchy type. The only person who'd ever made him lose his temper in the past had been his sister, Amelia. He'd never once gotten angry with Claire. Of course, Claire had always gone right along with everything Parker had suggested.

Smokey and Parker had set out early from the ranch to begin to search for men to hire on temporarily for a spring roundup. The Grizzly Bear had been empty at such an early hour, so Parker had told Smokey to wait around there while he went to see if the marshal had made any progress on his investigation.

He'd found Tichenor still at breakfast at the Grand, and the marshal had invited him to have some coffee while he waited for a man who had promised information on the lynching.

"Not on the lynching, exactly," he explained to Parker, "but rather on the murder of Johnny the Oyster."

Parker's eyes widened. "You mean Ole might not have been the murderer after all?"

"I don't know. I just got this message yesterday at the hotel. It said the man would meet me here this morning. There was no signature."

It was nearly noon, and they'd almost concluded that the message had been a hoax, when a cowboy in butterfly chaps and a silver-trimmed vest entered the dining room, looking around nervously. When he spotted the marshal he stopped for a minute, studying Parker. Then he walked over to their table.

"I wanted to talk to you alone, Marshal," he mumbled. It was hard to understand him. He had a front tooth missing and tried to keep his upper lip covering the gap while he talked.

"Mr. Prescott is involved in the investigation," Tichenor said vaguely. "You can speak in front of him." He motioned the man to a chair at the other side of the table.

The cowboy shook his head. "I ain't sittin' down with you, Marshal, no offense. I jest want to say my piece and get this off my conscience—so Johnny can rest quiet in his grave."

The marshal sat back in his chair and nodded calmly, giving no indication of the intense interest he was feeling at the man's words. Parker tried to emulate his demeanor. "What's your name, cowboy?" Tichenor asked.

"Taylor."

"And your first name?"

"Taylor's good enough. Do you want to hear what I come to say or not?"

The man had begun to look around the room again and a bead of sweat trickled from underneath his hat. "Yes, I do, Mr. Taylor. What do you know about your friend's death?"

"Murder, you mean."

"Yes, murder. He was shot in the back."

"That's the thing of it, Marshal. They shot him in the back like a low-down varmint. Johnny didn't deserve an end like that."

"Who shot him, Mr. Taylor?" Tichenor's voice was low, soothing.

"Dickerson. He done it himself."

Parker made a sudden movement in his chair, but Tichenor motioned him to be still. "Which Dickerson are we talking about—Jeremy?"

"Yeah. The mangy skunk."

"Did you see Mr. Dickerson shoot Johnny?"

"We all saw it. Johnny was saying as how he didn't want to be messing around anymore with the Lucky Stars cattle. Dickerson told him to shut his mouth, but when Johnny kept on about it, he just up and shot him."

"Where was this, Mr. Taylor?"

"Out at the ranch—the Lazy D. But then Mr. Jeremy says we've got to take the body into town and make it look like he was shot by some drunk."

Parker could no longer sit still in his chair. "Molly rode over to Dickerson's place this morning," he said grimly.

"Mr. Taylor," the marshal said, "I'm going to ask you to stay here at the hotel until we can put Mr. Dickerson under arrest and get a statement from you."

Taylor looked uneasy. "I don't know about any statement...."

"This is a murder case, Mr. Taylor. I'm afraid you have certain obligations here."

"I jest did it for Johnny. So's he could rest in peace."

"Well, you did the right thing. But it can't end here. If Mr. Dickerson committed a murder, he has to be brought to justice. That's the only way your friend will really be at peace."

Taylor rubbed his hands along the tops of his chaps and scuffled his feet. "I reckon," was all he said, but he didn't look happy about it.

The marshal stood up and said, "I guess I'll have to deputize you, Prescott. I'd be a damned fool to ride out to the Lazy D by myself."

Parker was still looking at the cowboy. "What did you mean by Johnny not wanting to mess with Lucky Stars cattle?"

Taylor looked at the ground. "You know...*messin'* with them. Spookin' them, cuttin' the calves away from their mamas. Things like that. Mr. Jeremy said it was fer the Hanks's own good—so they'd realize they needed a man around the place. A lot of the other hands agreed with him."

"What about poisoning heifers? Shooting mules?"

Taylor looked scared. "I don't know nothin' about that. All I ever done was the messin'."

"No one's accusing you of anything, Taylor." The marshal pulled a key from his pocket and handed it to him. "I want you to go on up and lock yourself in my hotel room until we get back here. I'll have them send you up a nice steak dinner, how's that?''

The frightened look faded from his eyes and he took the key. "You think they might find a couple of beers to go along with that?"

"I'll see to it," the marshal agreed with a nod.

Ned and Hiram Dickerson had obviously made their excuses after dinner to leave Molly and Jeremy alone in the Dickersons' parlor. Molly had not enjoyed the meal. She was still fuming about Parker's high-handed treatment of her that morning. Though underneath her anger, she had to admit, there was a touch of satisfaction in the idea that Parker didn't want her anywhere near Jeremy. He might couch it in fancy words, but it was jealousy, pure and simple. She discarded the notion that there was any other reason for her to stay clear of Jeremy. The supposed threats he had made had more than likely just been the two of them bristling at each other. They'd acted like two roosters in a single chicken coop since the first day they'd seen each other. It wasn't so terrible, after all, to have two strong-minded men both wanting her. Maybe she'd give Parker a chance to make amends when she got home that evening.

"What are you smiling about?" Jeremy asked as they sat together on the Dickersons' fancy brocade settee.

"Nothing. I should be getting on home. We have plenty of work to do now that spring's coming." Now was the moment to speak with Jeremy about the roundup she was planning. It had been the main reason she'd wanted to keep her appointment today, though she hadn't given that explanation to Parker.

She straightened her back. "In fact, I needed to talk to you about it. I have a favor to ask."

"Anything, my dear."

For a year she'd sworn that this moment would never come. She'd been afraid that asking for help meant showing weakness, proving that what the men said about her was true—a lady couldn't run a ranch. But the fact that she was sitting here with Jeremy, about to ask for his assistance, without so much as a rapid heartbeat, was an indication of how much she'd changed over these past few weeks. Part of the change had come with growing up—becoming truly the boss and manager she'd thought herself before her father died. And part of the change was due to Parker. He'd shown her that she could be a woman, fully a woman, and still be the same strong, independent person her father had helped her become. She could wear a dress if she chose and still command respect. She could love—and be loved—without sacrificing her own identity. No matter what happened between the two of them, she'd always be grateful to Parker for that lesson. She was quite sure things would have been different if Jeremy had been the one she had fallen in love with.

"What was it you wanted to ask me?" Jeremy prompted.

"You and your father were right. I need to get my cattle marked." She was pleased with the businesslike tone of her voice. "Parker and Smokey are trying to recruit some help in town, but I'm not sure how successful they'll be. If they don't find enough men, I'd like to hire on some of yours, just for a few days' roundup."

There was a look of satisfaction in Jeremy's black eyes. "I've made you the same offer in the past and you've always turned up your nose at me."

"I know. But I have a few more brains in my head than I used to have. In spite of what they say in town, there's no doubt in my mind that a woman can run a cattle ranch. But she can't run it by herself. *I* sure as heck can't. I'm asking for your help."

Jeremy leaned back against the rose-patterned damask. "Molly, I expect you know my feelings for you go beyond friendship."

Molly held up her hand. "Let's not mix up horses and mules here, Jeremy. We're talking a business deal. I'll pay you a commission on the men I hire, if you like."

His eyes were slightly hooded. "We can't talk about the one thing without the other, Molly. You realize that your ranch would be an excellent addition to the Lazy D holdings. If anyone else owned it and was having trouble keeping things under control, I'd just let them go bust and snatch the property up for myself."

"What about all your father's talk of being good neighbors?"

"My father's a little past his prime these days, to tell you the truth," he said with a bland smile.

"What exactly are you trying to tell me, Jeremy? Are you saying you won't let your men help me unless I agree that our relationship is to progress 'beyond friendship,' as you put it?"

She was holding her temper in check. Jeremy had gone to such pains to be nice to her lately, she hadn't anticipated that he would turn down her request.

"You make it sound sinister, my dear. I assure you I have nothing but honorable intentions. I hadn't planned to ask you formally so soon after your father's death, but I've always planned that you and I would be married."

He'd reached his arm along the back of the settee and put his hand around the back of her neck. It sent a shiver skittering down her spine. "As you say, Jeremy, it's not a good time for me to think about marriage. My first concern is getting the ranch back on its feet. I'm not thinking about anything else."

He ran one long, cold finger up and down the side of her jaw. "Perhaps it's time for you to start. If we were engaged, naturally the resources of the Lazy D would be at your disposal."

Molly pulled her neck away from his grasp. "I'm sorry, Jeremy. If you insist on asking the question at this time, the answer is no. I'm not interested in marrying you."

The only indication of his displeasure was a slight outward thrust of his thin lips. "Then I guess I won't ask the question yet. I'll give you time to consider the advantages ... and the disadvantages of turning me down."

"So does this mean you won't help me?" The air in the tiny parlor had grown stuffy. Molly took a deep breath. It would put more pressure on her to have to find the hands elsewhere, but in a strange way she felt almost relieved to think that she wouldn't, after all, be owing anything to the Dickersons.

"We'll discuss the whole picture again in a week or so. As I say, after you've had time to think. And there's another rather distasteful matter to consider."

"Which is?"

"I've been informed that you were talking to the territorial marshal about the night we both were involved in the...execution of a murderer."

"The lynching, you mean. Which I expect was a bit more than distasteful to Ole Pedersson."

"Pedersson was too pickled to know what hit him. And the hanging was perfectly legal. However, I understand that the marshal is still nosing around about it. I want you to promise not to get further involved."

She frowned. "I can hardly promise that. I was there, remember?"

"Yes, well, that was unfortunate, as I told you at the time. But it can be arranged for the others on the posse that night to conveniently forget your presence. I don't want you mixed up in this."

"You're too late, Jeremy. I've already told Marshal Tichenor exactly what went on that night. And if he wants me to swear to it in court, I'll do it."

He was silent for a long moment, his expression dark. Then he stood and held out his hand to help her up. "I'll let you get back to your duties, Molly. But I hope you'll give some serious consideration to my offer."

She took his hand reluctantly. She'd expected his proposal of marriage for some time, but she hadn't anticipated that it would sound so menacing. In fact, everything about Jeremy's oily manner was making her quite nervous. Perhaps Parker had been right this morning after all. It might just be her imagination, but at the moment she wanted nothing more than to ride away from the Lazy D and never come back.

"Why didn't you stop that blasted marshal from talking with Molly?" Jeremy asked furiously.

Sam Benton stood facing him, wringing the brim of his hat in his two hands. "There wasn't anything I could do about it. Hell, he's talked to everyone in the whole damn territory, it seems like. The man never wears down."

"Well, Molly's the one we need to worry about. The ranchers who were part of it should hold up all right. And I don't think I'll have any trouble with my men. They saw firsthand what happens to a dirty traitor."

"You shouldn't have shot the Oyster, Jeremy. You should've just turned him off the place."

"For him to go blabbing his story all over the territory? No, he had to be eliminated. And it served as a good lesson to the others."

"But if the marshal—"

"To hell with the marshal. The only person who can cause trouble is Molly, and once she's my wife, she'll cease to be a problem."

"When are you gonna marry her?"

"In due time. She may need a little more persuasion first. Her cattle problems have almost convinced her that she can't get on without my help. Perhaps something a little more drastic will push her the rest of the way."

"What do you have in mind?" Benton's flaccid face was wrinkled with worry. "'Cause I think Tichenor's going to keep after this—"

"Just shut up about him. We've got something else to think about."

"Something you want me to do?"

"No, you're too well-known. I'll use a couple of my men."

"What are you planning?"

Jeremy tapped his fingers together and smiled. "Perhaps Molly will be a little more willing to accept my help if the next thing to turn up missing at the Lucky Stars is not cattle, but one of her pretty sisters."

Mary Beth and Ned looked around the little room they'd used as a rendezvous through the cold winter. Their kisses and caresses had grown increasingly urgent as the season wore on, and that afternoon they'd come closer than they ever had before to giving themselves to each other completely.

"I don't care about waiting anymore," Mary Beth said with a touch of petulance.

But Ned gave a half-desperate laugh and said, "We've waited this long, Bethy. I guess we can make it to your birthday. It's only a week now."

"But that's just my birthday. Then we have to get engaged and set a date for the wedding . . ."

He leaned over and kissed her. "I'm telling your sister she has a month to make whatever plans you ladies seem to think necessary for a wedding."

"A month!"

"One month from your birthday. I'm not waiting another day."

"Or night," she agreed, snuggling against him. "Maybe we should come here for our honeymoon. I've grown awfully fond of this place."

"I want to give you a proper honeymoon—a suite in a fancy hotel in Denver."

"Molly's been to Denver, but I never got to go."

"Well, now you will. In a private sleeping car."

She gave a sigh of contentment. "I love you, Ned Dickerson."

He took a deep, calming breath. "I love you, too, Bethy, but I'm sending you home now before that honeymoon gets started a little too early."

"Just a little longer?" she pleaded, kissing the underside of his chin.

"No." He stood and lifted her to her feet alongside him. "It's getting dark, and I don't like the thought of you riding back all by yourself."

"Silly boy. One thing you should have learned by now, Ned. The Hanks sisters can take care of themselves."

Mary Beth had arrived late to supper several times recently, and Molly had resolved to speak to her about it. She knew that girls of Mary Beth's age sometimes needed time to themselves, but she was worried about having her out alone after dark.

"I need to talk with Mary Beth about these lone rides," she said as she and Susannah started to put together a supper of cold chicken and boiled potatoes. "And where in tarnation are Smokey and Parker? They should've been back hours ago."

Susannah hesitated a moment, then said, "Well, you know that Mary Beth's not really alone."

Molly's jaw dropped. "What in blazes are you talking about?"

"Honestly, Molly. Open your eyes. Do you think you're the only one in the family who can fall in love? Mary Beth and Ned Dickerson have been sneaking away together all winter."

"Mary Beth and Ned?"

Susannah nodded.

"But she's just a baby."

"A baby who's as old as our mother was when she was bouncing you on her knee with me in the oven."

"Well, hell's bells."

Susannah grinned. "It's not the end of the world, sis. We're just growing up—all of us. Mary Beth, too."

As they carried the plates to the table, Molly looked out the dark dining-room window. "So you think she's with Ned right now?"

"Probably. Young love, you know. You lose track of time. At least, that's what they tell me," she ended with a sour face.

"Your time will come soon enough." Molly laughed. "You certainly have enough offers these days."

"Yes, but all the young men in the area are so...boring. There's not a one who can hold a candle to Parker."

Molly tried to tamp down her feeling of jealousy. Susannah had never made a secret of her opinion of Parker. "That's because we haven't known him all our lives."

Susannah gave her an exasperated look. "No, Molly, it's not. It's because he's as charming and handsome as a prince with the wit of a scholar and the physique of a high-rigger lumberjack."

Molly smiled, but the little worm of jealousy squirmed around in her middle. "You'll find someone like that one of these days."

"Sure I will," Susannah said with a roll of her eyes.

"You will," Molly said firmly. "Should we go ahead and eat without them?"

Before Susannah could answer the question, the front door opened and Parker came in, followed by Smokey and Marshal Tichenor. "Good, you're just in time," Molly began, but she stopped as she saw their sober expressions. "What's the matter?"

"Did you go to the Lazy D today?" Parker asked.

Molly had almost forgotten that morning's argument. "You know I did."

"You were with Jeremy?"

She put her hands on her hips. "What's this all about?"

The marshal removed his hat and said, "We've just come from the Lazy D, Miss Hanks. We went to take Jeremy Dickerson into custody."

Molly braced herself against the thick oak table. "Because of the lynching?"

"No," the marshal answered. "We went to arrest him for the murder of the man known as Johnny the Oyster."

"There's an eyewitness who can testify against him," Parker added. With an angry glance at Molly he added, "I told you I didn't trust the guy."

"What about Ned?" Susannah asked.

Tichenor turned to her. "The brother? I don't think he was involved. He wasn't around the night of the lynching, from what I hear. I don't know about their father, though. He was there."

"Not Hiram," Molly said, still holding the edge of the table for support. "He couldn't have had anything to do with this."

The marshal shrugged. "Once we make an arrest the story usually starts to unravel. We'll see how it all plays out."

"But you haven't arrested him yet?" Molly asked.

"He wasn't there. We told his father we needed to talk with him and that we'd be back later this evening."

"I can't believe it," Molly said, shaking her head slowly.

"I can," Susannah said dryly.

Smokey had walked into the room and was eyeing the plates of cold food with disdain. "You call that a supper?" he asked.

"Smokey," Molly admonished. "Who can think about eating—"

Before she could finish there was a pounding on the front door. Parker and the marshal moved to one side as Susannah walked across the hall to open it.

It was the last person Molly wanted to see. "Jeremy!" she exclaimed, her eyes going from him to the marshal.

He was accompanied by Sheriff Benton, and both looked surprised to see Tichenor standing in Molly's front hall. But Jeremy recovered quickly. "I heard you were looking for me, Marshal," he said smoothly as Susannah stepped back and let him enter. "What can I do for you?"

Tichenor had moved slowly back against one side of the dining-room door frame, giving him a view of the front hall, the living room and the dining room. His right hand rested easily on the revolver strapped to his hip. Parker took up a position directly across the hall. For the first time Molly noticed that he, too, was wearing a gun belt under his jacket.

"This may be all a misunderstanding, gentlemen," she said, walking toward the group.

"Stay right where you are, Molly," Parker snapped.

Dickerson's eyes grew wary as he looked from her to the marshal. "What's going on?" he asked. Sheriff Benton was standing directly behind him as if ready to use Jeremy as a shield if things got violent.

"I'll ask you to stay calm, Mr. Dickerson," Tichenor said. "We're willing to hear your side of the story, and I can promise you that you'll receive a fair trial if it comes to that. But at the moment I'm putting you under arrest for the murder of Johnny the Oyster."

Jeremy moved so quickly, Molly didn't even see from where he'd pulled the gun. Suddenly he had an arm around Susannah's waist and a long-barreled revolver pressed to her temple. In a lightning second Tichenor had drawn his weapon and was aiming it at Jeremy, but with Susannah in front of him, there was no chance for a clear shot.

"Jeremy, no!" Molly yelled.

He looked over at her with a smile. "If you hadn't been so damned stubborn, Molly, none of this would have happened. I'd have married you, taken over the Lucky Stars and we'd all have lived happily ever after."

"Don't do this, Jeremy," she pleaded as he slowly backed toward the door, still holding Susannah. "Let her go and turn yourself in."

"Get the horses ready, Benton," Jeremy told the sheriff over his shoulder.

"If you had nothing to do with this, Benton, you'd better think twice about helping him," the marshal argued in a dispassionate tone. "It'll make you an accessory to murder."

Benton looked nervously from Dickerson to Tichenor. Finally he stepped inside the room and held up his hands. "I can't do it, Jeremy," he said. "Things have gone too far."

Jeremy cast him a glare of disgust. "As if I need your help, you fat old windbag. Just stay out of my way. All of you," he added, pressing Susannah's waist more tightly until she gave an involuntary groan.

"It's a sad day for your pa, Jeremy Dickerson," Smokey said.

"Shut up, old man." He half dragged Susannah across the threshold. "In case you have any ideas of getting a shot in while we're mounting up, I'd advise against it. You might have noticed that there's another Hanks sister missing at the moment. If you ever want to see her safe again, you'd better let me ride on out of here."

"Mary Beth? Where is she?" Susannah asked, trying to wriggle loose.

Dickerson pushed his arm brutally against her ribs. "Just stay clear away from me," he said, addressing the marshal and Parker. "Unless you want these ladies hurt."

Then he and Susannah faded from view in the blackness of the night.

Chapter Seventeen

Molly stared after them in stunned silence, but both Parker and the marshal went into action. Tichenor grabbed the sheriff's gun from his holster and slammed him up against the wall, while Parker ran to the front door to see which direction Dickerson was heading.

"What's he done with the other girl?" Tichenor demanded, pressing his forearm painfully against Benton's throat.

"Two of his men... Holding her..." Benton gurgled. The marshal eased his choke hold a little. "We found her riding back this way. Jeremy was going to have her turn up missing so that Miss Hanks would have to ask him for help finding her."

"Where is she?" Molly asked. Her body finally unfroze and she came running toward them. Parker caught her in his arms.

"Take it easy, Molly," he said. "We're going to find them. He won't dare hurt them."

Molly looked at him with anguish in her eyes. "He's a murderer."

With another disgusted shove, Tichenor released Benton. "Yes, ma'am," he said to Molly. "He's a murderer. And we're about to bring him to justice. As soon as I get this sorry excuse of a lawman locked up in his own jail, we'll get back over to the Lazy D. Someone there is going to know where we should start looking."

"I'm going with you," Molly said firmly.

The marshal looked doubtful, but before he could protest, Parker said, "They're her sisters. She has the right to come."

"That buffalo rifle of hers won't hurt none, either," Smokey added.

Tichenor looked around the group and made up his mind quickly. "Let's get on with it, then."

It seemed to take an agonizingly long time to ride to town, lock away the sheriff, then get out to the Lazy D. When they arrived, Hiram and Ned had already retired, unaware of the awful turn Jeremy's life had taken. A sleepy Ned answered the door, then listened with his father in stunned silence as Tichenor, in a blunt but not unsympathetic way, told them the story.

Hiram had to be seated, looking suddenly much older than his sixty-five years. Ned had the same look of shock that Molly had had at first. But finally, his usually pleasant face pulled into tight lines, he grimly told them that he knew where his brother and the sisters might be found.

"There's an old cabin up on our north forty. Nobody uses it these days. At least…" His voice cracked a little, then recovered. "We'll start looking for them there."

"You're coming with us?" the marshal asked.

Ned nodded.

"It might get rough for your brother."

Ned's eyes were hard. "If he's harmed Mary Beth, I'll kill him myself."

Hiram gave a moan from his seat on the sofa, but his son's expression remained implacable.

A quick trip to the Lazy D bunkhouse to talk with the cowhands confirmed that two of their number had ridden out with Jeremy and the sheriff earlier that afternoon. When the events of the day were explained to the remaining crew by a stone-faced Ned, every one of them volunteered to join the search party.

"Our main concern is the safety of the Hanks sisters," the marshal told them all in a loud voice. "Remember that Jeremy Dickerson is no longer your boss—he's a wanted man who by now should be considered unbalanced and dangerous. If you see any sight of him or the girls, you're to ride back here as fast as possible. We'll all meet up here again in three hours."

As the men headed out in opposite directions, the marshal's group followed Ned to the cabin he'd told them about. Molly rubbed Midnight's neck as if it would make her fly faster across the still-frozen grasslands. After what seemed like an eternity, Ned pulled up his horse and pointed. "That's it," he said in a low voice.

They all stopped riding and there was a moment of silence as they strained their eyes in the dark to make out a faint light in the distance. "Well, someone's there," the marshal said. "Now we just need to do this thing right so no one gets hurt."

He swung off his horse and motioned for the others to do the same. When they were standing around him, he said, "I need cool heads, now. If anyone feels like he can't handle that, I want you to stay behind."

He looked first at Molly, then at Ned, but neither one said a word.

"All right. We go in together."

The cabin had only one door, but there was a window around the back, so Tichenor sent Smokey to cover them from that side. Parker and Molly would each take one of the two front windows while the marshal and Ned went in through the door.

"I know those men, Marshal," Ned said in a low voice. "I'm sure they're only here because my brother ordered them to do it."

"Well, they're kidnappers now, good men or not."

"Once they see it's the law, I don't think they'll give us trouble."

"I hope you're right."

They left their horses behind and made their way quietly to the little house. There was no sound from inside and the only light appeared to be from a dying fire. Molly edged over to the window and felt her heart leap as she peered in and recognized the huddled forms of her sisters.

"Will the door be latched?" Tichenor whispered to Ned.

He shook his head. "The latch is broken. If I kick on the door, it'll open."

Smokey disappeared around the back of the cabin. Parker was ready at his window with his six-gun drawn. Molly held the rifle ready, pointed at the ground.

The marshal made a signal with his hand, then Ned kicked the door open with a crash and both men stepped into the room, guns up. Everything seemed to happen at once. There were shouts from inside, a scream from one of the sisters and the sound of broken glass as Parker and Smokey smashed in their windows. After a minute Molly followed suit, hammering at the glass with the barrel of her rifle.

The two Lazy D cowhands had been sleeping. One leapt to his feet, half babbling a question. The other stayed prone and stuck his hands above his head. "Don't shoot," he said.

Molly's eyes went directly to Mary Beth and Susannah, clutching each other against the far wall, their eyes big and scared. Mary Beth's long hair had fallen down around her shoulders. She looked haggard but unhurt.

Tichenor trained his gun unerringly on Jeremy, who was standing next to the fireplace, a log in his hand. "Nobody move," he ordered.

The log clattered to the floor. Mary Beth cried, "Ned!" and sat up on her knees, holding her arms toward him.

At a cautioning wave from the marshal, Ned stayed where he was, but he told her, "It's all right, Bethy. You just sit right there for a minute more."

"So you've turned against your own brother," Jeremy sneered at him. Molly hardly recognized his voice, and she suddenly realized that the marshal's comment about "unbalanced" might be close to the truth.

"It's over, Jeremy," Ned told his brother sadly. "I've covered up for you all our lives, it seems, but this time you've gone too far."

"You always were a little coward, Ned. The kind who would betray his own blood to a complete stranger just because he's wearing a tin badge."

"You're the one who's betrayed us, Jeremy, with your obsession for power. We never needed more land. The Lazy D was just fine—"

"The Lazy D's going to be the finest spread in Wyoming," Jeremy yelled. "And I'm not about to share it with a brother who goes sniveling off to the law." As he spoke, his hand suddenly snaked down to the revolver at his hip. It left the leather so fast the gun itself was a blur. There was another scream from Mary Beth, then a deafening blast from the window where Parker was positioned.

Jeremy grabbed his right hand with a cry of rage as his gun clattered to the floor, shot right out of his hand.

"Nice shooting, Prescott," the marshal said, quickly stepping over to retrieve the fallen weapon.

All at once Mary Beth was in Ned's arms. Molly threw down her rifle and raced inside, meeting Susannah in a sobbing embrace halfway across the room.

From the back window Smokey hollered at the two cowhands, "Don't you varmints even think about moving."

Parker echoed the sentiments, leaning in the front window over shards of glass. "I'll shoot off the first hand that reaches for a gun."

"Hell, Tichenor. I can't believe you take on ruthless killers without flinching, and then shuffle your feet like a bashful schoolboy about facing one pretty female."

Parker and the marshal had met for dinner at the Grand Hotel. It had been a long week for both of them. Tichenor had sent for two deputies to transport Dickerson and Sam Benton to Laramie for trial and had spent the rest of the week getting statements from everyone involved in all of Dickerson's illegal activities—Johnny the Oyster's murder, the poisoning of the Lucky Stars cattle and, finally, the kidnapping of Mary Beth and Susannah.

Parker hadn't had time to help him out. Once Hiram had understood what his son had done, he'd insisted that Molly would have the help of as many Lazy D hands as she needed to get her ranch back into operation. Characteristically, she hadn't taken time to brood about what had happened. As soon as she was sure that neither Mary Beth nor Susannah would suffer any lasting effects from their misadventure, she'd chosen a group of Lazy D cowhands and had started in rounding up the cattle that had gone unbranded last year.

Parker had joined the work party, though he didn't know that he'd been of much help. The men from the Lazy D were skilled and efficient. They did their jobs quickly, without much talk and without offering to give much advice to a tenderfoot from back East who was much too pretty to be a wrangler.

He'd done his best, but with Molly retreating into another of her distant, boss-lady humors, he was happy to get the summons from Harry.

"You're one to talk," the marshal answered him back. "You've been sick in love with that tough little cowgirl since I first met you, and now you say you're thinking about skedaddling off to California. So who's the bigger coward?"

Parker grinned. "I guess the bravest man's a coward when it comes to women. But, honestly, Susannah's a sweetheart. You ought to let her know how you're feeling."

"And just how do I do that, my Lothario friend? I can see how much luck you've had."

Parker gave a rueful shrug. "That quiet-mannered Ned Dickerson's shown us both up, I guess. We ought to ask him for advice."

"He's too busy planning his wedding," Tichenor noted.

"Yeah," Parker agreed glumly.

"So, will you talk to her for me or not?"

Parker gave an exasperated laugh. "Yes, my friend, I'll talk to her. I'll tell her you're quaking in your boots at the thought of speaking to her, but you think she's prettier than a field of primroses."

"You could leave out the quaking part, but the primrose sounds nice."

Parker slapped his friend on the shoulder. "You see, Harry? You *do* have a romantic soul. Susannah's as good as hooked."

Parker's mood grew gloomier as he rode back out to the ranch. Seeing tough Marshal Tichenor so smitten had given him a good laugh, but his friend's infatuation made Parker's apparent failure all the harder to take. It had been bad enough watching Ned and Mary Beth cooing like lovebirds all week long. Ned had practically moved into the Lucky Stars ranch house and was riding out with his men every day to help Molly with the branding.

She had plenty of help these days. Parker was superfluous, and evidently she'd come to that conclusion, too. She'd spoken to him only briefly the entire week. If he hadn't promised Mary Beth that he'd stay on for the wedding, he'd already be on his way to California.

Mary Beth and Ned had the big parlor to themselves when he came in the front door. They were snuggling on the sofa in front of the fireplace and barely acknowledged his entrance with two half-hearted waves.

He found Susannah in the kitchen, punching a big white mass of bread dough. "Who are you mad at?" he teased as she pummeled it with her slender fists.

She made a face at him. "I'm just getting this ready to rise overnight, but I could be mad at you, Parker Prescott."

"Why's that?"

"You were talking with Smokey about heading off to California," she accused.

"Guilty."

"I've never heard such plumb fool nonsense."

Parker frowned in confusion. "I always said that I'd stay as long as you all needed the help. Molly doesn't need me anymore—she's got lots of better cowhands."

She picked up the entire mass and slammed it down on the table. "What is it about you men that makes you so blind about the things that count the most?"

Parker sighed and pulled a chair out opposite her. When Susannah had something on her mind she was almost as relentless as Molly about getting it said. "All right, enlighten me. What am I blind about?"

"About Molly. 'She doesn't need me,'" she mimicked. "Tarnation, Parker, my sister's in love with you—how much more does a man have to be needed?"

Parker leaned his chin heavily on his hand. "I don't think so, Susannah. She's hardly talked to me."

"Because she's as mule headed as you are. You had a fight about her going over to Dickerson's. As things turned out, you were right, and now she says you think she's nothing but a difficult, stubborn boss lady and you want nothing to do with her."

"And just how did she come to this brilliant conclusion?"

"She says you've been paying all your attention this week to me and Mary Beth, which shows that what you really want in life is a sweet, docile female like the one you lost back in Deadwood."

That shut him up for a minute. Claire had been sweet and, yes, docile. And he wondered, suddenly, if that would have been enough for him if they had had a chance to spend a lifetime together. When he compared her now to Molly...

"Where is she?" he asked wearily.

Susannah gave the bread a final pummel and plopped it into the rising bowl. "I don't know. Out in the barn with her precious animals, I suppose."

Parker stood and turned toward the door. "Ned's horse isn't out there, is it?"

"No, it's hitched around at the side. Why?"

"Because we might not want to be disturbed for a while."

Susannah smiled. "You're not going off to California, are you, Parker?"

"Maybe not. If I can scare me up a better offer."

Her dimples deepened. "Good luck."

He half opened the door, then stopped. "Oh, Susannah, I almost forgot. Harry Tichenor's sweet on you and wants to know if you'll let him come courting. He should be here in about half an hour."

Then he swung out the door, leaving Susannah with her hands in the bread dough, her mouth hanging wide open.

* * *

Molly looked around the barn with some satisfaction. The three heifers who had stayed here all winter were gone—duly branded and off to join the big guys out on the range. The barn itself had been completely cleaned and spruced up by some of the Lazy D crew. In general the ranch was working at the moment the way Molly had always hoped and dreamed that it would. The men had taken her orders without a qualm. Of course, Ned had been around most of the time, but she'd sensed that once they had seen her riding out there with them, working as hard as anyone, the cowhands had begun to develop a measure of respect for her, in spite of her being a woman.

She should be happier.

She was happy, darn it. And she wasn't going to let anything spoil it. Not even the fact that Parker had spent most of the week hanging back with her sisters and was probably this very moment packing up his gear to leave.

"Evenin', boss lady."

She jumped. "You been trained by the Indians, Parker?" she asked, echoing the conversation they had had when he'd first come to the ranch—what now seemed like ages ago.

"Caught you daydreaming, did I? What were you dreaming about?"

She gripped the stall gate she'd just closed. "I wasn't dreaming. I was just thinking about how far the ranch has come in the past week."

"The Lazy D men have been very helpful."

Molly gave a rueful laugh. "As terrible as this has been for everyone, I guess it's turning out that Jeremy was right. I did need his help. Maybe if I'd admitted that a year ago, none of this tragedy would have happened.''

"Or maybe by now you'd be dead so he could really take control here.''

She turned around to face him directly. "I haven't thanked you for what you did that night. That was some mighty fine shooting, tenderfoot.''

"Yeah. At least I've learned a couple things since I came West.''

"You've learned a lot.''

"Not how to rope. Did you see me out there today?''

She'd seen little else, but she wasn't about to tell him that. Not if he was really thinking of leaving for California. "I understand you might be heading on out of here.''

He watched her eyes carefully as she said the words, her tone casual. She'd never make a good poker player. Susannah had been right again. "Well, with all the help you've got now, it doesn't appear as if I'm doing you much good.''

"So you *are* leaving?''

He walked up to her, very close, and spoke in a low voice. "I hear tell there's finally going to be a wedding on the Lucky Stars.''

She nodded, her face tensing as he drew near. She was wearing one of those linen shirts tucked into her buckskin trousers. The fabric stretched full over her breasts, then gathered at her small waist. Below her waist the buckskin clung to her hips like a second skin. She looked about as masculine as a pink ribbon. Parker licked his suddenly dry lips as sensitive portions of his body shared urgent messages.

"I still think Mary Beth's too young," she said. She glanced down, unavoidably seeing his obvious state of arousal. Her voice grew raspy. "What do you think?"

Parker kept coming, slowly, backing her flat against the gate. "I think if I don't kiss you right this minute, I'm going to explode."

His lips barely touched hers at first, then, when her arms crept up to encircle his neck, he took her mouth more fully, holding her very still, letting their lips and tongues do all the work. She made a move to caress him with one hand, but he grabbed her wrist and pinned it against the gate, all the while continuing the devastating kisses. It was long, hazy moments later that he loosened his hold, leaned his forehead against hers and said almost reverently, "I want you, Molly. I want you so bad that I can't even see straight. But I've also discovered that I'm head over heels in love. I thought I came out West to find something I was missing in my life back home. And it turns out I was right. Only it's not a gold mine—it's you."

Molly had felt the tears of happiness well up the moment he reached the word *love*. In one magical word, all her doubts, the insecurities, the jealousy of her sisters, all disappeared. She was loved. She was loved by a man who was handsome, charming, funny, a crack shot, a blatant flatterer, a terrible roper, a tenderfoot who knew nothing about ranching but would probably continue to try to order her around if he thought it was for her own good. "We'll fight," she said, but her heart was soaring.

He pulled his head away and looked at her, then wiped at one of the tears with the pad of his thumb. "We sure will, boss lady. And then we'll make up."

"And I'll get grouchy at roundup time and start to yell at you like I do all the cowboys."

He picked her up and gently nipped the side of her neck. "I know another couple of ways to make you yell," he said huskily.

He carried her to the pile of fresh hay at the back of the barn. "What are you doing?" she asked weakly.

"I'm going to make love to you, boss lady, all night if I need to, so you don't go tough on me again before I get you to agree to marry me."

They tumbled into the hay together and Molly rolled over, sitting up. "Truly, Parker?" she asked, the tears rolling again.

"It's all right if you take a lot of convincing," he said, pulling at the buttons of her shirt. "I've got all night."

"And you wouldn't rather have a wife who's sweet and pretty like . . . like Mary Beth or Susannah?"

He pretended to consider for a minute, until he saw the faintest hint of doubt creep into her eyes. Then he laughed and said, "Well, Mary Beth's taken already, and I have a feeling Susannah's about to be snatched up by the marshal, who's just a little faster on the draw than I am. So I guess that makes you the lucky bride."

She saw that he was teasing her, and threw a clump of straw at his head. "Don't do that to me, Parker. I was always the one who was never going to fall in love. It'll take me a while to believe it. You'll have to be patient with me."

He picked a piece of hay out of his hair and brushed some more off his shoulders. "And you'll have to be patient with me and those *cows* of yours. But in the meantime, neither one of us has to be patient about this."

He pushed her back into the hay, opening her shirt as they went. As usual, she had no female contraptions underneath so he was able to fasten his mouth immediately on a warm, full breast. "Dressing like a male does have its advantages," he murmured, moving to give equal attention to the other side.

Molly shifted beneath him, letting the waves build as he laved her with his tongue, then tugged at her nipples with increasingly demanding lips. His hand slipped under the pliant buckskin of her trousers, seeking the soft heat of her core. She drew in a quick breath when he touched her there, making tiny circles of arousal.

"Parker!" she said sharply.

He pulled himself up to her lips. "What is it, sweetheart?"

She pulled his head close and kissed him. "You did say I wouldn't have to be patient," she reminded him. The flush of passion was already creeping up her neck.

Swiftly he lifted her and adjusted both her trousers and his own to give him access to her open body. In only a few thrusts he brought them both to their peak and then tumbling, soaring over it.

They lay quiet for a few minutes, tangled with their clothes half on and half off. Finally he said, "I think I like impatient women."

She gave an embarrassed laugh. "Enough to marry one?"

"Yes, ma'am."

He started kissing her again, amazed that his body wasn't sated after what they'd just shared. She moved restlessly beneath him. "The hay prickles," she explained apologetically.

Parker smiled. "Ah, love in the Wild West. How could I ever even think about going back to New York City after this?" He reached out and dragged over a couple of horse blankets to put underneath her. "Is this all right, or should we go to my bunk?"

"We can't, Parker. Ned's here with Mary Beth and—"

Before she could start taking on the responsibilities of the world again, he silenced her mouth and her thoughts with another long kiss. "We'll just keep roughing it, then," he murmured.

Before long they both were once again out of breath. "I'm feeling impatient again," she said, only half teasing.

Parker took both her wrists and held them above her head, then looked down at her lean body. "Sorry, boss lady. When I said you didn't have to be patient..." He kissed just the tip of each swollen breast. "I only meant the *first* time."

Epilogue

Molly looked at herself in the cheval mirror that Susannah had moved into her big sister's bedroom for the occasion. The dress was perfect, just as she'd imagined. And, yes, her cheeks were rosy—the blushing bride. After all her talk of independence, Molly was to be the first Hanks sister to marry.

Ned and Mary Beth, now that they knew they had Molly's full support for their marriage, had decided that they could wait until after Jeremy's impending trial for the actual event. But Parker had been less patient.

"Hell, sweetheart, let's just go find a judge and get it done," he'd said the day following their reunion in the barn. But Molly, who'd sworn never to be one for those kind of things, had found herself with a peculiar desire to walk down the aisle as a beautiful bride in a true wedding with all the trimmings.

Parker, adamant, had given her a week. It had passed quickly, the house humming happily with activity. Susannah and Mary Beth had sewn feverishly on a blue silk wedding dress and Smokey had worked for two days on a wedding supper, complete with a tiered pound cake. Now that the day had arrived, he and Max had spent the afternoon rearranging the furniture in the big parlor. Max had brought a centerpiece of tin wedding bells for the table and a heart-shaped locket for the bride.

Susannnah and Mary Beth were with Molly in her tiny bedroom, fussing around her, giving last minute stitches to her dress and enjoying the unheard-of activity of primping their older sister's hair.

"Our neighbors won't believe it when they see you, Molly," Mary Beth said as she tucked the last errant strand into place with a satisfied nod.

"You're lovelier than any of us, sis," Susannah added. "Every man who ever turned his nose up at the boss of the Lucky Stars is going to be gnashing his teeth in frustration."

"The only one I want to impress is Parker," Molly said with a nervous laugh that sounded nothing like her.

As if she had conjured him, Parker's demanding voice suddenly spoke from behind the half closed door. "Where's my bride?"

"Go away," the three sisters shouted in unison.

"Not likely," he answered, pushing the door wide with a grin. "I'm afraid you three have got me here to stay."

"You should wait to see her downstairs," Susannah said with a frown.

"It's bad luck," Mary Beth added.

Parker's grin faded as he stopped and stared at Molly. The tucked bodice of her wedding dress emphasized her breasts and made her waist look impossibly tiny. Her hair was swept into a graceful twist that cascaded down to her bare shoulders, which were a tantalizing white in contrast to the sun-ripened skin of her face. Her smile for him was radiant.

"It couldn't possibly be bad luck," he said in a tightened voice. "There's going to be nothing but good luck around here from now on."

Molly looked up at the ceiling. "You hear that, Papa? Your lucky stars are happy at last."

"All right, lucky stars," boomed Max from the doorway behind Parker. "You'd better get a move on if we're going to have a wedding around here today." Then she too came to a dead stop. "Land, child. You're as pretty as a Scottish bluebell," she said, wiping a tear from her eye.

Smokey poked his head around her and gave a low whistle. "Mighty pretty," he confirmed. Then he twisted his head to look back at Max. "You crying, Maxie?"

"Of course I am, you old coot. Women always cry at weddings."

"Well, I'll be damned," Smokey marveled. "I never thought I'd see the day where a tough gal like you would go soft. It's weddings that do that, you say?"

Max nodded, wiping the other eye. "Every time."

Smokey gave Parker a poke in the ribs. "I suppose a fancy Eastern pup like you already knew that, right?"

Parker's eyes were still on his bride. "Weddings are one way to soften them up," he said, giving Molly one of his special smiles.

Smokey scratched at his beard. "That's something to think about. It surely is."

Finally breaking his gaze at Molly, Parker turned to Smokey and said in a stage whisper, "If weddings soften Max up, you're in luck, because I have a feeling there's going to be a slew of them around here. In fact, old timer, you might want to consider it yourself."

"Don't go giving him any more ideas, Parker," Max cautioned. "He's got plenty of them himself."

"I do *not*," Smokey protested.

They all laughed, then Smokey said grumpily, "Well, let's get on with it. The best man's down there pacing up and down the hall. You'd think *he* was the groom...."

"Harry's here?" Susannah interrupted, her face coloring.

"Yeah. He's all duded up pretty in a purple suit." Smokey gave a shudder. "It's amazing how quickly love can bring a good man low."

Susannah gave Molly a final quick embrace. "You're stunning, sis. I'll see you downstairs." Then she scooted past Parker and out the door.

"We should all be getting down there," Max said.

"I'm supposed to be giving this little filly away," Smokey said, putting out his arm.

Parker took hold of his elbow and steered him toward Max. "You can help Miz McClanahan down the stairs, Smokey—Mary Beth, too. We'll catch up to you in a minute."

The old cook looked at Molly, hesitating.

"It's all right, Smokey," she said with a nod. "We'll see you all downstairs."

When her sister and the older couple had left, Parker pulled her into his arms and bent to kiss the top of her breast, bare in the low-neck gown.

"I do like this dress," he whispered.

"Parker, everyone'll be waiting," she objected, her lips turned up in a smile.

"I'm probably going to like taking it off you even better."

"Mmm," she murmured, as he found a sensitive spot just under her ear.

He moved his arms down her back and pulled her tight against him. "Don't suppose there'd be time to try that theory out?"

Molly fought to bring herself back to sanity. She pushed on his chest, but he didn't budge. "We've got a wedding to go to, remember?"

He tipped his head back and grinned at her. "Is that so? And who's the lucky bride?"

The silk of her dress swished against the wool of his trousers as she swayed against him and said archly, "It's that lady rancher, Molly Hanks."

"Boss lady Hanks? I thought that little gal was too tough to want a man around."

"You thought wrong, cowboy." Molly pulled his head down and gave him a kiss. It started sedately, but as Parker seized her up against him until her feet left the floor, the kiss became a devastating fusion of lips and tongue.

"Lord almighty, Molly," Parker said, finally breaking the embrace and setting her down. "After that, we'd darn well better go on down and get ourselves hitched."

Molly stepped back and clasped her hands together to stop the trembling in her arms. She took in a deep breath, then looked up into Parker's adoring eyes. "Hitched? I thought you didn't like roping, tenderfoot."

Parker pulled her hands gently apart, then tucked one into his arm. "Well, now, it's like I told you, boss lady," he said, turning them toward the door, "I'm a fast learner."

* * * * *

This January, bring in the New Year
with something special from

WYOMING RENEGADE
by
Susan Amarillas

"Susan Amarillas is well on her way to becoming queen
of the frontier romance." —*Affaire de Coeur*

Available wherever Harlequin Historicals are sold.

Look us up on-line at: http://www.romance.net

BIGB97-

Heartbreak RANCH

Four generations of independent women...
Four heartwarming, romantic stories of the West...
Four incredible authors...

Fern Michaels
Jill Marie Landis
Dorsey Kelley
Chelley Kitzmiller

Saddle up with Heartbreak Ranch, an outstanding
Western collection that will take you on a whirlwind
trip through four generations and the exciting,
romantic adventures of four strong women who
have inherited the ranch from Bella Duprey,
famed Barbary Coast madam.

Available in March,
wherever Harlequin books are sold.

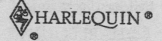

HARLEQUIN ®

HTBK

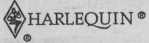